TELL MY HORSE

Ascending the sacred waterfalls at Saut d'Eau

TELL MY HORSE

VOODOO AND LIFE

IN HAITI AND

JAMAICA

ZORA NEALE HURSTON

WITH A NEW FOREWORD BY ISHMAEL REED
SERIES EDITOR: HENRY LOUIS GATES, JR.

Harper & Row, Publishers, New York
Grand Rapids, Philadelphia, St. Louis, San Francisco
London, Singapore, Sydney, Tokyo, Toronto

A hardcover edition of this book was originally published by J. B. Lippincott, Inc.

TELL MY HORSE. Copyright © 1938 by Zora Neale Hurston. Renewed 1966 by Joel Hurston. Foreword © 1990 by Ishmael Reed. Afterword, Selected Bibliography, and Chronology © 1990 by Henry Louis Gates, Jr. All rights reserved. Printed in the United States of America. No part of this book may be used or reproduced in any manner whatsoever without written permission except in the case of brief quotations embodied in critical articles and reviews. For information address Harper & Row, Publishers, Inc., 10 East 53rd Street, New York, N.Y. 10022.

First PERENNIAL LIBRARY edition published 1990.

Designed by Cassandra J. Pappas

LIBRARY OF CONGRESS CATALOG CARD NUMBER 89-45673

ISBN 0-06-091649-4

99 00 01 02 RRD-H 30 29 28 27 26 25 24 23 22 21

To
Carl Van Vechten
God's image of a friend

CONTENTS

�

Part III
VOODOO IN HAITI

ILLUSTRATIONS

✦

FOREWORD

✵

A line from Countee Cullen's famous poem "Heritage" typifies the attitudes of many "educated" white and black Americans for whom African and Neo-African religions are exotic faiths whose gods, "quaint . . . outlandish . . . ," and "heathen," are "naught" to them. It took the restless intellect of Zora Neale Hurston to make Neo-African religion, and its gods, more than "naught." The result was *Tell My Horse,* a major work of the Voodoo bibliography, which includes books written in Spanish, French, Portuguese, and Creole as well as English. The majority of these works have yet to be translated, which makes Hurston's work a treasure for the English reader who is curious about the subject. Though Voodoo had been driven underground by the time *Tell My Horse* was published, there has been a resurgence recently, due to the arrival in the United States of many of its followers from South and Central America and the Caribbean. Since white American readers are suspicious of the scholarship of those they deem to be aliens—they seem to need one of their own to translate—the efforts of such scholars as Robert Thompson, Robert Gover, and Michael Ventura and musicians like Kip Hanrahan and David Byrne have been invaluable in defusing some of the hysteria with which Neo-African religion has been regarded in the United States, a Protestant country. The contemporary misunderstanding of Voodoo was recently shown by the harsh criticism that African priests and Americans like Rev. George A. Stallings, Jr., received from the Catholic hierarchy as a result of their incorporation of the African style into western Catholic rites—even though such blending of styles has been long established in the Caribbean, Central and South America, and Haiti, where it is said that the people are ninety-five per cent Catholic and one hundred per cent Voodoo. It is against this background that Zora Neale Hurston's pioneer work can be appreciated, though one can understand why a writer tackling such a taboo subject would have appeared odd to the intellectually slothful of her time.

But *Tell My Horse,* the result of Hurston's travels to Jamaica and Haiti, is more than a Voodoo work. She writes intelligently about the botany, sociology, anthropology, geology, and politics of these nations in a style that is devoid of pompous jargon and accessible to the general reader. It is an entertaining book.

Hurston's gift for storytelling is immense, whether writing about the hunting of a wild boar by the Maroons at Accompong ("Men who had thrown off the bands of slavery by their . . . courage and ingenuity"), or an account of the extraordinary steps that Jamaicans take to appease a "duppy," lest it return from the grave and do harm to the living. In one of the book's very good interviews an informant tells Hurston that "the duppy . . . is the most powerful part of any man. Everybody has evil in them, and when a man is alive, the heart and the brain controls him and he will not abandon himself to many evil things. But when the duppy leaves the body, it no longer has anything to restrain it and it will do more terrible things than any man ever dreamed of. It is not good for a duppy to stay among living folk."

Part travelogue, *Tell My Horse* invokes the beauty of Jamaica and Haiti and the sacred zones where African gods continue to dwell—the "good" ones, the Rada group, and the "bad" ones, the Petros. The enemies of Voodoo have exploited rumors associating the Secte Rouge, a Petro sect, with human sacrifice in order to defame Voodoo, less a religion than the common language of slaves from different African tribes, thrown together in the Americas for commercial reasons. This common language was feared because it not only united the Africans but also made it easier for them to forge alliances with those Native Americans whose customs were similar. Voodoo has been the inspiration for the major slave revolts in this hemisphere, including the one that ousted the French from Haiti, but just as Christianity has been used by tyrants as a means for persecuting their opponents, Voodoo has been similarly abused.

Hurston's account of the Neo-African religion practiced in Haiti is fascinating. She gives a thorough description of the main loas (gods), their needs, their desires, and their powers. The details about art and dance are informative, though she describes the dance as "barbaric." But the most interesting discussion in *Tell My Horse* concerns possession, that strange phenomenon during which a mortal is taken over by a god. (One wonders what would happen if "possession," this amazing phenomenon, were as available to the millions of anxiety-ridden Americans as are the billions of toxic stress-reducing pills that are shoveled across drugstore counters and the illegal substances consumed by Americans that make ours a nation of junkies.)

It is interesting to note that a growing number of psychiatrists and physicians are beginning to trace the mental and physical health problems of many blacks—in particular the lack of self-esteem—to the symbolic annihilation to which their culture is subjected by the white-pride school curricula and media. Perhaps another cause of this depression is the severance of any link to the images of their ancient religion. One wonders how the millions of Catholics and Protestants who came to these shores or the followers of Buddhism and Confucianism would have fared had their faiths been driven underground, depriving them of spiritual nourishment, or if their religions had been exposed to the kind of pillorying that Neo-African religion receives in the media and from the mo-

tion picture industry. Typical of the treatment accorded Voodoo was NBC anchorman Tom Brokaw's sensational announcement that the drug murders occurring in Mexico in
1988 were the result of Voodoo rites; it was revealed later that
the so-called drug cult had been inspired by a Hollywood
"Voodoo" film entitled *The Believers*.

Contemporary myths about black literature proliferate, but
the fate of the average black writer, male or female, is the
same: the nonavailability of their books; reviews that are often
influenced by racist ideology or that exhibit a double standard;
the difficulty in getting their views aired—these are just some
of the problems that hamper their careers. Most would agree
with Countee Cullen's assessment that a black writer in a
country in which they are treated as aliens is "a curious thing."
For Hurston, though, the human family has room for a
President Jean Vilbrun Guillaume Sam, a "greedy detestable
criminal," as well as his son, known by the peasants of his time
as "fine" and "intelligent." In her novel *Their Eyes Were
Watching God,* despite their flaws, the men are productive and
talented. In *Tell My Horse,* Hurston describes, without sermon-
izing, the Jamaican practice of cultivating geishas for the de-
light of prospective grooms and comments in passing on the
practice of polygamy. When commenting about the status of
women in the United States, she sounds more like Phyllis
Schlafly than Bell Hooks or Michelle Wallace: "The majority
of men in all the states are pretty much agreed that just for
being born a girl-baby you ought to have laws and privileges
and pay and perquisites. And so far as being allowed to voice
opinions is concerned, why, they consider that you are born
with the law in your mouth, and that is not a bad arrangement
either. The majority of the solid citizens strain their ears trying
to find out what it is that their womenfolk want so they can
strain around and try to get it for them, and that is a *very* good
idea and the right way to look at things." Ironically, many of
today's feminists would consider such thinking to be "retrograde." Zora Neale Hurston has also gained the reputation of

a racial chauvinist. She reserves some of her harshest opinions for black nationalists (Race Men), whom she dismisses as "windbags" and "demagogues."

The Zora Neale Hurston of *Tell My Horse* is skeptical, cynical, funny, ironic, brilliant, and innovative. With its mixture of techniques and genres, this book, originally published in 1938, is bound to be the postmodernist book of the nineties. But her greatest accomplishment is in revealing the profound beauty and appeal of a faith older than Christianity, Buddhism, and Islam, a faith that has survived in spite of its horrendously bad reputation and the persecution of its followers.

ISHMAEL REED

PART I

JAMAICA

CHAPTER 1

THE ROOSTER'S NEST

Jamaica, British West Indies, has something else besides its mountains of majesty and its quick, green valleys. Jamaica has its moments when the land, as in St. Mary's, thrusts out its sensuous bosom to the sea. Jamaica has its "bush." That is, the island has more usable plants for medicinal and edible purposes than any other spot on earth. Jamaica has its Norman W. Manley, that brilliant young barrister who looks like the younger Pitt in yellow skin, and who can do as much with a jury as Darrow or Liebowitz ever did. The island has its craze among the peasants known as Pocomania, which looks as if it might be translated into "a little crazy." But Brother Levi says it means "something out of nothing." It is important to a great number of people in Jamaica, so perhaps we ought to peep in on it a while.

The two greatest leaders of the cult in Jamaica are Mother Saul, who is the most regal woman since Sheba went to see Solomon, and Brother Levi, who is a scrontous-looking man himself.

Brother Levi said that this cult all started in a joke but worked on into something important. It was "dry" Pocomania when it began. Then it got "spirit" in it and "wet." What with the music and the barbaric rituals, I became interested and took up around the place. I witnessed a wonderful ceremony with candles. I asked Brother Levi why this ceremony and he said, "We hold candle march after Joseph. Joseph came from cave where Christ was born in the manger with a candle. He was walking before Mary and her baby. You know Christ was not born in the manger. Mary and Joseph were too afraid for that. He was born in a cave and He never came out until He was six months old. The three wise men see the star but they can't find Him because He is hid in cave. When they can't find Him after six months, they make a magic ceremony and the angel come tell Joseph the men wanted to see Him. That day was called 'Christ must day' because it means 'Christ must find today,' so we have Christmas day, but the majority of people are ignorant. They think Him born that day."

I went to the various "tables" set in Pocomania, which boils down to a mixture of African obeah and Christianity enlivened by very beautiful singing. I went to a "Sun Dial"—that is a ceremony around the clock (24 hours long). The place was decorated from the gate in, with braided palm fronds and quacca bush. Inside the temple, the wall behind the altar was papered with newspapers.

There, the ceremony was in the open air. A long table covered with white. Under this table, on the ground, lighted candles to attract the spirits. There was a mysterious bottle which guaranteed "the spirit come." The Shepherd entered followed by the Sword Boy, carrying a wooden sword. After him came the Symbol Boy with a cross, chanting. Then came the Unter Boy with a supple jack, a switch very much like a rattan cane in his hand. During the ceremony he flogged those who were "not in spirit" that is, those who sat still. They are said to "cramp" the others who are in spirit. The Governess followed the Unter Boy. She has charge of all the women, but otherwise she functions something like the Mambo of Haiti. She aids the Shepherd and generally fires the meeting by leading the songs and whipping up the crowd. There followed

4

then the Shepherd Boy who is the "armor-bearer" to the Shepherd.

Their ceremony is exciting at times with singing, marching, baptisms at sacred pools in the yard. Miraculous "cures" (Mother Saul actually sat down upon a screaming Chinese boy to cure him of insanity); and the dancing about the tables with that tremendous exhalation of the breath to set the rhythm. That is the most characteristic thing of the whole ceremony. That dancing about the lighted candle pattern on the ground and that way of making a rhythmic instrument and of the breathing apparatus—such is Pocomania, but what I have discussed certainly is not all of it.

These "Balm yards" are deep in the lives of the Jamaican peasants. A Balm Yard is a place where they give baths, and the people who operate these yards are to their followers both doctor and priest. Sometimes he or she diagnoses a case as a natural ailment, and a bath or series of baths in infusions of secret plants is prescribed. More often the diagnosis is that the patient has been "hurt" by a duppy, and the bath is given to drive the spirit off. The Balm Yard with a reputation is never lacking for business. These anonymous rulers of the common people have decreed certain rules and regulations for events in life that are rigidly adhered to. For instance the customs about birth and death. The childbed and the person of the newborn baby must be protected from the dead by marks made with bluing. When it is moved from this room, the open Bible must precede it to keep off the duppies, and so on.

Tables are usually set because something for which a ceremony has been performed is accomplished. The grateful recipient of favor from the gods then sets a table of thanksgiving. No one except the heads of the Balm Yard and the supplicants are told what it is for. Most of the country products are served with plenty of raw rum. The first and most important thing is a small piece of bread in a small glass of water as a symbol of plenty.

And then Jamaica has its social viewpoints and stratifications which influence so seriously its economic direction.

5

Jamaica is the land where the rooster lays an egg. Jamaica is two per cent white and the other ninety-eight per cent all degrees of mixture between white and black, and that is where the rooster's nest comes in. Being an English colony, it is very British. Colonies always do imitate the mother country more or less. For instance some Americans are still aping the English as best they can even though they have had one hundred and fifty years in which to recover.

So in Jamaica it is the aim of everybody to talk English, act English and *look* English. And that last specification is where the greatest difficulties arise. It is not so difficult to put a coat of European culture over African culture, but it is next to impossible to lay a European face over an African face in the same generation. So everybody who has any hope at all is looking out for the next generation and so on. The color line in Jamaica between the white Englishman and the blacks is not as sharply drawn as between the mulattoes and the blacks. To avoid the consequences of posterity the mulattoes give the blacks a first class letting alone. There is a frantic stampede white-ward to escape from Jamaica's black mass. Under ordinary circumstances the trend would be towards the majority group, of course. But one must remember that Jamaica has slavery in her past and it takes many generations for the slave derivatives to get over their awe for the master-kind. Then there is the colonial attitude. Add to that the negro's natural aptitude for imitation and you have Jamaica.

In some cases the parents of these mulattoes have been properly married, but most often that is not the case. The mixed-blood bears the name with the bar sinister. However, the mulatto has prestige, no matter how he happened to come by his light skin. And the system of honoring or esteeming his approach to the Caucasian state is so elaborate that first, second, third and fourth degrees of illegitimacy are honored in order of their nearness to the source of whiteness. Sometimes it is so far fetched, that one is reminded of that line from "Of Thee I Sing," where the French Ambassador boasts, "She is the illegitimate daughter of the illegitimate son of the illegitimate nephew of the great Napoleon." In Jamaica just substitute the word Englishman for Napoleon and you have the situation.

Perhaps the Jamaican mixed bloods are logical and right, perhaps the only answer to the question of what is to become of the negro in the Western world is that he must be absorbed by the whites. Frederick Douglass thought so. If he was right, then the strategy of the American Negro is all wrong, that is, the attempt to achieve a position equal to the white population in every way but each race to maintain its separate identity. Perhaps we should strike our camps and make use of the cover of night and execute a masterly retreat under white skins. If that is what must be, then any way at all of getting more whiteness among us is a step in the right direction. I do not pretend to know what is wise and best. The situation presents a curious spectacle to the eyes of an American Negro. It is as if one stepped back to the days of slavery or the generation immediately after surrender when negroes had little else to boast of except a left-hand kinship with the master, and the privileges that usually went with it of being house servants instead of field hands. Then, as in Jamaica at present, no shame was attached to a child born "in a carriage with no top." But the pendulum has swung away over to the other side of our American clock. Even in His Majesty's colony it may work out to everybody's satisfaction in a few hundred years, if the majority of the population, which is black, can be persuaded to cease reproduction. That is the weak place in the scheme. The blacks keep on being black and reminding folk where mulattoes come from, thus conjuring up tragi-comic dramas that bedevil security of the Jamaican mixed bloods.

Everywhere else a person is white or black by birth, but it is so arranged in Jamaica that a person may be black by birth but white by proclamation. That is, he gets himself declared legally white. When I used the word black I mean in the American sense where anyone who has any colored blood at all, no matter how white the appearance, speaks of himself as black. I was told that the late John Hope, late President of

Atlanta University, precipitated a panic in Kingston on his visit there in 1935, a few months before his death. He was quite white in appearance and when he landed and visited the Rockefeller Institute in Kingston and was so honored by them, the "census white" Jamaicans assumed that he was of pure white blood. A great banquet was given him at the Myrtle Bank Hotel, which is the last word in swank in Jamaica. All went well until John Hope was called upon to respond to a toast. He began his reply with, "We negroes—." Several people all but collapsed. John Hope was whiter than any of the mulattoes there who had had themselves ruled white. So that if a man as white as that called himself a negro, what about them? Consternation struck the banquet like a blight. Of course, there were real white English and American people there too, and I would have loved to have read their minds at that moment. I certainly would.

The joke about being white on the census records and colored otherwise has its curious angles. The English seem to feel that "If it makes a few of you happy and better colonials to be officially white, very well. You are white on the census rolls." The Englishman keeps on being very polite and cordial to the legal whites in public, but ignores them utterly in private and social life. And the darker negroes do not forget how they came to be white. So I wonder what really is gained by it. George Bernard Shaw on his recent tour observed this class of Jamaicans and called them "those pink people" of Jamaica.

That brings us to the matter of the rooster's nest again. When a Jamaican is born of a black woman and some English or Scotsman, the black mother is literally and figuratively kept out of sight as far as possible, but no one is allowed to forget that white father, however questionable the circumstances of birth. You hear about "My father this and my father that, and my father who was English, you know," until you get the impression that he or she *had* no mother. Black skin is so utterly condemned that the black mother is not going to be mentioned nor exhibited. You get the impression that these virile Englishmen do not require women to reproduce. They

8

just come out to Jamaica, scratch out a nest and lay eggs that hatch out into "pink" Jamaicans.

But a new day is in sight for Jamaica. The black people of Jamaica are beginning to respect themselves. They are beginning to love their own things like their songs, their Anansi stories and proverbs and dances. Jamaican proverbs are particularly rich in philosophy, irony and humor. The following are a few in common use:

1. Rockatone at ribber bottom no know sun hot. (The person in easy circumstances cannot appreciate the sufferings of the poor.)
2. Seven year no 'nough to wash speckle off guinea hen back. (Human nature never changes.)
3. Sharp spur mek maugre horse cut caper. (The pinch of circumstances forces people to do what they thought impossible.)
4. Sickness ride horse come, take foot go away. (It is easier to get sick than it is to get well.)
5. Table napkin want to turn table cloth. (Referring to social climbing.)
6. Bull horn nebber too heavy for him head. (We always see ourselves in a favorable light.)
7. Cock roach nebber in de right befo' fowl. (The oppressor always justifies his oppression of the weak.)
8. If you want fo' lick old woman pot, you scratch him back. (The masculine pronoun is always used for female. Use flattery and you will succeed.)
9. Do fe do make guinea nigger come a' Jamaica. (Fighting among themselves in Africa caused the negroes to be sold into slavery in America.)
10. Dog run for him character; hog run for him life. (It means nothing to you, but everything to me.)
11. Finger nebber say, "look here," him say "look dere." (People always point out the shortcomings of others but never their own.)
12. Cutacoo on man back no yerry what kim massa yerry. (The basket on a man's back does not hear what he hears.)

9

Up until three years ago these proverbs and everything else Jamaican have been lumped with black skins and utterly condemned.

There is Mrs. Norman W. Manley, a real Englishwoman who is capturing Jamaican form in her sculpture. Her work has strength of conception and a delicate skill in execution. Because she used native models, she has been cried down by the "census whites" who know nothing about art but know that they do not like anything dark, however great the art may be. Mrs. Manley's work belongs in New York and London and Paris. It is wasted on Kingston for the most part, but the *West Indian Review,* which is the voice of thinking Jamaica, has found her. That is a very hopeful sign. And there is the yeast of the Bailey Sisters and the Meikle Brothers and their leagues, and influences like the Quill and Ink Club which is actively inviting Jamaica's soul to come out from its hiding place. The Rooster's Nest is bound to be less glamorous in the future.

CHAPTER 2

❖

CURRY GOAT

The very best place to be in all the world is St. Mary's parish, Jamaica. And the best spot in St. Mary's is Port Maria, though all of St. Mary's is fine. Old Maker put himself to a lot of trouble to make that part of the island of Jamaica, for everything there is perfect. The sea is the one true celestial blue, and the shore, the promontories, the rocks and the grass are the models for the rest of the world to take pattern after. If Jamaica is the first island of the West Indies in culture, then St. Mary's is the first parish of Jamaica. The people there are alert, keen, well-read and hospitable.

They did something for me there that has never been done for another woman. They gave me a curry goat feed. That is something utterly masculine in every detail. Even a man takes the part of a woman in the "shay shay" singing and dancing that goes on after the feed.

It was held on a Wednesday night at the house of C. I. Magnus. His bachelor quarters sat upon a hill that overlooked his large banana plantation. I heard that Dr. Leslie, Claude Bell, Rupert Meikle and his two big, handsome brothers and Larry Coke and some others bought up all those goats that

11

were curried for the feed. I have no way of knowing who all chipped in to buy things, but the affair was lavish.

We set out from Port Maria in Claude Bell's car, containing Claude, Dr. Leslie and I. Then Larry Coke overtook us and we ambled along until we ran into something exciting. Just around a bend in the road we came to an arch woven of palm fronds before a gate. There were other arches of the same leading back to a booth constructed in the same manner. It was not quite finished. Men were seated in the yard braiding more palm fronds. A great many people were in the yard, under the palm booth and in the house. Three women with elaborate cakes upon their heads were dancing under the arch at the gate. The cakes were of many layers and one of the cakes was decorated with a veil. The cake-bearers danced and turned under the arch, and turned and danced and sang with the others something about "Let the stranger in." This kept up until an elderly woman touched one of the dancers. Then the one who was touched whirled around gently, went inside the yard and on into the house. Another was touched and turned and she went in and then the third.

"What is going on here?" I asked Claude Bell, and he told me that this was a country wedding. That is, it was the preparation for one. Claude Bell is the Superintendent of Public Works in St. Mary's, so that everybody knows him. He went over and said that we wished to come in and the groom-to-be made us welcome. I asked how was it that they all knew at once who the groom was and they said that he would always be found out front being very proud and expansive and doing all the greeting and accepting all the compliments.

We went inside the house and saw the cakes arranged to keep their vigil for the night. A lighted candle was placed beside the main cake, and it was kept burning all that night. It did add something to the weight of the occasion to drape that bride's cake in a white lace veil and surround it with lights for a night. It made one spectator at least feel solemn about marriage. After being introduced to the shy little bride and shaking hands with the proud groom we went off after promis-

12

ing to come back to the wedding next day.

So on to the Magnus plantation and the curry goat feed. It was after sundown when we arrived. Already some of the others were there before us. Around a fire under a clump of mango trees, two or three Hindoos were preparing the food. Magnus was setting out several dozen quarts of the famous T. T. L. rum, considered the best in Jamaica. They told me that a feed without T. T. L. was just nothing at all. It must be served or it is no proper curry goat feed. The moon rose full and tropical white and under it I could see the musicians huddled under another clump of trees waiting until they should be told to perform.

Finally there were about thirty guests in all including some very pretty half-Chinese girls. The cooks announced and we went inside to eat. Before that everybody had found congenial companions and had wandered around the grounds warming themselves by the moonlight.

It appeared that there must be a presiding officer at a curry goat. Some wanted the very popular Larry Coke, but it seemed that more wanted the more popular Dr. Leslie, so it went that way. He sat at the head of the table and directed the fun. There was a story-telling contest, bits of song, reminiscences that were side splitting and humorous pokes and jibes at each other. All of this came along with the cock soup. This feast is so masculine that chicken soup would not be allowed. It must be soup from roosters. After the cock soup comes ram goat and rice. No nanny goat in this meal either. It is ram goat or nothing. The third spread was banana dumpling with dip-and-flash. That is, you dip your boiled banana in the suruwa sauce, flash off the surplus and take a bite. By that time the place was on fire with life. Every course was being washed down with T. T. L. Wits were marvelously sharpened; that very pretty Lucille Woung was eating out of the same spoon with J. T. Robertson; Reginald Beckford kept on trying to introduce somebody and the others always howled him down because he always got wound up and couldn't find his way out. Finally Dr. Leslie asked him why he never finished and he said "Being a banana man, I have to go around the corner before I get my target." The award for the best story-teller went to Rupert Meikle, but his brother H. O. S. Meikle ran him a close second.

The band began playing outside there in the moonlight and we ran away from the table to see it. You have to see those native Jamaica bands to hear them. They are doing almost as much dancing with the playing as they are playing. As I said before no woman appears with the players, though there is a woman's part in the dancing. That part is taken by a man especially trained for that. The whole thing is strong meat, but compelling. There is some barbaric dancing to magnificent rhythms. They played that famous Jamaican air "Ten Pound Ten," "Donkey Want Water," "Salaam," and "Sally Brown." All strong and raw, but magnificent music and dancing. It is to be remembered that curry goat is a strong feed, so they could not have femalish music around there.

We got home in time to sleep a little before going on to the wedding the next afternoon.

The wedding was at the church and the guests all finally got there by sending one car back and forth several times. The bride came in the last load. There were many, many delays, but finally the couple were married and everybody went back to the house for the reception.

At the house it came to me what a lot of trouble these country people were taking to create the atmosphere of romance and mystery. Here was a couple who were in late middle life, who had lived together so long that they had grown children and were just getting married. Seemingly it all should have been rather drab and matter of fact. Surely there could be no mystery and glamor left for them to find in each other. But the couple and all the district were making believe that there was. It was like sewing ruffles on fence rails. The will to make life beautiful was strong. It happens this way frequently in Jamaica. That is, many couples live together as husband and wife for a generation and then marry. They explain that they always intended to marry, but never had the

14

money. They do not mean by that that they did not have the price of the marriage license. They mean that they did not have the money for the big wedding and all that it means. So they go on raising their children on the understanding that if and when they can afford it they will have the wedding. Sometimes, as in this case, the couple is along in years and with grown children before the money can be spared. In the meanwhile, they live and work together like any two people who have been married by the preacher.

Back at the house everything was very gay with cake and wine and banter. There was a master of ceremonies. The bride's face was covered with her veil. In fact it had never been uncovered. She was made to stand like that and the master of ceremonies received bids on who was to lift her veil first. The highest bidder got the first peep. The first man to peep had bid six shillings. I thought that that was very high for a poor man until I found that on such occasions it was agreed that the word shilling is substituted for pence. It would sound too poor to say pence. He paid his sixpence amid great applause and lifted the bride's veil and peeped and put it back in place. Then the bidding began again and kept up until the master of ceremonies put a stop to it. The bidding had gone on for some time and everyone pretended a curiosity about the youth and glamor they imagined to be hidden under the veil.

After the unveiling of the bride we left. The groom made us promise that we would be present at the "turn thanks." That is a ceremony held at the church on the Sunday after the eighth day after the wedding. Again everybody goes to the church to see the bride again in her finery. The pastor and the Justice of the Peace are there and give the happy couple a lecture on how to live together. But the bride does not wear her veil this time, she is resplendent in her "turn-thanks" hat. The couple are turning thanks for the blessing of getting married.

But we did not go to the turn-thanks. Something happened

in Claude Bell's summer house that rushed me off in another direction.

The next morning after the wedding I was lounging in the summer house and looking at the sea when a young man of St. Mary's dropped in. I do not remember how we got around to it, but the subject of love came up somehow. He let it be known that he thought that women who went in for careers were just so much wasted material. American women, he contended, were destroyed by their brains. But they were only a step or two worse off than the rest of the women of the Western world. He felt it was a great tragedy to look at American women, whom he thought the most beautiful and vivacious women on earth, and then to think what little use they were as women. I had been reclining on my shoulder-blades in a deck chair, but this statement brought me up straight. I assured him that he was talking about what he didn't know.

"Oh, yes, I do," he countered, "I was not born yesterday and my light has not been kept under a bushel, whatever that is."

"You are blaspheming, of course, but go ahead and let me see what you are driving at."

"Oh, these wisdom-wise Western women, afraid of their function in life, are so tiresomely useless! We men do not need your puny brains to settle the affairs of the world. The truth is, it is yet to be proved that you have any. But some of you are clever enough to run mental pawnshops, that is you loan out a certain amount of entertainment and hospitality on some masculine tricks and phrases and later pass them off as your own. Being a woman is the only thing that you can do with any real genius and you refuse to do that."

I tried to name some women of genius but I was cut short. The man was vehement.

"You self-blinded women are like the hen who lived by a sea-wall. She could hear the roar of the breakers but she never flew to the top of the wall to see what it was that made the sound. She said to herself and to all who would listen to her,

16

'The world is something that makes a big noise.' Having arrived at that conclusion, she thought that she had found a great truth and was satisfied for the rest of her life. She died without ever hopping upon the sea-wall to look and see if there was anything to the world besides noise. She had lived beside the biggest thing in the world and never saw it."

"So you really feel that all women are dumb, I see."

"No, not all women. Just those who think that they are the most intelligent, as a rule. And the Occidental men are stupid for letting you ruin yourselves and the men along with you."

Of course I did not agree with him and so I gave him my most aggravating grunt. I succeeded in snorting a bit of scorn into it. I went on to remark that Western men, especially American men, probably knew as much about love as the next one.

Then *he* snorted scornfully. He went on to say that the men of the West and American men particularly knew nothing about the function of love in the scheme of life. I cut in to mention Bernarr McFadden. He snorted again and went on. Even if a few did have some inkling, they did not know how to go about it. He was very vehement about it. He said we insulted God's intentions so grossly that it was a wonder that western women had not given up the idea of mating and marriage altogether. But many men, and consequently women, in Jamaica were better informed. I wanted to know how it was that these Jamaicans had been blessed beyond all others on this side of the big waters, and he replied that there were oriental influences in Jamaica that had been at work for generations, so that Jamaica was prepared to teach continental America something about love. Saying this, he left the summer house and strode towards his car which was parked in the drive. But he could not say all that to me and then walk off like that. I caught him on the running board of his car and carried him back. When I showed a disposition to listen instead of scoffing, we had a very long talk. That is, he talked and I listened most respectfully.

Before he drove away he had told me about the specialists

who prepare young girls for love. This practise is not universal in Jamaica, but it is common enough to speak of here. I asked to be shown, and he promised to use his influence in certain quarters that I might study the matter at close range. It was arranged for me to spend two weeks with one of the practitioners and learn what I could in that time. There are several of these advisors scattered about that section of Jamaica, but people not inside the circle know nothing about what is going on.

These specialists are always women. They are old women who have lived with a great deal of subtlety themselves. Having passed through the active period and become widows, or otherwise removed from active service, they are re-inducted in an advisory capacity.

The young girl who is to be married shortly or about to become the mistress of an influential man is turned over to the old woman for preparation. The wish is to bring complete innocence and complete competence together in the same girl. She is being educated for her life work under experts.

For a few days the old woman does not touch her. She is taking her pupil through the lecture stages of instruction. Among other things she is told that the consummation of love cannot properly take place in bed. Soft beds are not for love. They are comforts for the old and lack-a-daisical. Also she is told that her very position must be an invitation. When her lord and master enters the chamber she must be on the floor with only her shoulders and the soles of her feet touching the floor. It is *so* that he must find her. Not lying sluggishly in bed like an old cow, and hiding under the covers like a thief who has snatched a bit of beef from the market stall. The exact posture is demonstrated over and over again. The girl must keep on trying until she can assume it easily. In addition she is instructed at length on muscular control inside her body and out, and this also was rehearsed again and again, until it was certain that the young candidate had grasped all that was meant.

The last day has arrived. This is the day of the wedding. The old woman gives her first a "balm bath," that is, a hot herb bath. Only these old women know the secret of which herbs to use to steep a virgin for marriage. It is intended, this bath is, to remove everything mental, spiritual and physical that might work against a happy mating. No soap is used at this point. It is a medicinal sweating tub to open the pores and stimulate the candidate generally. Immediately that the virgin leaves the bath she is covered and sweated for a long time. Then she is bathed again in soapy water.

Now the subtleties begin. Jamaica has a grass called khus khus. The sweet scent from its roots is the very odor of seduction. Days before the old woman has prepared an extract from these roots in oil and it is at hand in a bowl. She begins and massages the girl from head to foot with this fragrant unction. The toes, the fingers, the thighs, and there is a special motional treatment for every part of the body. It seemed to me that the breasts alone were ignored. But when the body massage is over, she returns to the breasts. These are bathed several times in warm water in which something special had been steeped. After that they are massaged ever so lightly with the very tips of the fingers dipped in khus khus. This fingertip motion is circular and moves ever towards the nipple. Arriving there, it begins over and over again. Finally the breasts are cupped and the nipples flicked with a warm feather back and forth, back and forth until there was a reaction to stimulation. The breasts stiffened and pouted, while the rest of the body relaxed.

But the old woman is not through. She carries this same light-fingered manipulation down the body and the girl swoons. She is revived by a mere sip of rum in which a single leaf of ganga has been steeped. Ganga is that "wisdom weed" which has been brought from the banks of the sacred Ganges to Jamaica. The girl revives and the massage continues. She swoons again and is revived. But she is not aware of the work-a-day world. She is in a twilight state of awareness, cushioned on a cloud of love thoughts.

Now the old woman talks to her again. It is a brief summation of all that has been said and done for the past week.

19

"You feel that you are sick now but that is because the reason for which you were made has not been fulfilled. You cannot be happy nor complete until that has happened. But the success of everything is with you. You have the happiest duty of any creature on earth and you must perform it well. The whole duty of a woman is love and comfort. You were never intended for anything else. You are made for love and comfort. Think of yourself in that way and no other. If you do as I teach you, heaven is with you and the man who is taking you to his house to love and comfort him. He is taking you there for that reason and for no other. That is all that men ever want women for, love and softness and peace, and you must not fail him."

The old instructor ran over physical points briefly again. She stressed the point that there must be no fear. If the girl experienced any pain, then she had failed to learn what she had been taught with so much comfort and repetition. *There was nothing to fear.* Love killed no one. Rather it made them beautiful and happy. She said this over and over again.

Still stressing relaxed muscles, the old woman took a broad white band of cloth and wound it tightly about the loins of the girl well below the navel. She circled the body with the band perhaps four times and then secured it with safety pins. It was wound very tightly and seemed useless at first. All the time that this was being done the girl was crying to be taken to her future husband. The old woman seemingly ignored her and massaged her here and there briefly.

They began to put her wedding clothes upon the girl. The old woman was almost whispering to her that she was the most important part of all creation, and that she must accept her role gladly. She must not make war on her destiny and creation. The impatient girl was finally robed for her wedding and she was led out of the room to face the public and her man. But here went no frightened, shaking figure under a veil. No nerve-racked female behaving as if she approached her doom. This young, young thing went forth with the assurance of infinity. And she had such eagerness in her as she went!

CHAPTER 3

❖

HUNTING THE WILD HOG

If you go to Jamaica you are going to want to visit the Maroons at Accompong. They are under the present rule of Colonel Rowe, who is an intelligent, cheerful man. But I warn you in advance not to ride his wall-eyed, pot-bellied mule. He sent her to meet me at the end of the railroad line so that I would not have to climb that last high peak on foot. That was very kind of Colonel Rowe, and I appreciate his hospitality, but that mule of his just did not fall in with the scheme somehow. The only thing that kept her from throwing me, was the fact that I fell off first. And the only thing that kept her from kicking me, biting me and trampling me under foot after I fell off was the speed with which I got out of the way after the fall. I think she meant to chase me straight up that mountain afterwards, but one of Colonel Rowe's boys grabbed her bridle and held her while I withdrew. She was so provoked when she saw me escaping, that she reared and pitched till the saddle and everything else fell off except the halter. Maybe it was that snappy orange-colored four-in-hand tie that I was wearing that put her against me. I hate to think it was my face. Whatever it was, she started to rolling her

21

pop-eyes at me as soon as I approached her. One thing I will say for her, she was not deceitful. She never pretended to like me. I got upon her back without the least bit of co-operation from her. She was against it from the start and let me know. I was the one who felt we might be sisters under the skin. She corrected all of that about a half mile down the trail and so I had to climb that mountain into Accompong on my own two legs.

The thing that struck me forcefully was the feeling of great age about the place. Standing on that old parade ground, which is now a cricket field, I could feel the dead generations crowding me. Here was the oldest settlement of freedmen in the Western world, no doubt. Men who had thrown off the bands of slavery by their own courage and ingenuity. The courage and daring of the Maroons strike like a purple beam across the history of Jamaica. And yet as I stood there looking into the sea beyond Black river from the mountains of St. Catherine, and looking at the thatched huts close at hand, I could not help remembering that a whole civilization and the mightiest nation on earth had grown up on the mainland since the first runaway slave had taken refuge in these mountains. They were here before the Pilgrims landed on the bleak shores of Massachusetts. Now, Massachusetts had stretched from the Atlantic to the Pacific and Accompong had remained itself.

I settled down at the house of Colonel Rowe to stay a while. I knew that he wondered about me—why I had come there and what I wanted. I never told him. He told me how Dr. Herskovits had been there and passed a night with him; how some one else had spent three weeks to study their dances and how much money they had spent in doing this. I kept on day by day saying nothing as to why I had come. He offered to stage a dance for me also. I thanked him, but declined. I did not tell him that I was too old a hand at collecting to fall for staged-dance affairs. If I do not see a dance or a ceremony in its natural setting and sequence, I do not bother. Self-experience has taught me that those staged affairs are never the same as the real thing. I had been told by some of the Maroons that their big dance, and only real one, came on January 6th. That was when they went out to the wooded peaks the day before and came back with individual masques and costumes upon them. They are summoned from their night long retreat by the Abeng, or Conk-shell. Then there is a day of Afro-Karamante' dancing and singing, and feasting on jerked pork.

What I was actually doing was making general observations. I wanted to see what the Maroons were like, really. Since they are a self-governing body, I wanted to see how they felt about education, transportation, public health and democracy. I wanted to see their culture and art expressions and knew that if I asked for anything especially, I would get something out of context. I had heard a great deal about their primitive medicines and wanted to know about that. I was interested in vegetable poisons and their antidote. So I just sat around and waited.

There are other Maroon settlements besides Accompong, but England made treaty with Accompong only. There are now about a thousand people there and Colonel Rowe governs the town according to Maroon law and custom. The whole thing is very primitive, but he told me he wished to bring things up to date. There is a great deal of lethargy, however, and utter unconsciousness of what is going on in the world outside.

For instance, there was not a stove in all Accompong. The cooking, ironing and whatever else is done, is done over an open fire with the women squatting on their haunches inhaling the smoke. I told Rowe that he ought to buy a stove himself to show the others what to do. He said he could not afford one. Stoves are not customary in Jamaica outside of good homes in the cities anyway. They are imported luxuries. I recognized that and took another tack. We would build one! I designed an affair to be made of rock and cement and Colonel Rowe and some men he gathered undertook to make it. We sent out to the city and bought some sheet tin for the stove pipe and the pot-holes. I measured the bottoms of the pots and

23

designed a hole to fit each of the three. The center hole was for the great iron pot, and then there were two other holes of different sizes. Colonel Rowe had some lime there, and he sent his son and grandchildren out to collect more rocks. His son-in-law-to-be mixed the clay and lime and in a day the furnace-like stove was built. The kitchen house lacking a floor anyway, the stove was built clear across one side of the room so that there was room on top of it for pots and pans not in use. The pot-holes were lined with tin so that the pots would not break the mortar. Then we left it a day to dry. We were really joyful when we fired it the next day and found out that it worked. Many of the Maroons came down to look at the miracle. There were pots boiling on the fire; no smoke in the room, but a great column of black smoke shooting out of the stove pipe which stuck out of the side of the house.

In the building of the stove I came to know little Tom, the Colonel's grandson. He is a most lovable and pathetic little figure. He is built very sturdy and is over strong for his age. He lives at the house of his grandfather because he has no mother and his father will not work for himself, let alone for his son. He is not only lazy and shiftless, he is disloyal to Colonel Rowe who has wasted a great deal of money on him. Little Tom is there among more favored grandchildren and his life is wretched. The others may strike him, kick him, I even saw one of them burn him without being punished for it. He is fed last and least and is punished severely for showing any resentment towards the treatment he gets from his cousins. They are the children of the Colonel's favorite child, his youngest daughter, and she is there to watch and see that her three darlings are not in any way annoyed by Tom. He was so warmed by the little comfort he got out of me that I wished very much to adopt him. He is just full of love and goodwill and nowhere to use it. It was most pointedly scorned when he offered it. When I asked why all this cruelty to such a small child, they answered with that excuse of all cruel people, "He is a very bad child. He has criminal tendencies. If we do not treat him harshly he will grow up to be nothing but a brute."

So they abuse him and beat him and scorn him for his future good.

It was not long before I noticed people who were not Maroons climbing the mountain road past the Colonel's gate. I found that they were coming to Accompong for treatment. Colonel Rowe began to tell me about it and soon after that I met the chief medicine man. Colonel Rowe told me he was a liar and over ambitious politically, but that he really knew his business as a primitive doctor. Later I found that to be true. He was a wonderful doctor, but he wanted to be the chief. At one time he had seized the treaty that was signed long ago between England and the Maroons and attempted to make himself the chief. This had failed and he was still not too sincere in his dealings with Colonel Rowe, but their outward relations were friendly enough. So he took to coming around to talk with me.

First we talked about things that are generally talked about in Jamaica. Brother Anansi, the Spider, that great cultural hero of West Africa who is personated in Haiti by Ti Malice and in the United States by Brer Rabbit. About duppies and how and where they existed, and how to detect them. I learned that they lived mostly in silk-cotton trees and in almond trees. One should never plant either of those trees too close to the house because the duppies will live in them and "throw heat" on the people as they come and go about the house. One can tell when a duppy is near by the feeling of heat and the swelling of the head. A duppy can swell one's head to a huge thing just by being near. But if one drinks tea from that branch of the snake weed family known as Spirit Weed, duppies can't touch you. You can walk into a room where all kinds of evil and duppies are and be perfectly safe.

The Whooping Boy came up. Some say that the Whooping Boy is the great ghost of a "penner" (a cow-herd). He can be seen and heard only in August. Then he can be heard at a great distance whooping, cracking his whip and "penning" his ghost cows. He frightens real cows when he "pauses" (cracks) his whip.

25

The Three-leg-Horse manifests himself just before Christmas, a woman said that "him drag hearse when him was alive" (he was used to pull a hearse when he was alive) and that he did not appear until one in the morning. From then until four o'clock he ranged the highways and might attack a wayfarer if he chanced to meet one. If he chases you, you can only escape by running under a fence. If you climb over it, he will jump the fence after you.

But the men all looked at each other and laughed. They denied that the Three-leg-Horse ever hurt any one. Girls, they said, were afraid of it, but it was not dangerous. He appeared around Christmas time to enjoy himself. When the country people masque with the horse head and cow head for the parades, the three-legged-Horse wrapped himself up in a sheet and went along with them in disguise. But if one looked close he could be distinguished from the people in masques, because he was two legs in front and one behind. His gait is a jump and a leap that sounds "Te-coom-tum! Te-coom-tum!" In some parts of Jamaica he is called "The Three-legged Aurelia," and they, the people, dance in the road with the expectation that the spirit horse will come before seven o'clock at night, and pass the night revelling in masquerade. Two main singers and dancers lead the rest in this outdoor ceremony and it is all quite happy.

All in all from what I heard, I have the strong belief that the Three-legged-Horse is a sex symbol and that the celebration of it is a fragment of some West African puberty ceremony for boys. All the women feared it. They had all been told to fear it. But none of the men were afraid at all. Perhaps under those masques and robes of the male revellers is some culture secret worth knowing. But it was quite certain that my sex barred me from getting anything more than the other women knew. (I found the "Société Trois-jambe" in Haiti also but could learn nothing definite of its inner meaning.)

But the Rolling-Calf is the most celebrated of all the apparitions in Jamaica. His two great eyes are balls of fire, he moves like lightning and "he has no abiding city." He wanders all over Jamaica. The Rolling-Calf is a plague put upon the earth to trouble people, and he will always be here. He keeps chiefly to the country parts and comes whirling down hills to the terror of the wayfarer. But the biggest harm that he does is to spoil the shape of the female dog. He harms the dog; she squeals and the owner goes into the yard and sees nothing but a flame of fire vanishing in the distance. The dog's shape is ruined, and she will never have puppies again. Rolling-Calf can be seen most any moonlight night roving the lanes of the countryside.

After a night or two of talk, the medicine man began to talk about his profession and soon I was a spectator while he practised his arts. I learned of the terrors and benefits of Cow-itch and of that potent plant known as Madame Fate. "It is a cruel weed," he told me, and I found he had understated its powers. I saw him working with the Cassada bean, the Sleep-and-Wake, Horse Bath and Marjo Bitters. Boil five leaves of Horse Bath and drink it with a pinch of salt and your kidneys are cleaned out magnificently. Boil six leaves and drink it and you will die. Marjo Bitter is a vine that grows on rocks. Take a length from your elbow to your wrist and make a tea and it is a most excellent medicine. Boil a length to the palm of your hand and you are violently poisoned. He used the bark of a tree called Jessamy, well boiled for a purgative. Twelve minutes after drinking the wine glass of medicine the purge begins and keeps up for five days without weakening the patient or griping.

I went with him to visit the "God wood" tree (Birch Gum). It is called "God Wood" because it is the first tree that ever was made. It is the original tree of good and evil. He had a covenant with that tree on the sunny side. We went there more than once. One day we went there to prevent the enemies of the medicine man from harming him. He took a strong nail and a hammer with him and drove the nail into the tree up to the head with three strokes; dropped the hammer and walked away rapidly without looking back. Later on, he sent me back to fetch the hammer to him.

27

He proved to me that all you need to do to poison a person and leave them horribly swollen was to touch a chip of this tree to their skin while they were sweating. It was uncanny.

We went to see a girl sick in bed. The medicine man was not in high favor with the mother; but Accompong is self-sufficient. They keep to their primitive medicine particularly. He went in and looked down on the sick girl and said that it was a desperate case, but he could cure her. But first the mother must chop down the papaya tree that was growing just outside of the bed-room window. The mother objected. That was the only tree that she had and she needed the fruit for food. The medicine man said that she *must* cut it down. It was too close to the house to begin with. It sapped the strength of the inmates. And it was a tall tree, taller than the house and she ought to know that if a paw paw or papaya tree were allowed to grow taller than the house, that somebody would die. The mother hooted that off. That tree had nothing to do with the sickness of her daughter. If he did not know what to do for her, let him say so and go on about his business and she would call in someone else. If he knew what to do, get busy and stop wasting time on the paw paw tree.

Day by day the young woman grew weaker in spite of all that was done for her. Finally she called her mother to the bed and said, "Mama, cut the tree for me, please."

"I will do anything to make you well again, daughter, but cutting that tree is so unnecessary. It is nothing but a belief of ignorant people. Why must I cut down the tree that gives us so much food?"

Several times a day, now the girl begged her mother to cut the tree. She said if she were strong enough she would find the machete and chop it down herself. She cried all the time and followed her mother with her eyes pleading.

"Mama, I am weaker today than I was yesterday. Mama, please chop down the tree. Since I was a baby I have heard that the paw paw was an unlucky tree."

"And ever since you were a baby you have been eating the fruit," the mother retorted. "I spend every ha' penny I can find to make you well, and now you want me to do a foolish thing like killing my tree. No!"

"Mama, if it is cut I will live. If you don't cut it I will die."

The girl grew weaker and finally died. The grief stricken mother rushed outside with the machete and chopped down the tree. It was lying in the yard full of withered leaves and fruit when the girl was buried. But even then the woman was not completely convinced. She thinks often that it might have been coincidence. I passed her house on my way to visit the daughter of Esau Rowe, who is the brother of the Colonel. The mourning mother was looking down at the great mass of withered fruit when I spoke to her. She did not exactly ask me for a little money, but she opened the way for me to offer it. I gave her three shillings with the utmost joy because I knew she needed it.

"Thank you," she said half choked with tears. "My girl is dead. I—I don't know—" she looked down at the tree, "I don't know if it was I who could have saved her. I wish I could know. Have you noticed how hungry a person can be the next day after a funeral? But I don't suppose you could know about such things at all."

One night Colonel Rowe, Medicine Man and I sat on what is going to be a porch when the Colonel finds enough money to finish it, looking down on the world and talking. The tree frogs on the mountainside opposite were keeping up a fearful din. Colonel Rowe said it was a sign of rain. I said I hoped not, for then all Accompong would become a sea of sticky mud. I expressed the wish that the frogs shut up. Colonel Rowe said that Medicine Man could make them hush but that would have no effect upon the weather.

"He can stop those frogs over on that other peak?" I asked.

"Yes, he can stop them at will. I have seen him do it, many times."

"Can you, really?" I turned to Medicine Man.

"That is very easy to do."

"Do it for me, then. I'd like to see that done."

He stood up and turned his face toward the mountain peak

29

opposite and made a quick motion with one hand and seemed to inhale deeply from his waist up. He held this pose stiffly for a moment, then relaxed. The millions of frogs in the trees on that uninhabited peak opposite us ceased chirping as suddenly as a lightning flash. Medicine Man sat back down and would have gone on telling me the terrible things that the milk from the stalk of the paw paw tree does to male virility, but I stopped him. I had to listen to this sudden silence for a while.

"Oh, they will not sing again until I permit them," Medicine Man assured me. "They will not sing again until I pass the house of Esau on my way home. When I get there I will whistle so that you will know that I am there. Then they will commence again."

We talked on awhile about the poisonous effect of Dumb Cane and of bissy (Kola nut) as an antidote, and how to kill with horse hair and bamboo dust. I was glad, however, when Medicine Man rose to go.

"Oh, you need not worry," Colonel Rowe told me, "he can do what he says."

He walked out of Colonel's tumbledown gate and began to climb the mountain in that easy way that Maroons have from a life time of mountain climbing, and grew dim in the darkness. After a few minutes we heard the whistle way up the path and like an orchestra under the conductor's baton, the frog symphony broke out. And it was certainly going on when I finally dropped off to sleep.

I kept on worrying the Colonel about jerked pig. I wanted to eat some of it. The jerked pig of the Maroons is famous beyond the seas. He explained to me that the Maroons did not jerk domestic pork. It was the flesh of the wild hog that they dressed that way. Why not kill a wild hog then, and jerk it, I wanted to know.

"Mama! That is much harder than you think. Wild hog is very sensible creature. He does not let you kill him so easily. Besides, he lives in the Cock-Pit country and that is hard travelling even for us here who are accustomed to rocks and mountains."

30

"And there are not so many now as there use to be. We have killed many and then the mongoose also kill some," Medicine Man added.

"A mongoose kill a wild hog? I cannot believe it!" I exclaimed.

"Oh, that mongoose, he a terrible insect," Medicine Man said. "He is very destroyfull, Mama! If the pig is on her feet she will tear that mongoose to pieces, Mama! But when she is giving birth the mongoose run there and seize the little pig as it is born and eat it. So we do not have so many wild pig now."

But I kept on talking and begging and coaxing until a hunting party was organized. A hunting party usually consists of four hunters, the dogs and the baggage boy, but this one was augmented because few of the men had much work to do at the moment, and then I was going, and women do go on hog hunts in Accompong. If I had had more sense I would not have gone either, but you live and learn. The party was made up of Colonel Rowe, his brother Esau, Tom Colly, his two sons-in-law, his prospective son-in-law, his son who acted as baggage boy and your humble servant.

The day before, old machetes were filed down to spear heads and made razor sharp. Then they were attached to long handles and thus became spears. All of this *had* to be done the day before, especially the sharpening of all blades. If you sharpen your cutting weapons on the day of the hunt, your dogs will be killed by the hog.

We were up before dawn the day of the hunt, and with all equipment, food for several days, cooking utensils, weapons, and the like, we found our way by stealth to the graveyard. Medicine Man was to meet us there and he was true to his word. There the ancestors of all the hunters were invoked to strengthen their arms. The graves are never marked in Accompong for certain reasons, and thus if a person does not himself know the graves of his relatives there is no way of finding out. One of the men had been away in Cuba for several years and could not find his father's grave. That was consid-

31

ered not so good, but not too bad either. No attempt was made to guess at it for fear of waking up the wrong duppy, who might do him harm. So the ceremony over, it was necessary for us to be out and gone before anyone in Accompong should speak to us. That would be the worst of luck. In fact, we were all prepared to turn back in case it happened to us. Some of us would be expected to be killed before we returned.

The baggage-boy was carrying our food which was not very heavy for the Maroons are splendid human engines. Not a fat person in all Maroon town. That comes, I suppose, from climbing mountains and a simple diet. They are lean, tough and durable. They can march, fight or work for hours on a small amount of food. The food on the hunt was corn pone, Cassada-by-me (Cassava bread), green plantain, salt, pimento and other spices to cure the hog when and if we caught him, *and* coffee. The baggage boy carried the iron skillet and the coffee pot also. The hunters carried their own guns and blades. I stumbled along with my camera and note book and a few little womanish things like comb and tooth brush and a towel.

We struck out back of the cemetery and by full sun-up we were in the Cock-Pit country. There is no need for me to try to describe the Cock-Pits. They are great gaping funnel-shaped holes in the earth that cover miles and miles of territory in this part of Jamaica. They are monstrous things that have never been explored. The rock formations are hardly believable. Mr. Astly Clerk is all for exploiting them as a tourist lure. But very few tourists have the stamina necessary to visit even one of them let alone descend into these curious, deep openings. They are monstrous.

By the time we reached the first of the Cock-Pits I was tired but I did not let on to the men. I thought that they would soon be tired too and I could get a rest without complaining. But they marched on and on. The dogs ran here and there but no hog sign. As the country became more rocky and full of holes and jags and points and loose looking boulders, I thought more and more how nice it would be to be back in Accompong.

Around noon, we halted briefly, ate and marched on. I suggested to Colonel Rowe that perhaps all the hogs had been killed already and we might be wasting our time. I let him know that I would not hold the party responsible if they killed no hogs. We had tried and now we could return with colors flying. He just looked at me and laughed. "Why," he said, "this is too soon to expect to find hog sign. Sometimes we are out four days before we even pick up the sign. If we pick up the hog sign tomorrow before night, we will have a luck."

And four more hours till sun-down!

We picked up no hog sign that day, but the men found a nest of wild bees in a tree growing out of the wall down inside a Cock-Pit. Everybody was delighted over the find. I asked them how would they get it. They tried several times to climb down to it but the wall was too sheer and the tree leaned too far out to climb into it. So Colly let himself be swung head foremost over the precipice by his heels and he was pulled up with the dripping honey combs. I had to look away. It was too much for my nerves, but no one else seemed to think anything of the feat.

While they were eating the honey, I sprawled out on a big hot rock to rest and the Colonel noticed it and ordered the men to build a hut for the night. It was near sun-down anyway.

The men took their machetes and chopped down enough branches to make a small shack and inside of an hour it was ready for use.

We found no hog sign the second day and I lost my Kodak somewhere. Maybe I threw it away. My riding boots were chafing my heels and I was sore all over. But those Maroons were fresh as daisies and swinging along singing their Karamante' songs. The favorite one means "We we are coming, oh." It says in Karamanti, "Blue Yerry, ai! Blue Yerry Gallo, Blue Yerry!"

It was near dark on the third day the dogs picked up the hog sign. No sight of him, you understand. They struck a scent and began to dash about like ferrets hungry for blood. But it was too late for even a Maroon to do anything about it. The men built the hut dead on the trail and we settled down for the night. Esau explained that they built the hut on the trail for a purpose. He said that the wild hog is an enchanted beast. He has his habits and does not change them. He has several hiding places along one trail and works from one to the other. When he reaches the limit of his range, he is bound to double back on his trail, seeking one of his other hideaways. He can go a long time without food but he must have water. And so if the dogs keep after him he has no time to hunt water. When there is little rain and the waterholes are dried up, he will climb the rocks and drink the water from Wild Pines (a species of orchid). But it takes time for him to find these plants. He cannot do it with dogs at his heels. The hunters must not sleep too soundly during the night as the hog will repass and they will not know it. He is very shrewd. When he gets near the camp and smells the smoke he will climb higher and pass the camp higher up the mountain and be lost before morning.

We did not sleep much that night. And I suppose it was mostly my fault that we didn't. I was inside the hut by myself for one thing and I was a little scared because the men had told me scary things about hogs. They had said that when a wild boar, harassed by the dogs and hunter, turns back down the trail, you must be prepared to give him the trail or kill him. His hide was tough and unless the bullet struck squarely and in a vital spot, it might be deflected. Then the men had to go in with their knives and spears and kill or be killed. I was afraid that the men would go to sleep and the boar be upon us before we knew it. So I kept awake and kept the others awake by talking and asking questions. We could hear the dogs at a distance, barking and charging and parrying. So the night passed.

The next day the chase was really hot. About noon the party divided. Colonel Rowe with three men went ahead to catch up with the dogs and see if the hog had made a stand. Esau, Colly and Tom stayed with me. That is, they stayed back to tackle the brute in case he doubled back on his track. We heard a great deal of noise far ahead, but no sound of shots nor anything conclusive. By three o'clock, however, the sounds were coming nearer, and the men looked after their guns. Then we heard a terrific and prolonged battle and the barking of the dogs ceased.

"Sounds like he has killed the dogs," said Esau.

"Killed five dogs?" I asked.

"If he is a big one, that would not be hard for him to do," Esau said. "When he gets desperate he will kill anything that stands in his way. But he will not kill the dogs if he can get at the hunter. He knows that the hunter is his real enemy. Sometimes he will charge the dogs, and swerve so fast that the hunter is caught off guard, and attack. A man is in real danger there."

It was not long after that, that we heard deep panting. It was a long way off but it seemed upon us. There was a huge boulder over to the right and I moved nearer to it so that I might hide behind it if necessary after seeing the wild boar approach and pass. The panting came nearer. Now we could hear him trotting and dislodging small stones. The men got ready to meet the charge. The boar with his huge, curving tusks dripping with dogs' blood came charging down upon us. I had never pictured anything so huge, so fierce nor so fast. Everybody cleared the way. He had come too fast for Esau to get good aim on a vital spot.

Just around a huge rock he whirled about. He made two complete circles faster than thought and backed into a small opening in the rock. He had made his stand and resolved to fight. Only his snout was visible from where we were. The men crept closer and Esau chanced a shot. The bullet nicked his nose and the shocking power of it knocked the hog to his knees. We rushed forward, the men expecting to finish him off with the knives. At that moment he leaped up and charged the crowd. I raced back to the big rock and scrambled up. What was going on behind my back I did not know until I got on top of the rock and looked back. Tom had scurried to safety

35

also. Colly had not quite made it. The hog had cut the muscle in the calf of his leg and he was down. But Esau rushed in and almost pressed the muzzle of his rifle against the head of the boar and fired. The hog made a half turn and fell. Esau shot him again to make sure and he scarcely twitched after that.

While we were doing the best we could for Colly, the others came. They had heard the shooting. As soon as Colly was made as comfortable as possible, the men supported him and all made a circle around the fallen boar. They shook each other's hand most solemnly across the body of the hog and kissed each other for dangers past. All this was done with the utmost gravity. Finally Colonel Rowe said, "Well, we got him. We have a luck."

Then all of the men began to cut dry wood for a big fire. When the fire began to be lively, they cut green bush of a certain kind. They put the pig into the fire on his side and covered him with green bush to sweat him so that they could scrape off the hair. When one side was thoroughly cleaned, they scraped the other side and then washed the whole to a snowy white and gutted the hog. Everything was now done in high good humor. No effort was made to save the chitterlings and hasslets, which were referred to as "the fifth quarter," because there was no way to handle it on the march. All of the bones were removed, seasoned and dried over the fire so that they could be taken home. The meat was then seasoned with salt, pepper and spices and put over the fire to cook. It was such a big hog that it took nearly all night to finish cooking. It required two men to turn it over when necessary. While it was being cooked and giving off delicious odors, the men talked and told stories and sang songs. One told the story of Paul Bogle, the Jamaican hero of the war of 1797 who made such a noble fight against the British. Unable to stop the fighting until they could capture the leader, they finally appealed to their new allies, the Maroons, who some say betrayed Bogle into the hands of the English. Paul Bogle never knew how it was that he was surprised by the English in a cave and taken. He was hanged with his whole family and the war stopped.

Towards morning we ate our fill of jerked pork. It is more delicious than our barbecue. It is hard to imagine anything better than pork the way the Maroons jerk it. When we had eaten all that we could hold, the rest was packed up with the bones and we started the long trek back to Accompong. My blistered feet told me time and time again that we would never get there, but we finally did. What was left of the wild pig was given to the families and friends of the hunters. They never sell it because they say they hunt for fun. We came marching in singing the Karamante' songs.

> Blue yerry, ai
> Blue yerry
> Blue yerry, gallo
> Blue yerry!

CHAPTER 4

✣

NIGHT SONG AFTER DEATH

The most universal ceremony in Jamaica is an African survival called "The Nine Night." Minor details vary according to parish and district, but in the main it is identical all over the island. In reality it is old African ancestor worship in fragmentary form. The West African tradition of appeasing the spirit of the dead lest they do the living a mischief.

Among the upper classes it has degenerated into something that approximates the American wake, with this one difference: when the people who attend wakes leave the house of mourning they always call out a cheerful goodbye to the family. In Jamaica any form of goodbye is taboo. Even the family and housemates, after everyone else is gone, go to their separate rooms without taking leave of each other. Then one by one the windows and doors are slowly closed in silence. The lights in the various rooms go out in the same way so that the house is gradually darkened. The dead is dismissed.

But the barefoot people, the dwellers in wattled huts, the donkey riders, are at great pains to observe every part of the ancient ceremony as it has been handed down to them. Let me speak of one that I saw in St. Thomas.

This man had died in the hospital some distance from home. He was as poor in death as he had been in life. He had walked barefooted all his days so now there would be no hearse, no car, no cart—not even a donkey to move this wretched clay. Well then, a rude stretcher was made out of a sheet and two bamboo poles and men set out on foot to bring the body home. There are always more men than donkeys.

According to custom, several people from the district went along with the body-bearers to sing along the road with the body. The rest of the district were to meet them halfway. It is a rigid rule that the whole district must participate in case of death. All kinds of bad feelings are suspended for the time being so that they sing together with the dead.

The news of his death had come to his woman near sundown so that many things had to be done at night that are usually done in daylight. That is, make coffee, mix butter-dough, provide rum and bread for the "set up." Some folks had to stay behind to look after this.

The bearers and these folks had been gone a long time when we others set out to meet them half way. Two or three naked lights or flambeaux were among us but nobody felt the need of them. A little cement bridge had been agreed upon as the halfway mark, so we halted there to wait. Perhaps it seemed longer than it really was because people saved up the entertainment inside them for the time when the body would arrive. So we were a sort of sightless, soundless, shapeless, stillness there in the dark, wishing for life.

At last a way-off whisper began to put on flesh. In the space of a dozen breaths the keening harmony was lapping at our ears. Somebody among us struck matches and our naked lights flared. The shapeless crowd-mass became individuals. A hum seemed to rise from the ground around us and became singing in answer to the coming singers and in welcome to the dead.

The corpse might have been an African monarch on safari, the way he came borne in his hammock. The two crowds became one. Fresh shoulders eagerly took up the burden and

40

all voices agreed on one song. Then there was a jumbled motion that finally straightened out into some sort of a marching order with singing. Harmony rained down on sea and shore. The mountains of St. Thomas heaved up in the moonlessness; the smoking flambeaux splashed the walking herd; bare feet trod the road in soundless rhythm and the dead man rode like a Pharaoh—his rags and his wretchedness gilded in glory.

The less fortunate of the district who for one reason or another could not help with the singing on the road were waiting for us at the house. The widow stood in the inner door and cried in a ceremonial way. Her head was draped in a bath towel in such a way that at a short distance it looked like a shaggy white wig.

Everything that could be done was already done because the Nanas, or old nurses of the district, had charge. There was a strong flavor of matriarchal rule about the place. Unconscious or not, an acknowledgment of the priestess ran through it all. There was one who seemed especially to have authority over the rest. She conferred with the wife in a whisper for a moment and then ordered several women to make a shirt for the dead man out of cloth that she produced from nowhere it seemed. She turned from that to other things. But even in the midst of the much-do she had time to observe that only one woman was working on the shirt. To be sure the lone worker was most skillful with her needle, but the Nana stopped her and glared all about her at the other women.

"One woman no make shirt for dead." She accused the others with a look. "What for do?" (What can I do about it?) asked the efficient seamstress. "Them don't help me."

Everybody knew it was bad luck for only one woman to sew a garment for the dead. It exposed her to spite-work from the ghost of the departed. They were being a little lazy, that was all. But they did go to work with a will when the Nana got in behind them. "I tell you to make shirt, and you *make* shirt!" she scolded. "My word must stand for dominate." (My word must rule.)

41

The other nanas were washing the body. The Nana-Superior stopped them while the body was being dried with a towel. They did nothing right unless she watched them every minute, she complained. Where were the lime and the nutmeg, she demanded to know? Could a person be called ready for burial when his nose, mouth, under his arms and between his legs had not been rubbed with slices of lime and a nutmeg? Of course not! The women explained to her that lime and nutmeg had not been provided by the wife of the deceased. What could they do about it? Nana ran somebody out to pick some off of anybody's tree. The messenger was not to come back without it. The body must be prepared in the ceremonial way, and no other, Must do!

The burial was to take place in the yard as is usual among the common people of Jamaica, but the grave could not be opened until morning. So Nana sent men out to gather lumber for the coffin. Boards were bought until there was no more money. Then the rest were gifts from backyards, or just scraped up from here and there until the coffin was ready for the body.

When it came time to place the body in the coffin there was a great deal of talk back and forth. Some few said that he had been a fairly good man and that they were sure that once buried, he would not return. All the trouble of keeping the ghost, or duppy, in the grave was unnecessary. But the majority were for taking no chances. Every precaution for keeping duppies in graves must be taken. So as soon as the body was placed in the coffin, the pillow with the parched peas, corn and coffee beans sewed inside it was placed under his head. Then they took stronger methods. They took four short nails and drove one in each cuff of the shirt as close to the hand as possible to hold the hands firmly in place. The heel of each sock was nailed down in the same way. Now the duppy was "nailed hand and foot."

The brother of the corpse was summoned and he spoke to the dead and said, "We nail you down hand and foot. You must stay there till judgment. If we want you we come wake you." Some salt mixed with "compellance" powder was sprinkled in the coffin and it was finally closed.

Followed activities of the set-up. The leader tracked out sankeys. (Methodist hymns.) Then he looked about him and asked, "Who is the treble?" That is, who is raising the hymns? A willing volunteer obliged and the rest of us sang. There were periods of short prayers, a little story-telling, a period of eating and the like until the last cock-crow (5 A.M.).

Several bottles of rum were handed over to the gravediggers early that morning and after sprinkling the ground with rum they all drank some and began digging with a will. After that, every bottle that was opened, the first drink out of it was poured into the grave for the dead. Soon the grave was opened, the parched corn and peas thrown in and the coffin lowered with proper rituals and patted to rest in the earth. The trail of salt and ground coffee was laid from the grave to the house door to prevent the return of the duppy and people went on home.

A sort of wake is held every night after this until the ninth night after death, but it is understood that practically no one except the family and old friends will bother to come again until the "nine night." But all being new to me, I decided to miss nothing. So each night I came bringing some white rum for folks to talk by, I made bold to ask the reason for the nine night. With everybody helping out with detail they told me.

It all stems from the firm belief in survival after death. Or rather that there *is no death*. Activities are merely changed from one condition to the other. One old man smoking jackass rope tobacco said to me in explanation: "One day you see a man walking the road, the next day you come to his yard and find him dead. Him don't walk, him don't talk again. He is still and silent and does none of the things that he used to do. But you look upon him and you see that he has all the parts that the living have. Why is it that he cannot do what the living do? It is because the thing that gave power to these parts is no longer there. That is the duppy, and that is the most powerful part of any man. Everybody has evil in them, and when a man

43

is alive, the heart and the brain controls him and he will not abandon himself to many evil things. But when the duppy leaves the body, it no longer has anything to restrain it and it will do more terrible things than any man ever dreamed of. It is not good for a duppy to stay among living folk. The duppy is much too powerful and is apt to hurt people all the time. So we make nine night to force the duppy to stay in his grave."

"Where is the duppy until nine night?" I asked. "Doesn't it stay in its grave at all until then?"

"Oh, yes. The duppy goes into the grave with the body and it stays in there the first day and the next. But the third day at midnight it rises from the grave."

The eyes of a youngish matron flew wide open. "Eh, eh!" she exclaimed, "True, sah?" (Is that true?)

"Sure, I see it myself," said the narrator.

"Eh, eh," the matron said sliding forward in her seat, "Tell, make see." (Explain it to us.)

"It was when I was a pickney (small child) my uncle died and was buried in the yard. I had heard tell that the duppy rises on the third night at cock-crow, so I got up out of my bed and went into the yard on the third night after his death and climbed a big mango tree where I could see the grave. I heard the cock-crow and felt the midnight breeze. Then I saw some thick mist come from the grave and make a huge white ball that lifted itself free from the earth for a moment, then sat down on top of the grave. I was just a pickney, so I got frightened and I climbed down from the mango tree and ran into the house. The duppy, him go dream to mama (appeared to her in a dream) and tell her and she told me not to do that again. One must never spy on a duppy, because it vexes him. The duppy told mama that if I had not been a part of the family he would have hurt me."

This narrative excited everybody. They all began to tell what they knew about duppies.

"A pickney duppy is stronger than the duppy of a man," one said.

"Oh, no. A coolie duppy is stronger than all other duppies."

"No, man, a Chinee duppy is strongest of all."

"Well," the man who started it all summed up, "all duppies got power to hurt you. He can breathe on you and make you sick. If he touches you, you will have fits."

"But," somebody defended the duppies, "duppies will never come inside your yard to hurt you unless somebody send him. It is a rude [wicked] person who set duppies on folks."

"Oh, many people are cruel, man. Some goes to the cemetery with rum and threepence and a calabash stick. They throw the rum and the money on the grave for the duppy and then they beat the grave with the calabash stick. Then they throw themselves down upon the grave and they roll on the grave and they beat it and call the duppy and tell him, 'You see what advantage so-and-so takes of me! You see how I punish [how I suffer]. I want you to follow so-and-so. I want you to lick him! I want you to lick him so!' [The grave is beaten violently with the stick.] And the duppy comes out of the grave and does what he is paid to do. Otherwise he would stay in his grave."

"But some duppy is rude, man. Some duppy will come even if nobody don't send call him. If he is not tied down he will come. Some duppy take a big strong chain to hold him down. I see a grave chained like that up in Manchester. They have to send to England to get a chain strong enough to tie him.

"Duppy is strong, but no matter how strong he is, he can't come in the house if you put tobacco seed over the door. He can't come in until he count all the seed, and duppy can't count more than nine. If you put more than ten, duppy will never come inside. The duppy counts with a jerk and when he gets to nine he wails, 'Lord, I miss!' And then he have to start all over again. He will keep that up until last cock-crow and then duppy *must* go back to his grave."

Somebody contends that duppies *can* count and do anything else if they have salt. Salt, they said, makes sense. That is why nobody gives salt to duppies because with salt, they are too strong for mortals. Somebody else shouts that that is not the reason at all. Duppies, he says, do not like salt. Salt gives "temper" to mortal food and duppies are not mortal any longer so they do not need salt. When he leaves off being mortal, the duppy does not need anything to temper his vittles. Another says that salt is *not* given because salt is heavy. It holds duppies to the ground. He cannot fly and depart if he has salt. Once Africans could all fly because they never ate salt. Many of them were brought to Jamaica to be slaves, but they never were slaves. They flew back to Africa. Those who ate salt had to stay in Jamaica and be slaves, because they were too heavy to fly. A woman was positive that duppies do not like salt. She said that salt vexed duppies. If a duppy sees salt around a place he will keep away. He will run right back to his grave.

The Nana said that was true and moreover, a duppy was in bad danger if he did not get back to his grave. He positively must be there by last cock-crow. And that is how a duppy can be punished for leaving the grave to hurt people. She said that if you meet a duppy in the road and you are wearing a felt hat, take off the hat and fold it four times and sit on it and the duppy cannot come close enough to you to hurt you, and neither can he run back to his grave. He is tied until you let him go. So you can hold him from his grave until after cock-crow and make him a homeless duppy forever.

"I never heard of sitting on a hat to hold a duppy," an old man said, "so I would not trust a hat. A river stone is what will tie a duppy." There was a great groan of agreement to this. "You take two river stones. You must have one stone from the bed of the river to sit on, and one little flat river stone to place on top of your head and the duppy cannot come up to you and he cannot go back to his grave."

"True, true, that is very true," the room agreed. So the man went on.

"One worthless woman died and soon after her duppy came to harm the family in the next yard to where she use to live. The family had a daughter, and she being a very young girl, they sent her always for water. One night they sent her for water after dark. Soon she run back in the house and fell in

46

a fit. She had many fits and foamed at the mouth."

"If they foam at the mouth, that is a sign of duppy."

"Eh, eh, that sure is duppy."

"So the father gave her salt to eat and made a cross on her forehead with chalk. Then he rubbed under her arms with garlic and she got better and was able to talk. She said that she saw the old woman who had died and the duppy came up to her and laughed in her face and threw heat on her and touched her. Then she had fits and knew nothing until she was revived. The father grew very mad when he heard this. He went outside and got two river stones to trap the duppy. He sat very still with the river-stones on his head and under him. The duppy came and saw him and tried to run back to the grave, but she could not go. Then the duppy tried to rush upon him and hurt him, but she could not do that either. So the duppy advanced, and the duppy backed up. This went on for quite a while. Then she began to plead, 'Do, Bucky Massa, let me go! Let me go back to the grave. I won't do it again! Do, Bucky Massa, please let me go!' But the man said, 'No, you worthless duppy, I'll keep you until day.' He meant to do so, but he fell asleep after awhile and the top rock fell off of his head. The duppy saw it and quick as lightning, it ran back to the grave and never came out again. Nobody ever saw that duppy again."

"But some duppies wish to stay in their graves," Nana said, "and it is a most cruel thing to wake them after they are gone. Let them rest. They don't need to come back for nothing after they are gone. God gives the duppy nine days after death to do and take with him what he wants. After that let him rest."

Then I wanted to ask a question. "You tell me that the duppy rises on the third night after death and that he does not depart until the ninth night. But where is he all this time?" I asked.

"Oh, the duppy goes back and forth from the grave to his house where he use to live. He is in the yard and he visits all the places where he use to go. On the ninth night he goes back to the apartment [room] where he lived last and where he breathed his last breath and takes with him the shadow of everything he wants. We know that he is there, so we prepare everything for him in that dead room that he wants so that he will go away happy and not come back and harm us. We know that he likes singing and to see his family and friends for the last time. The whole district comes to make him happy so that he will rest well and not come back again."

The talk went on and on all about duppies caught in bottles; duppies caught in pimento sticks to make a terrible weapon; duppies sitting on beds of the sick and "throwing heat" on them; duppies paid to throw the sick out of bed; duppies raining showers of stones in the houses; duppies forcing men to turn around and walk with them from town to town. So the nights ran together and made nine.

On that ninth night Joe Forsythe and I came to the familiar yard. People stood about in small collections talking. A great table at the far left was loaded with foodstuffs. Fried fish, rice, rum, bread, coffee, wet sugar for the coffee, fowl, and what not. A sizable tarpaulin had been stretched on tall poles from one house wall. Chairs and boxes were spaced around the edge of the covered area and boards were laid between these to make plenty of seats. A small deal table was in the center and a four-spouted naked light hung directly over the table. There was a chair for the leader when the time should arrive for him to "track out" the hymn for the rest to sing. The beginning of everything was there, but nothing had shaped up yet. I went inside to pay my respects to the widow.

Most of the patriarchs had already arrived and were in the dead room. The feast for the duppy was spread. There was white rum and white rice without salt and white fowl also saltless. The wooden bath bowl was full of water and placed in the center of the floor. A glass of drinking water was on the white draped table with the food which was not in plates at all, but spread on banana leaves. The bed was snowy white in its cleanliness.

The intimates sat and talked casually. Now and then one of the old women looked out of the door and bawled at some girl whom she considered too free with the boys. But mostly they had the air of just waiting around for something. I could hear a great hub-bub of talking from the outside and looked out to find that the yard was full of people.

Suddenly one Nana removed her clay pipe from her lips and stared pointedly at the door for a moment, then nudged her neighbor to look. She looked in the same direction and in turn nudged her neighbor. Calling-attention gestures swept the room in the silence. Everything was conveyed by gesture. The first Nana led the "seeing." Her eyes went from door to bed, from bed to bath bowl, from bath bowl to table, and all eyes followed hers. Little nods of gratification as the duppy was observed to eat or drink, or bathe, or take the shadow of his bed and meal. Finally he was seen to take a seat to enjoy the evening. Then the leader arose and spoke to him.

"We know you come," he said with gracious courtesy. "We glad you come. Myself two times."

All others nod and murmur in agreement. The duppy is assured of a welcome in every way. "We do the best we can."

The leader went outside and took his place under the four-pronged naked light and began tracking out the songs. The "treble" raised the song. He had a dramatic falsetto with uncanny qualifications. It could not be called a good voice, but it did things to those who could sing. It seemed to search out the hidden roads to harmony so the others could find them. The night song had begun. It kept up hour after hour. The monotony varied only by the new inventions in melody and harmony on the same song.

Way late the leader cried "Sola!" That was an invitation for those who had special or favorite songs to track the verses out for the others to sing the chorus. Ten or more people were instantly tracking out. The leader gave precedence to a girl. She was a penny brown girl with high lights in her eyes. She acted out the verses of a song and raised the singing to a frenzied pitch.

Inside the room the old ones kept the duppy entertained with Anansi stories. Now and then they sang a little. A short

49

squirt of song and then another story would come. Its syllables would behave like tambour tones under the obligato of the singing outside. It fitted together beautifully because Anansi stories are partly sung anyway. So rhythmic and musical is the Jamaican dialect that the tale drifts naturally from words to chant and from chant to song unconsciously. There was Brer Anansi and Brer Grassquit; Brer Anansi and the Chatting Pot; Brer Frog's dissatisfaction with his flat behind and Anansi's effort to teach him how to make stiffening for it. And how all the labor was lost on account of Brer Frog's boasting and ingratitude. "So Frog don't learn how to make him behind stick out like other animals. Him still have round behind with no shape because him don't know how to make the stiffening." A great burst of laughter. This is the best liked tale and it is told more than once.

Eleven o'clock arrives and "tea" is served. When this is over it is still a half hour till midnight. Plaintive tunes, mournful songs are sung now. A new and most doleful arrangement of "Lead Kindly Light" fairly drips tears. Then "Good Night" sung over and over. Finally the leader signals a halt. He then solemnly invites all the family and close friends together in the dead room to help discharge the dead.

I was signalled to come too so I went. Inside the tiny room it was very crowded and solemn. The brother of the dead man was selected to preside. He tracked out, "There is rest for the Weary," and after that he prayed:

"Lord, we come to send off the spirit of our dear one to thee. We know him is with thee for him is thy child and not Satan child. So him is not with Satan in Hell but with thee in Heaven. Accept him there, Lord. Don't drive him out of thy Kingdom. And whether him is gone to thee or to Satan, help we to discharge him from this house forever. The living has no right with the dead. Amen." He tracked out a sankey and then addressed the duppy directly.

"We know you come and we make you welcome. We give you white fowl; we give you rice and leave your bed for you. We leave you water and we do *everything* for you. Done!!! Go

50

on to your rest now and no do we no harm. We no want to see you again. You must left and you not to come again. *No come back!* Mind now, you come again we plant you!"

Now this closest male relative of the dead man seizes the sheet from the bed and casts it to the floor. The mattress follows. Eager hands help gather up the slats and take the bed down completely. The slats are thrown to the floor with a great clatter. The brother takes one of the slats and beats the pile of bedding on the floor before it is taken outdoors. The women seize the banana leaves with the food heaped on them and throw them out of the window. The water follows. A Nana looks at the door and nudges. They all "see" the duppy depart. The duppy that was once a man can have no more friendly relationship with mortals.

Instantly outside the tempo changes. They grow jubilant. A "village lawyer" holds up his hand in restraint. "It no finish yet! It no finish yet!"

"Yes, man, it finish. Him gone. Bed is outside."

"Then what about the chalk marks? Make I see." (Show them to me.)

In their eagerness to begin play, some have overlooked or forgotten this last necessity. The know-it-all takes a piece of white chalk and with an air of importance makes a cross mark on all the windows and doors. The recent activities inside have driven the duppy out. The cross marks are meant to keep him out. It is finished.

A play spirit seized the yard. Men hunted up rocks with which to play "Dollyman." A game where fingers get crushed and fights commence. Temporary love affairs were developing right and left. In spite of the older women who tried to keep an eye on the girls, there were numerous love-lit excursions into the outer darkness. Two men with cow-cords under their arms swaggered about very conscious of the weapon they carried. But a "bad stick" under the arm of a stocky, grim looking fellow was regarded with awe.

This was one of the far-famed "Ebolite" sticks. They are made from pimento wood, which becomes "prementa" on the

51

lips of the peasant. A stick of pimento about a yard long is cut. It is roasted in a fire with great skill so that the bark sheds completely without injuring the wood beneath. A little more roasting and the stick becomes a beautiful, dark, glistening thing. The stick is buried in a grave, a coolie grave is the preference, and allowed to remain there for two or three weeks. In this time, the duppy of the person buried there has come to live in the stick. After it is dug up it is polished and the two ends and sometimes the middle of the stick is wound with brass wire. The stick is ready for its baptism after the wire and it is given a name. This name is always feminine. It is named for some mule or horse or obeah woman. Soon everyone in the district knows this stick just as well as if it were justice of the peace. People whisper its name as if it were a person. "Me see Alice in the yard," and no man however full of rum would jostle the owner of Alice in the yard. But rum was talking thru several men there. "Red men licking a black man," is the way one woman spoke of it.

I was standing in the swirl of all this when Joe touched my arm. "Let's go," he said.

"No, I don't want to go. Look, one man has got his fingers mashed over there at the dollyman game. I think it's going to be a fight. I want to see it."

"Plenty fight, man. But I take you to see Koo-min-ah. That's the best kind of nine night. It don't happen often. It's a nine night but it don't happen until the person been dead a year and a half. The Africans do this with the Maroons. I take great trouble to fix it so you can come see. Come on. They make two 'house' tonight."

When we reached the yard where the Koo-min-ah was being held we found that we were early for the Koo-min-ah but late for a magnificent Congo. Both the drumming and the muscular subtleties were extraordinary.

Zachariah, "The Power," came forward and received me and later explained that they built the house for the duppy after he was gone eighteen months because it was not certain that the spirit had definitely settled down in his new home

52

before then. If the house which in reality is a cement tomb were built earlier than that, it might be closed while the duppy happened to be out, and then he would become a wandering spirit.

Back of us was an elaborate palm booth. Off to one side the Maroons were jerking a pig. Close by the Africans were preparing a goat with all fragrant herbs. Four or five persons in full ceremonials appeared out of a house there in the back. The Power hurriedly left us and went into the house. The intriguing monotony of the Congo died down and people began to collect around the great booth. There is a bustle inside there but the flambeau hanging from a palm stem is not yet lighted.

The Power appears for a moment at the door and the light flares. Four men who look like African nabobs I find are the drummers, and the four less panoplied men with them are the "rackling" men. That is the men who play the triple rhythm on the back of the drum with little sticks. There are two "shuckers," the men who play the cha cha.

There under the booth are two "houses" for the dead. Between them is a wooden bath bowl which contains a large calabash full of water. That is all. I wonder about the bowl and the calabash but the time is past for asking questions, because the drummers are pounding the drumheads with hammers and turning pegs in tuning their instruments.

There is the thunder of drums subtly rubbed with bare heels, and the ferocious attack of the rackling men. The thing has begun. They are "making house for duppy." The hands of the drummers weave their magic and the drums speak of old times and old things.

A few warming-up steps by some dancers. Then a woman breaks through the dancers with a leap like a lioness emerging from cover. Just like that. She sings with gestures as she challenges the drummers, a lioness defying the tribesmen.

"Ah minnie wah oh, Ah minnie wah oh!"

And the men at the instruments reply:

"Saykay ah brah ay."

53

She makes some liquid movements of her upper body and cries again:

"Yekko tekko, yekko tekko, Yahm pahn sah ay!"

The men:

"Ah yah yee-ai, Ah yah yee-ai, ah say oh!"

She danced thru one furious movement and cried again:

"Yekko tekko, ah pah ahah ai!"

This whole thing was repeated many times with more singers and dancers entering into it each time. Now the scores of dancers circled the tombs. It was asymmetric dancing that yet had balance and beauty. It was certainly most compelling. There was a big movement and a little movement. The big movement was like a sunset in its scope and color. The little movement had the almost imperceptible ripple of a serpent's back. It was a cameo in dancing.

One male dancer suddenly ceases and demands rum. All the others join him. Zachariah hesitates and fools around a bit, but they insist and he produces a bottle. The oldest man among the Africans is summoned. It is the law that he must have the first drink that is poured. It is handed to him with deference. Zachariah takes the next drink himself, then the woman singer-dancer who I learn is called "The Governess." Then the drummers, then the rackling men and the shuckers, then the dancers. Lastly, these who just stand and sing. They don't really belong, so if nothing is left for them no harm is done.

The dancing begins in earnest now. The Governess is like an intoxicating spirit that whips up the crowd. Those rackling men become fiends from hell. The shuckers do a magnificent muscle dance which they tell me is African. The drums and the movements of the dancers draw so close together that the drums become people and the people become drums. The pulse of the drum is their shoulders and belly. Truly the drum is inside their bodies. More rum, more fire.

"Hand a' bowl, Knife a' throat
Rope a' tie me, Hand a' bowl

"Hand a' bowl, Day a' light
Wango doe, doe, Knife a' throat

"Hand a' bowl, Knife a' throat
Want ingwalla, Fum dees ah"

Now Zachariah proved the magnificent dancer that he was.
He dominated the group with his skill. The whole perform-
ance rose to a pitch. They all followed him in spirit and ferocity if not in skill. It was the goat song that was being sung. The
Governess was speaking for the sacrificial one, and Zachariah
was dancing the priest. Women began to "cramp." They flung
themselves about and fell quivering. It is law that they be not
allowed to lie on the ground and they were instantly seized up
by men and the tempo increased. Clothes were torn away
unconsciously. Two or three hot, wet bodies collided with me.
I saw women picked up by their buttocks, their bodies bent
backwards so limply that their heads and heels trailed the
ground. Their faces were bathed in rum to revive them. If it
took too long, they were carried outside of the lighted circle
somewhere to be revived. The drummers, the shuckers, the
rackling men had played their faces into ferocious masks. Ec-
static body movements went with every throb.

Zachariah leaped over both graves, over the seated drummers, whirled his body in mid-air, fell on his back, arched his
back until only his head and toes touched the ground, held the
pose in trembling ecstasy for a long moment, then hurled his
lower body up and seized a cramping woman with his thighs
and brought her down. Somebody rushed in and broke his
scissors hold and the dance went on.

Too late I saw the goat dragged up between the tombs and
the knife in Zachariah's hand. In a flash he was catching the
blood from its throat in a glass. There was a great pressing
forward for a drop of his wonder-working blood, but the
crowd was driven back. Still in motion, Zachariah took a deep
drink from the glass, then allowed each drummer a little sip.
"The Power" then danced with the glass and finally with a

55

leap and a cry, hurled it as far from him as he could. Some of the crowd motioned to follow the glass and take it up, but "The Power" shook his head in warning and chanted without ceasing to dance, "Who want to take it up, take it up, but it is trouble to do so." That halted the rush instantly. Not a soul ventured to go.

After a magnificent flourish that coincided with sounds of the drums, "The Power" went into a cramp himself and sank to the ground. Nobody touched him. Then I saw the rising calabash. There before my eyes the calabash full of water rose from the bath bowl and slowly mounted to the top of the palm booth and as slowly sank again. The drums went on and on. They sang on and on.

Hand a' bowl. . . . Cocks crowing raucously. . . . Day a' light. . . . Night took on a deathly look. . . . Want ingwalla. . . . The spirit went out of the drums. . . . Fum dee ah. . . . The sun came up walking sideways.

CHAPTER 5

✧

WOMEN IN THE CARIBBEAN

I t is a curious thing to be a woman in the Caribbean after you have been a woman in these United States. It has been said that the United States is a large collection of little nations, each having its own ways, and that is right. But the thing that binds them all together is the way they look at women, and that is right, too. The majority of men in all the states are pretty much agreed that just for being born a girl-baby you ought to have laws and privileges and pay and per-quisites. And so far as being allowed to voice opinions is concerned, why, they consider that you are born with the law in your mouth, and that is not a bad arrangement either. The majority of the solid citizens strain their ears trying to find out what it is that their womenfolk want so they can strain around and try to get it for them, and that is a *very* good idea and the right way to look at things.

But now Miss America, World's champion woman, you take your promenading self down into the cobalt blue waters of the Caribbean and see what happens. You meet a lot of darkish men who make vociferous love to you, but otherwise pay you no mind. If you try to talk sense, they look at you right pitifully as if to say, "What a pity! That mouth that was made to supply some man (and why not me) with kisses, is spoiling itself asking stupidities about banana production and wages!" It is not that they try to put you in your place, no. They consider that you never had any. If they think about it at all, they think that they are removing you from MAN's place and then granting you the privilege of receiving his caresses and otherwise ministering to his comfort when he has time to give you for such matters. Otherwise they flout your God-given right to be the most important item in the universe and assume your prerogatives themselves. The usurpers! Naturally women do not receive the same educational advantages as the men.

This sex superiority is further complicated by class and color ratings. Of course all women are inferior to all men by God and law down there. But if a woman is wealthy, of good family and mulatto, she can overcome some of her drawbacks. But if she is of no particular family, poor and black, she is in a bad way indeed in that man's world. She had better pray to the Lord to turn her into a donkey and be done with the thing. It is assumed that God made poor black females for beasts of burden, and nobody is going to interfere with providence. Most assuredly no upper class man is going to demean himself by assisting one of them with a heavy load. If he were caught in such an act he probably would become an outcast among his kind. It is just considered down there that God made two kinds of donkeys, one kind that can talk. The black women of Jamaica load banana boats now, and the black women used to coal ships when they burned coal.

The old African custom of polygamy is rampant down there. The finer touches of keeping mistresses come from Europe, however. The privileges those men have of several families at the same time! And their wives don't like it a bit better than we do, but the whole national set-up favors him and crushes her. If one woman is protected in breaking into her husband's arrangements and regulating his pleasures, what is to hinder the others? The thing might become general and that would

58

be a sad state of affairs! No, selfish, jealous wives must be discouraged.

Women get no bonus just for being female down there. She can do the same labors as a man or a mule and nobody thinks anything about it. In Jamaica it is a common sight to see skinny-looking but muscular black women sitting on top of a pile of rocks with a hammer making little ones out of big ones. They look so wretched with their bare black feet all gnarled and distorted from walking barefooted over rocks. The nails on their big toes thickened like a hoof from a life time of knocking against stones. All covered over with the gray dust of the road, those feet look almost saurian and repellent. Of course their clothing is meager, cheap and ugly. But they sit by the roadside on their enormous pile of rocks and crack down all day long. Often they build a slight shelter of palm leaves to protect them from the sun. The government buys the crushed rock to use in road-building and maintenance. It is said that a woman who sticks to her business with the help of a child or two can average about one dollar and a half per week. It is very hard, but women in Jamaica must eat like everywhere else. And everywhere in the Caribbean women carry a donkey's load on their heads and walk up and down mountains with it.

But the upper class women in the Caribbean have an assurance that no woman in the United States possesses. The men of her class are going to marry inside their class. They will have their love affairs and their families wherever they will or may. But seldom does one contract a marriage outside of his class. Here in the United States a man is liable to marry whenever he falls in love. The two things are tied together in his mind. But in the Caribbean it is different. Love and marriage need not be related at all. What is shocking to an American mind is that the man has no obligation to a girl outside of his class. She has no rights which he is bound to respect. What is worse, the community would be shocked if he did respect them. Fatherhood gives no upper class man the license to trample down conventions and crash lines, nor shades-of-color

59

lines, by marrying outside his class.

Here is an example of this from Jamaica. A pretty girl, but definitely brown, boarded a train to come down to Kingston to work for the United Fruit Company as a typist. A young man, a mulatto, was already on the train travelling in the same class as the girl. He was immediately attracted to the girl's lush appeal and laid siege. This went on for months after she was established in Kingston and her mother had come to join her. The girl was thrilled at his attentions even though he never took her out to meet his friends. She began to dream the impossible, that this mulatto of good family had honorable intentions towards her mama's daughter. Now then, her girl friend in whom she confided her great hope and greater love, began to tell her that rumors were about that he was engaged to a girl of his own set. The lovelorn little country bird charged him but he denied it in the most positive manner. She believed him and kept up the female game of advance and retreat to lure him into the golden circle of matrimony.

Then one Sunday night he did not call to take her for a country ride as usual. He did not come until Tuesday night. He did not come into the house then. He stayed in the car and called her to come and go for a ride. As soon as she was in the car she said, "George, my friend says that you are going to be married. She says that the girl's mother came to borrow cake pans from my friend's mother early Monday morning, saying that you were going to marry her daughter tomorrow. Is it true?" "No, it is not true, darling, I love no one but you. Do you think I would be taking you for a drive tonight if I expected to marry someone else tomorrow?" He drove faster up into the wooded heights and away from Kingston.

Up in a safe little spot he induced her to leave the car after a struggle and possessed her. Afterwards, standing above her he said humbly, "I lied to you, dear. I *am* getting married tomorrow as they told you. But I just had to have you. I could have no peace of mind for thinking of you. I had to do it tonight because tomorrow I will be married and I can not continue calling on you. Come on, get into the car. I've got to get on back to town and attend to several things for to-morrow."

And he drove like the wind to her door and never even alighted to help her, but rushed her out of the car. In the struggle before getting out of the car before her seduction she had lost one of her pumps. Evidently not wishing to leave any clues for his bride to find, he discovered the shoe a short distance from the house of the ravished girl and threw it in the road where it was found later by her friend and returned to her.

His wedding, next day, was considered one of the great social events of the year. But that is not the end. A year or two later this same man heard that the girl he had ravished was about to marry. He told the other man of his own experience with her and asked in a scornful tone, "You don't want second-hand goods, do you?" The other man did not. She is still around Kingston drinking too much and generally being careless of herself. But what becomes of her is unimportant. The honor of two men has been saved, and men's honor is important in the Caribbean.

In Haiti the law says that a woman may accuse no man of being the father of her child unless she is married to him. Thus unattached men who have been out for a few nights of pleasure need fear no embarrassment from girls who come to complain of consequences. Furthermore several intelligent Haitian women have told me that a man may marry a girl but if he wishes to do so, he can return her to her parents by saying simply, "I was not the first." Then he can vindicate his honor by getting a divorce and marry the woman he prefers. So far as the discarded bride is concerned, she has no redress. She cannot refute his statement. What could she offer as proof? The marriage would have to be consummated before the husband could have grounds for his complaint. And after that the bride is in a difficult position to make out a case for her virginity before marriage. It is barely possible that some girls, not really wanted as wives, but unattainable otherwise, have been traduced out of their good names and their husband's homes at the same time after satiation. Who knows?

Take the case of Mr. A. He was a widower in his late forties. A spinster in her early thirties worked in a store very near his place of business. They fell in love and he proposed marriage. They married quietly and went to Leogane to spend their honeymoon. Leogane is a small town about twelve miles south of Port-au-Prince. During the night he accused her of having lost her virgin status and not only drove her from the bed, but he also drove her from the house. She, in this great distress of mind, started out to walk back to Port-au-Prince because she had no other way of getting there, turned out penniless and barehanded the way she was. But her virtuous husband considered that she was getting off too light. He went outside himself and gathered up a band of rowdies and paid them to follow her all the way to Port-au-Prince beating drums, and dish pans and five-gallon cans, while they made announcements about the state of affairs to everyone they met. This outraged man whose honor had nearly been tampered with secured a divorce and married a sister of a well known physician in Port-au-Prince. The allegedly unvirtuous wife hid around a year or two and died. Perhaps she suffered some but then he was a man and therefore sacred and his honor must be protected even if it takes forty women to do it.

PART II

POLITICS AND
PERSONALITIES
OF HAITI

CHAPTER 6

✢

REBIRTH OF A NATION

For four hundred years the blacks of Haiti had yearned for peace. For three hundred years the island was spoken of as a paradise of riches and pleasures, but that was in reference to the whites to whom the spirit of the land gave welcome. Haiti has meant spilt blood and tears for blacks. So the Haitians got no answer to their prayers. Even when they had fought and driven out the white oppressors, oppression did not cease. They sought peace under kingdoms and other ruling names. They sought it in the high, cold, beautiful mountains of the island and in the sudden small alluvial plains, but it eluded them and vanished from their hands.

A prophet could have foretold it was to come to them from another land and another people utterly unlike the Haitian people in any respect. The prophet might have said, "Your freedom from strife and your peace shall come when these symbols shall appear. There shall come a voice in the night. A new and bloody river shall pour from a man-made rock in your chief city. Then shall be a cry from the heart of Haiti—a great cry, a crescendo cry. There shall be survivors, and they shall have a look and a message. There shall be a Day and the

Day shall mother a Howl, and the Howl shall be remembered in Haiti forever and nations beyond the borders shall hear it and stir. Then shall appear a Plume against the sky. It shall be a black plume against the sky which shall give fright to many at its coming, but it shall bring peace to Haiti. You who have hopes, watch for these signs. Many false prophets shall arrive who will promise you peace and faith, but they are lacking in the device of peace. Wait for the plume in the sky."

THE VOICE IN THE NIGHT

A whisper ran along the edge of the dawn. A young girl heard rifle shots spattering the darkness of a night that was holding its breath. The girl stirred in fright and went to waken her father and her family where they were, but there was no need. All Haiti was awake and listening for shots. The father ordered the family to dress in haste and questioned the girl nervously. "Your ears are younger than mine. Did it seem to you that those shots came from the direction of the palace? For if they came from the palace or *near* the palace, the people in the prison—go see if the door is secure."

The girl went to the door but instead of seeing to the fastening, she eased the door open and crept outside. A band of Cacos passed swinging machetes. There were signs on many gates announcing that foreigners occupied those houses.

"But this is a street of foreigners," said one of the Cacos to his fellows. "Let us go into a street of Haitians so that we may kill some people." The girl drew her Haitian face back into the shadows and the little band of knife-men went on the business of hunting work.

The girl crept out onto the sidewalk again straining to translate the whisper of the night. Outside the ominous pulsation of the city was more definite. The voice of the night rose higher to say what it would. This night *must* say something, the political situation was too tense to pass another day undefined, and every house in Haiti had an ear strained with fear or with hope. Behind her, Fannie heard her father find the

66

unlatched door by his gasp of terror. Across the street she saw someone all but crawling along the sidewalk as close to the wall as possible. She found that it was the son of a neighbor around her own age. She hailed him in a whisper, and he beckoned her to cross the street to where he was. He seemed to be afraid for her.

"What are you doing outside, Fannie?"

"I heard shots, Etienne. Why are you outside tonight? It is very dangerous. I saw Cacos walking."

The boy crept close to her in the dark to give tongue to the speechless something that was reeking in the air.

"Sh-sh-Fannie. The people in the prison are dead!"

"How do you know that, Etienne?"

"A whisper came to our door. A Voice—nobody saw who spoke. But it is certain. The people in the prison are dead."

THE BLOODY RIVER

The people and the women of Port-au-Prince came to the prison that dawn morning. Winged tongues had whispered at every door, "The people in the prison are dead! Our people in the prison are dead!" A very few worried the bone of whether Jean Vilbrun Guillaume Sam was still President in the palace or a fugitive in the French Legation. But nobody listened to them talk. The collected mass said, "The people in the prison are dead." Or some said it like a question, "Are our people dead in the prison?"

Some blamed the political foes who had harried President Sam to the point where he had seized nearly two hundred men, all members of good families, and imprisoned them more as hostages for the good behavior of the leaders than as politicians suspected of plotting the overthrow of the Sam administration. Some denounced the machinations of Sam and his adherents. President Sam, they said, was a cheat and a fraud. He was a man of no honor. He had not the politesse. He had no regard for established rules of occupying the palace. He did not respect the conventions. He was a greedy and

67

detestable criminal. He had been in the palace for five months, or nearly so. That was sufficient time for him to "assure his future," if he had been alert and intelligent about the national funds. Why then must the monster resist the efforts of other desiring men to improve their fortunes? When Sam had captured the principal cities, had not Theodore sailed away like a gentleman? Now that General Bobo had marched from the north and invested the capitol, why did Sam ignore the conventions governing the situation? Clearly the man was a greedy, stupid pig lacking in good manners. A man like that deserved no loyalty and allegiance from cultured folk. He must expect revolution. The men in the prison were heroes for having resisted him. This was the opinion of the majority. A few still felt that Sam having gained the presidency should not be deposed by violence, and that his resistance was justified. Moreover, the nation wanted peace. The people were weary of the "generals" and their endless revolutions and counter-revolution. Their greed and ambition were destroying the nation. They breathed a great prayer for Peace! But where in Haiti?

They had heard shots and the President had issued orders to kill the political prisoners in the prison at the first shots of the opposing forces. And now it was generally agreed that the shots had come from the Champ de Mars and that the President's Caco army on which he had depended, had answered weakly before it deserted the President's cause. So now the families of the prisoners were there and they must go into the jail. Screams and groans had been reported with muffled shots. The families must know if the unhappy sounds pertained to their own. Someone said that fifteen bloody men with bloody blades had just left the jail. But Charles Oscar Etienne, Chief military officer of the government, could not be found to be questioned. Chocotte and Paul Herard were inside, rumor said, but no one could enter to question them. But dawn discovered a drain from the inside of the prison flowing with gouts and clots of blood. The doors crashed open before the fury of families and friends of families and they surged to the cells of their relatives to be reassured of their safety.

THE CRESCENDO CRY

There in the cells in huddled stillness were shot bodies and cut bodies. Skulls crushed in by machetes' blows and bowels ripped away by blades. Men with machetes had been ordered to follow the rifle men. The finished youth of the three sons of Polynice in their helplessness called out to pity and retribution. The hunks of human flesh screamed of outrage. The blood screamed. The women screamed. The great cry went up from the bloody cells and hung over Haiti like smoke over a ruin. And the sun rushed up from his slot in the horizon to listen.

THE SURVIVORS

They lifted the heaps of the dead and found a man. He screamed and muttered and screamed. He was mad. Another one could talk, "I heard them when they said, 'Fifteen men, forward march!' " Then he whispered, "I heard Chocotte, the adjutant, say, 'Fire close to the ground. A bullet in the head for each man. Every one of the political prisoners must die. The arrondissement's orders are that not one be left standing. They don't know the kind of man that General Vilbrun is.' But I am still alive, am I not? The slaughter of July twenty-seventh is past and I am still alive." They led out Stephen Alexis; they led out a mad man and they led out another. These three had survived the massacre. "But where is the body of Charles Oscar Etienne?" Polynice cried. "He cannot be alive or this butchery could not have happened. He is the Chief military officer of Haiti with the care and protection of these unarmed and helpless people."

"He is the friend of Guillaume Sam," someone answered him.

"But honor lays a greater obligation than friendship; and if

69

friendship made such a monster of a man, then it is a thing vile indeed. No, Oscar Etienne is dead. Only over his dead body could such a thing have happened. Show me the body of Etienne. Look near the bodies of my three young sons. It must be there. He could not have betrayed them out of their young lives in so wretched a manner. Look well and find the body of this honorable man who died in defense of his own honor and the helplessness of his prisoners. We must bury him with honor like our great ones. Like L'Ouverture he died defending Haiti from brutality and butchery."

So Polynice went about among the dismembered parts of bodies to which no one could give a name, searching for one small piece of the protector of the helpless that he might do it honor and thus wash his own grief, which was a terrible thing. After a while someone told him, "But Oscar Etienne is not dead. He was seen to leave the prison before five o'clock. It was he who ordered the massacre. He has taken refuge in the Dominican legation. He will not come out for any reason at all."

"Then I must go and bring him out. It will be a great kindness to him after this terrible end of my sons. He will not wish to live and remember his defeat in the carrying out of his duty. I must hurry to relieve him of his memories."

Polynice rushed to the Dominican legation and dragged out the cringing Etienne who went limp with terror when he saw the awful face of the father of the Polynices. He mumbled "mistakes" and "misunderstanding" and placed the blame upon President Vilbrun Sam. But it is doubtful if Polynice heard a word. He dragged him to the sidewalk and gave him three calming bullets, one for each of his murdered sons and stepped over the dead body where it lay and strode off. The crowd followed him to the home of Etienne where they stripped it first and then levelled it to its foundation. In their rage they left nothing standing that one might say "Here is the remains of the house of Etienne who betrayed and slaughtered defenseless men under his protection for the crime of difference of politics." His heart retched terribly as he went through

70

the city that was weeping and washing the dead as he made his way to the French legation to see if he might not speak with General Sam. The weepers and Polynice were the survivors with the mad man and Stephen Alexis and that other one who did not die.

THE DAY AND THE HOWL

All that day of the massacre the families washed bodies and wept and hung over human fragments asking of the bloody lumps, "Is it you, my love, that I touch and hold?" And in that desperate affection every lump was carried away from the prison to somebody's heart and a loving burial. They knew that Vilbrun Guillaume Sam hid in the French legation after fighting his way out of the palace with something of the courage of Christophe and the ferocity of Dessalines. But this day was the day of the dead. It was not the day of thinking of Vilbrun Sam. This was the day of feeling. The next day the one hundred and sixty-seven martyrs would be buried. With their bodies out of sight, perhaps they could think again. So another night of whispers and sleeplessness and the funeral processions streamed to the churches from all directions. People fell into the processions as they passed grim and solemn. Men called out encouragement from houses along the way. Women wept at windows. Body after body climbed toward the great church of the Sacred Heart. Funeral met funeral at the door. Peasant women with their weeping handkerchiefs tied tight about their loins wailed all about the doors along the routes. The people who had not been able to get into the church stopped the processions of bodies as they were carried from the church and wept over them.

One black peasant woman fell upon her knees with her arms outstretched like a crucifix and cried, "They say that the white man is coming to rule Haiti again. The black man is so cruel to his own, *let the white man come!*"

With the bodies in the earth, with the expectation of American intervention, with the prong of such cries in their hearts,

71

the people moved toward the French legation. They were not to be balked. For this day and this act amenities national and inter-national were suspended. The outraged voice of Haiti had changed from a sob to a howl. They dragged General Jean Vilbrun Guillaume Sam, until the dawn of the day of the massacre, president of the Republic, from his hiding place. They chopped his hand that tried in its last desperation to save him from the massed frenzy outside the legation gates. They dragged him through the door into the court and there a woman whose dainty hands had never even held a broom, struck him a vicious blow with a machete at the root of his neck, and he was hurled over the gate to the people who chopped off his parts and dragged his torso in the streets.

THE PLUME AGAINST THE SKY

They were like that when the black plume of the American battleship smoke lifted itself against the sky. They were like that when Admiral Caperton from afar off gazed at Port-au-Prince through his marine glasses. They were so engaged when the U.S.S. *Washington* arrived in the harbor with Caperton in command. When he landed, he found the head of Guillaume Sam hoisted on a pole on the Champ de Mars and his torso being dragged about and worried by the mob. This dead and mutilated corpse seemingly useless to all on earth except those who might have loved it while it was living. But it should be entombed in marble for it was the deliverer of Haiti. L'Ouverture had beaten back the outside enemies of Haiti, but the bloody stump of Sam's body was to quell Haiti's internal foes, who had become more dangerous to Haiti than anyone else. The smoke from the funnels of the U.S.S. *Washington* was a black plume with a white hope. This was the last hour of the last day of the last year that ambitious and greedy demagogues could substitute bought Caco blades for voting power. It was the end of the revolution and the beginning of peace.

CHAPTER 7

✢

THE NEXT
HUNDRED YEARS

Peeps at personalities in the Black Republic.

Haiti has always been two places. First it was the Haiti of the masters and slaves. Now it is Haiti of the wealthy and educated mulattoes and the Haiti of the blacks. Haiti of the Champ de Mars and Haiti of the Bolosse. Turgeau against the Salines. Under this present administration, the two Haitis are nearer one than at any time in the history of the country. The mulattoes began their contention for equality with the whites at least a generation before freedom for the blacks was even thought of. In 1789 it was estimated that the mulattoes owned at least ten per cent of the productive land and held among them over 50,000 black slaves. Therefore when they sent representatives to France to fight for their rights and privileges, they would have been injuring themselves to have asked the same thing for the blacks. So they fought only for themselves.

In 1791 under Boukmann, Biasson and Jean-François, the blacks began their savage lunge for freedom and in 1804 they were free. Their bid for freedom had to have lunge and it had to be savage, for every man's hand was against them. Certainly their kinfolks, the mulattoes, could see no good for themselves in freedom for the blacks. Thus the very stream of Haitian liberty had two sources. It was only the white Frenchman's scorn of the mulattoes and his cruelty that forced Pétion and his followers into the camp of the blacks.

Since the struggle began, L'Ouverture died in a damp, cold prison in France, Dessalines was assassinated by the people whom he helped to free, Christophe was driven to suicide, three more presidents have been assassinated, there have been fourteen revolutions, three out-and-out kingdoms established and abolished, a military occupation by a foreign white power which lasted for nineteen years. The occupation is ended and Haiti is left with a stable currency, the beginnings of a system of transportation, a modern capitol, the nucleus of a modern army.

So Haiti, the black republic, and where does she go from here? That all depends. It depends mostly upon the action of a group of intelligent young Haitians grouped around Dividnaud, the brilliant young Minister of the Interior. These young men who hold the hope of a new Haiti because they are vigorous thinkers who have abandoned the traditional political tricks.

In the past, as now, Haiti's curse has been her politicians. There are still too many men of influence in the country who believe that a national election is a mandate from the people to build themselves a big new house in Pétionville and Kenscoff and a trip to Paris.

It is not that Haiti has had no able men in the presidential chair in the past. Several able and high minded men have been elected to office at various times. But their good intentions have been stultified by self-seekers and treasury-raiders who surrounded them. So far there has been little recognition of compromise, which is the greatest invention of civilization and its corollary, recognition of the rule of the majority which is civilization's most useful tool of government. Of course, it is more difficult to discover the will of the majority in a nation where less than ten per cent of the population can read and write. Still there is a remarkable lack of agreement among those few who do read and write.

Of course Haiti is not now and never has been a democracy according to the American concept. It is an elected monarchy. The President of Haiti is really a king with a palace, with a reign limited to a term of years. The term republic is used very loosely in this case. There is no concept of the rule of the majority in Haiti. The majority, being unable to read and to write, have not the least idea of what is being done in their name. Haitian class consciousness and the universal acceptance of the divine right of the crust of the upper crust is a direct denial of the concept of democracy. Neither is the Haitian chambers of Senate and deputies the same sort of thing as our Senate and House. No man may seek either of those offices in Haiti unless he has the approval of the Palace.

In addition to the self seekers who continually resorted to violence to improve their condition—they always called themselves patriots—Haiti has suffered from another internal enemy. Another brand of patriot. Out of office, he continually did everything possible to chock the wheels of government. In office himself, he spent his time waving the flag and orating on Haiti's past glory. The bones of L'Ouverture, Christophe and Dessalines were rattled for the poor peasants' breakfast, dinner and supper, never mentioning the fact that the constructive efforts of these three great men were blocked by just such "patriots" as the present day patriots. No one mentioned that all three died miserably because of their genuine love of country. Less worthy men have lived to rob, oppress, and sail off to Jamaica on their way to Paris and the boulevards. These talking patriots, who have tried to move the wheels of Haiti on wind from their lungs, are blood brothers to the empty wind bags who have done so much to nullify opportunity among the American Negroes. The Negroes of the United States have passed through a tongue-and-lung era that is three generations long. These "Race Men's" claim to greatness being the ability to mount any platform at short notice and rattle the bones of Crispus Attucks; tell what great folks the

Rex Hardy, Jr.

The American Minister and President Stenio Vincent (right)

thirteenth and fourteenth amendments to the constitution had made out of us; and *never* fail to quote, "We have made the greatest progress in sixty years of any people on the face of the globe." That always brought the house down. Even the white politicians found out what a sure-fire hit that line was and used it always when addressing a Negro audience. It made us feel so good that the office seeker did not need to give out any jobs. In fact I am told that some white man way back there around the period of the Reconstruction invented the line. It has only been changed by bringing it up to date with the number of years mentioned. Perhaps the original demagogue reared back with one hand in his bosom and the other one fumbling in his coat tails for a handkerchief and said, "You have made the greatest progress in ten years, etc." But America has produced a generation of Negroes who are impatient of the orators. They want to hear about more jobs and houses and meat on the table. They are resentful of opportunities lost while their parents sat satisfied and happy listening to crummy orators. Our heroes are no longer talkers but doers. This leaves some of our "race" men and women of yesterday puzzled and hurt. "Race leaders" are simply obsolete. The man and woman of today in America is the one who makes us believe he can make our side-meat taste like ham.

These same sentiments are mounting in Haiti. But they have not spread as rapidly as in the United States because so few of the Haitian population can read and write. But it is there and growing. There is a group of brilliant young men who have come together to form a scientific society under the leadership of Dr. Camille Lherisson, who is a great grandson of a Lowell of Massachusetts. He is a graduate of Magill University in Canada and Harvard, and head of the Department of Biology in the Medical School at Port-au-Prince, and on the staff of the hospital. Dr. Dorsainville, Dr. Louis Mars, and several other men of high calibre meet in the paved court of Dr. Lherisson's home once every week to listen to foreign scientists who happen to be visiting Haiti at the time, or to provoke discussion among themselves. These men with Divid-

77

naud, who is the most politically conscious of them all, are the realists of Haiti. Dr. Rulx Léon, Director General of the Public Health Department, is definitely of these thinking men who hold the future of Haiti in their hands. One has only to look through the Service d' Hygiene and visit the hospitals to realize what a great man is Dr. Léon. The finest medical men in Haiti are on his staff. He does not even permit his own feelings toward the men to influence him. Every one in Port-au-Prince knows that he is the personal enemy of the most brilliant man of his staff and yet he retains him. "The man is a genius. Haiti needs his talents," Dr. Léon explained. "It is not for me to thrust my personal disagreements before the welfare of the country. I am trying to keep this department up to the standard set by the American doctors of the Occupation. Unfortunately there is so little money with which to work." And the man in question is just as big as Dr. Léon. He gives everything in him to his work. Everywhere in the National Medical Service there is evidence of great talent and high character.

It is touching to go through the hospital and visit the maternity ward. Young Dr. Sam has charge there. He is the son of the President Guillaume Sam, whose horrible death brought on the Occupation in 1915. Nowhere is there a more earnest physician than Dr. Sam. How he loves those babies that are delivered under his care! This is real devotion. His face is so fine and intelligent, and he is so careful with the very poorest of the peasant mothers who come to his out-patient clinic! Nothing is finer in all Haiti than Dr. Sam at work. The same thing, but not so obvious, is felt about Dr. Seide. The Service d'Hygiene is full of character and talent and that is another way of saying that Dr. Leon is a big man. Any little-souled man would be too petty to hire such men. The man evidently has no fear of being dwarfed by his subordinates.

Among these men, and Elie Lescot, Haitian minister at Washington, is of them, one sees the real tragedy of Haiti. Here are clear headed, honest men of ability who see what is to be done for the salvation of Haiti, but there are "so many

Rex Hardy, Jr.

Dr. Rulx Léon and family

ways that wind and wind" and there is so much red tape, so many bad political habits that must be forgotten before they can be at all effective. People are beginning to say that the most promising man in Haiti to untangle this snarl-upon-snarl in government is the dynamic young Dividnaud. He is not only intelligent, he has force in his makeup and a world of courage. He conducts the affairs of his department with a brisk celerity. He is no dreamer, no rattler-of-bones, no demagogue. The Minister of the Interior is a man of action if ever one lived. And he is continually spoken of as the most audacious man in all Haiti. It has been proven conclusively that he cannot be bluffed and bullied. The President knows that and the people know that the President knows it. There is a spirit in him and others that is opposed to the old-style Haitian who has his eyes closed to fact and keeps chanting to himself that Haiti has a glorious past and that everything is just lovely. They know that everything is *not* lovely; that what happened in 1804 was all to Haiti's glory, but this is another century and another age. The patriots of 1804 did what was necessary then. It is now another time that calls for patriotism. They feel that they must do those things which will prove that they deserve their freedom. It is said over and over that they are weary of the type of politician who does everything to benefit himself and nothing to benefit his country but who is the first to rush to press to "defend" Haiti from criticism. These "defenses" are the only returns that Haiti receives for the money the "defender" is allowed to squander and the opportunities for national advancement that he ignores or prostitutes to his own advantage. The honest and earnest of Haiti do not want Haiti apologized for. They want to make these apologies unnecessary. So they are now laying the groundwork for greater unity and progress in the future.

They realize that internal matters are not so glory-getting as foreign wars, but they are even more necessary. They see that all is *not* well, that public education, transportation and economics need more attention, much more than do the bones of Dessalines. The peasants of Haiti are so hungry, and relief would not be difficult with some planning. They are refusing to see the glorified Haiti of the demagogue's tongue. These few intellectuals must struggle against the blind political pirates and the inert mass of illiterates.

That brings us to the most striking phenomenon in Haiti to a visiting American. That habit of lying! It is safe to say that this art, pastime, expedient or whatever one wishes to call it, is more than any other factor responsible for Haiti's tragic history. Certain people in the early days of the Republic took to deceiving first themselves and then others to keep from looking at the dismal picture before them. For it was dismal, make no mistake about that, if it is looked at from the viewpoint of the educated mulatto and the thinking blacks. This freedom from slavery only looked like a big watermelon cutting and fish-fry to the irresponsible blacks, those people who have no memory of yesterday and no suspicion of tomorrow. L'Ouverture, Christophe, Pétion and Dessalines saw it as the grave problem it was. No country has ever had more difficult tasks. In the first place Haiti had never been a country. It had always been a colony so that there had never been any real government there. So that the victors were not taking over an established government. They were trying to make a government of the wreck of a colony. And not out of the people who had at least been in the habit of thinking of government as something real and tangible. They were trying to make a nation out of very diffident material. These few intelligent blacks and mulattoes set out to make a nation out of slaves to whom the very word government sounded like something vague and distant. Government was something, they felt, for masters and employers to worry over while one rested from the ardors of slavery. It has not yet come to be the concern of the great mass of Haitians.

It must have been a terrible hour for each of the three actual liberators of Haiti, when having driven the last of the Frenchmen from their shores, they came at last face to face with the people for whom they had fought so ferociously and so long. Christophe, Dessalines and Pétion were realists. Every plan

81

they laid out attests this. They tried to deal with things as they were. But Dessalines was murdered; Christophe killed himself mercifully to prevent the people for whom he had fought so valiantly from doing it in a more brutal manner. Pétion saw his co-leaders fall and abandoned his great plans for restoration of the coffee and sugar estates and other developments that had once brought such great wealth to the colony of Saint Dominique.

Perhaps it was in this way that Haitians began to deceive themselves about actualities and to throw a gloss over facts. Certainly at the present time the art of saying what one would like to be believed instead of the glaring fact is highly developed in Haiti. And when an unpleasant truth must be acknowledged a childish and fantastic explanation is ready at hand. More often it is an explanation that nobody but an idiot could accept but it is told to intelligent people with an air of gravity. This lying habit goes from the thatched hut to the mansion, the only differences being in the things that are lied about. The upper class lie about the things for the most part that touch their pride. The peasant lies about things that affect his well-being like work, and food, and small change. The Haitian peasant is a warm and gentle person, really. But he often fancies himself to be Ti Malice, the sharp trickster of Haitian folk-lore.

The Haitian people are gentle and lovable except for their enormous and unconscious cruelty. It is the peasants who tie the feet of chickens and turkeys together and sling the bundle over their shoulders with the heads of the fowls hanging down and walk for miles down mountains to the market. The sun grows hot and the creatures all but perish of thirst and they do faint from their unnatural and unhappy position. I have bought chickens from women who came into my yard and found them unconscious. Sometimes the skin would be rubbed from their thighs from being tied too tight. They bore holes in the rumps of the donkeys by prodding them with sharp sticks to make them hurry when they have been driving donkeys for centuries and should know by now that the little animals are not inclined to speed. I have seen great pieces of hide scraped off the rumps and thighs of these patient little beasts, yet they were still being driven. There are thousands of donkeys in Haiti whose ears have been beaten off in an effort to hurry them. I have seen horses raw from their withers to their rumps, scalded by saddles and still being worked.

I say Haitian people are unconsciously cruel instead of merely the peasants. I know that the upper classes do not sell chickens nor drive donkeys, but they do rule the country and make the laws. If they were conscious of the cruelty of the thing, they would forbid it. I spoke of this one day to Jules Faine when I visited him and found him chasing some boys away who were trying to kill birds with stones. I said that he was the first Haitian whom I had noticed who seemed to care about such things.

"Why should these peasants be tender with animals?" he asked gently. "No one has been tender with them."

"Why do you Americans always speak of our cruelty to animals?" The editor of the *Le Matin* asked me. "You are cruel also. You boil live lobsters."

"Yes," I said, "but the people who sell them would not be permitted to drag them by the legs from Massachusetts to Virginia, nor to half-skin them on the way."

"It is all the same." He shied away from actuality and went on.

Then again under the very sound of the drums, the upper class Haitian will tell you that there is no such thing as Voodoo in Haiti, and that all that has been written about it is nothing but the malicious lies of foreigners. He knows that is not so and should know that you know that it is not true. Down in his heart he does not hate Voodoo worship. Even if he is not an adept himself he sees it about him every day and takes it for a matter of course, but he lies to save his own and the national pride. He has read the fantastic things that have been written about Haitian Voodoo by people who know nothing at all about it. Consequently, there are the stereotyped tales of virgin worship, human sacrifice and other elements borrowed from European origins. All this paints the Haitian as a savage and he does not like to be spoken of like that. So he takes refuge in flight. He denies the knowledge and the existence of the whole thing. But a peasant who has been kindly treated will answer frankly if he is not intimidated by the presence of a Gros Negre or a policeman. That is, if the policeman is strange to him or is known to be self-conscious about Voodoo. But that same peasant who answered you so freely and so frankly about Voodoo, if you paid him in advance for the simplest service would not return with your change. The employer class in Haiti continually warn their foreign friends not to pay for any service in advance nor to send anyone off with change. The peasant does not consider this as stealing. He prides himself on having put over a smart business deal. What he might lose by it in future business never occurs to him. And while this applies particularly to the servant class, it is just as well not to pay any money in advance to *anyone* in Haiti unless you know them very well indeed.

This self-deception on the upper levels takes another turn. It sounds a good deal like wishful thinking out loud. They would like to say that Haiti is a happy and well-ordered country and so they just say it, obvious facts to the contrary. There is the marked tendency to refuse responsibility for anything that is unfavorable. Some outside influence, they say, usually the United States or Santo Domingo, is responsible for all the ills of Haiti. For example in June and July I learned that thousands of Haitian laborers were being expelled from Cuba and returned to Haiti. Knowing that work was scarce and hunger plentiful already I asked what was going to be done about providing jobs for these additional hands. Among answers I got was "What can we do? We are a poor country that has been made poorer by an Occupation forced upon us by the United States. So now we have no money to provide work for our laborers." "But," I countered, "you and many others have told me that the Occupation brought a great deal of money here which you were sorry to lose." "Oh, perhaps they did make jobs for a few hundred people, but what is that when they robbed the country so completely? You *see* that we have nothing left, and besides they are still holding our customs and so we cannot sell our coffee to any advantage. France will always buy our coffee if only they would make decent terms with France. Then there would be work for all our people."

"But I have just heard that France has attempted to collect more for her debt than your country actually owed her and the American fiscal agents would not permit it. Is that not true?"

"We know nothing, Mademoiselle. All we know is that the Marines saw that our country was rich and so they came and robbed us until we grew tired of it and drove them away."

"You evidently were very slow to wrath because they stayed here nineteen years, I believe," I said.

"Yes, and we would have let them stay here longer but the Americans have no politeness so we drove them out. They knew that they had no right to come here in the beginning."

"But, didn't you have some sort of disturbance here, and were you not in embarrassing debt to some European nations? It seems that I heard something of the sort."

"We never owed any debts. We had plenty of gold in our bank which the Americans took away and never returned to us. They claimed that we owed debts so that they could have an excuse to rob us. When they had impoverished the country they left, and now our streets are full of beggars and the whole country is very poor. But what can a weak country like Haiti do when a powerful nation like your own forces its military upon us, kills our citizens and steals our money?"

"No doubt you are correct in what you say. However, an official of your own government told me that Haiti borrowed $40,000,000 to pay off these same foreign debts which you tell never existed at all."

"Mlle., I swear on the head of my mother that we had no debts. The Americans did force us to borrow the money so that they could steal it from us. That is the truth. Poor Haiti has suffered much."

All this was spoken with the utmost gravity. There was a dash of self pity in it. He was patently sorry for himself and all of the citizens who had suffered so much for love of country. If I did not know that every word of it was a lie, I would have been bound to believe him, his lies were that bold and brazen. His statements presupposed that I could not read and even if I could that there were no historical documents in existence that dealt with Haiti. I soon learned to accept these insults to my intelligence without protest because they happened so often.

With all the grave problems in Haiti to be dealt with, President Stenio Vincent, himself, finds time to indulge in the national pastime of blowing up a hurricane with his tongue. He has fabricated a conqueror's role for himself and struts as the second deliverer of Haiti, thus ranking himself with L'Ouverture, Dessalines and Christophe. He goes about it by having himself photographed with the frowning mien of a conqueror and looking for all the world like a ferocious rabbit. Without cracking a smile he announces himself as the Second Deliverer of Haiti. He bases his claim on the fact that President Roosevelt, in keeping with his good-neighbor policy, withdrew the Marines from Haiti during Vincent's administration. He knows that the N.A.A.C.P., The Nation and certain other organizations had a great deal more to do with the withdrawal of the Marines than Vincent did and much more than they are given credit for. In fact they are never mentioned when Vincent orates about Second Independence and honors himself as the Second Liberator. The story of how he drove out the Marines all by himself is a great one, the way he tells it. He even holds a celebration about it every year on August 21st. For the 1937 celebration he is supposed to have spent 80,000 gourds (about $16,000) to illumine the city of Port-au-Prince in celebration of an event that never took place.

But in spite of the great cost, something seemed lacking. Not a great number of people turned out and those who did come did not effervesce. It went off with more spirit in 1936 when the people were not so hungry as they had become a year later. The Haitian people naturally love fetes, and under

86

normal circumstances they are happy to join in celebrating anything at all. No one in Haiti actually believes that President Vincent drove out the Marines, because even the humblest peasant knows that there was no fighting on the occasion of their departure and from past experience they know if there had been any fighting the Marines would have been on top as usual. But if the President wished to celebrate something, why not? After all the imagination is a beautiful thing.

Now in 1937 hunger and want were stalking the land. There were people who did not have a garment of any kind to cover their nakedness so that they could not come out of doors at all. As far back as November 1936 there were scared whispers about prisoners starving to death in the prison in Port-au-Prince. The jobless peasant still felt hungry after his meal of sour oranges. They had nothing really against a celebration for any reason whatsoever, but some "pois rouge et dee wee" (red beans and rice) would have suited their mood better than the electric lights, especially in celebration of a fiction. A great many expressed resentment toward the whole thing. Why celebrate the leaving of the Marine Corps when nobody wanted the Marines to go anyway? Their era of prosperity had left with the Marines. If President Vincent had arranged for them to go, then he was no friend to the people. The man they wanted to honor was the one who could bring them back. A great many of them had their doubts as to whether the $16,000 stated actually was spent. "They don't spend all of this money as they tell us. The Gros Negre only find more excuse to take money for themselves." The Champ de Mars was full of suspicion and doubt that night.

It is a well known fact, and freely acknowledged in Haiti, that before the withdrawal of the American Marines, Colonel Little and the officers of the Occupation prepared a Haitian fighting force of three thousand men under Colonel Calixe. With so many trained men, and with the equipment left by the Americans plus that bought by the Haitian government, it would seem that some effective resistance could be made to an invasion from Santo Domingo if necessary. Therefore it is astonishing to read the recent statements of President Vincent that Haiti is defenseless before the onslaughts of Santo Domingo. That statement is far from true and very puzzling until one considers the reports of starvation among the Haitian peasants and the rumors of uprisings. One revolt was reported definitely under way at Cayes in the south when the massacre took place on the border. That whole department was said to be seething with revolt at the results of hunger. Does President Vincent think it better to allow the Dominicans to kill a few thousand Haitian peasants than to arm the peasants and risk being killed himself? Does he fear that if the stores of ammunition in the basement of the palace were issued to the army that his own days in the palace would be numbered? From actual conditions in Haiti these questions are not too far fetched. President Vincent practically acknowledged it himself in his statement to Quentin Reynolds in which he said that the Garde d'Haiti was only large enough to police Haiti. Are his own people more to be feared than Trujillo? Does he reason that after all those few thousand of peasants are dead and gone and he is still President in the palace? But if the arms and the ammunition in the basement of the palace ever got out of his control in his attempt to avenge their massacre, he might find himself "sailing for Jamaica" like many other Haitian ex-presidents have done?

Another significant figure in Haitian life is Colonel Calixe, chief of the Garde d'Haiti, which means that he is the number one man in the military forces of Haiti. He is a tall, slender black man around forty with the most beautiful hands and feet that I have ever beheld on a man. He is truly loved and honored by the three thousand men under him. His officers are well-trained professional men—doctors, engineers, lawyers and the like. There is no doubt that the military love their chief. But it is apparent that others fear his influence. Perhaps they think he might be moved to seize executive power, for he is bound by a curious oath. Not only must he refrain from moving against the Palace, he is further under threat of punishment of death if anything should happen to the President in any way at all. More than that, the ammunition is kept in the basement of the Palace under the special eye of Col. Armand, mulatto choice of the President for military chief. But the Garde d'Haiti was trained and established under the American military officers of the Occupation, and it is said that Colonel Little selected Calixe as the most able of all the Haitian officers available and had insisted on him as chief. Someone told me that the American officers had preferred Calixe, but also that President Vincent had felt that the appointment was wise because Colonel Calixe was a hero among the blacks and also because he is from the North. He is a native of Fort Liberty, a small town near Cape Haitian, and the North has always played an important part in the history of Haiti. This was then an attempt to soften the differences between the blacks and the mulattoes and recognize the importance of the North. Otherwise the administration would have preferred the mulatto Colonel André or La Fontant if Armand was not appointed. To his great credit it must be said that in the face of great opposition, the President has taken many steps to destroy this antagonism between the mulattoes and the blacks which has been the cause of so much bloodshed in Haiti's past and has been one of the major obstacles to national unity. But the end is not yet in sight. Anyway, there is Colonel Calixe with his long tapering fingers and his beautiful slender feet, very honest and conscientious and doing a beautiful job of keeping order in Haiti. If he is conscious of the jitters he inspires in other office holders and men of ambitions, he does not show it. He has told me that he is a man of arms and wishes no other job than the one he has. In fact we have a standing joke between us that when I become President of Haiti, he is going to be my chief of the army and I am going to allow him to establish state farms in all of the departments of Haiti, a thing which he has long wanted to do in order to eliminate the beggars from the streets of Port-au-Prince, and provide food for the hospitals, jails and other state institutions, since there is not enough tax money to do these things well. He is pathetically eager to clear the streets of Haiti of beggars and petty thieves and to make his department shine generally. If he has ambitions outside of his office, he dissembles well. And what a beautifully polished Sam Brown belt on his perfect figure and what lovely, gold-looking buckles on his belt!

There is somebody else in Haiti that the people cannot forget. He is not there in person, but his shadow walks around like a man. That is the shadow of Trujillo, President of neighboring Santo Domingo. Trujillo is not in Haiti; he is not even a Haitian but he has connections that reach all around. He has relatives there and numerous friends and admirers. All day long, Haitians are pointing to the Man of Santo Domingo. Some of them with fear, the rest with admiration. Some Haitians even speak of him with hope. They reason that if he can bring peace and advancement to Santo Domingo, he can contrive something of the kind in Haiti. They remember his resplendent visit to Haiti in 1936 and afterwards his gift of food and provisions to the Haitian peasants. Trujillo is *really* among those present in Haiti. Moreover, the Haitian who cannot find work in his own country, immediately thinks of migrating to Santo Domingo. Before the recent border trouble, there were thousands of Haitians in Santo Domingo because of better working and living conditions. With this condition in mind, Trujillo is supposed to have made a speech in which he threatened in a veiled manner to clean up the Haitian end of the island. His contention being, perhaps, that his own country always had to share the burden of Haiti's poor economic arrangement. So that Santo Domingo's own strides toward advancement were being shortened by having to absorb great numbers of the unemployed of her practically static neighbor. So the poor people of Haiti see more in Trujillo than just the President of a neighboring country.

Among the whispered angles of the notorious case of Joseph Jolibois, Fils, is the one that Jolibois, Fils, was the friend of Trujillo, and that when the President of Santo Domingo learned of his mysterious death in jail, he burst into a rage and expelled the Haitian Minister from his country. He is said to have accused someone very high in Haitian national life of murdering his friend Jolibois, Fils, to get him out of the way because he was becoming too popular with the people and too open in his opposition to the Administration. That was in 1936. Since then people whisper: "They say that Jolibois was poisoned in that prison. Jolibois was accused of shooting Elie Elius to death but there was no proof. They say that both men were troublesome and were liquidated for that reason. They say that Trujillo is in a great rage over the death of his friend and means to avenge him. Soon now, perhaps, he will come with his great army to punish the Haitian government for the death of Jolibois. Who knows?"

These new and vigorous young Haitian intellectuals feel that Santo Domingo's great advancement should spur Haiti out of her fog of self-deception, internal strife and general backwardness. They are advocating universal free grammar schools as in the United States and a common language. As things stand, the upper class Haitians speak French and the peasants speak Creole. M. Sejourne' rightfully contends that the barrier of language is a serious thing in a nation. It makes for division and distrust through lack of understanding. He thinks that either French must speedily be taught to all, or that Haiti must adopt Creole as its official language and commission some of its scholars like Jules Faine to reduce the patois to writing. Then there is the matter of religion. Nominally Haiti is a Catholic country, but in reality it is deeply pagan. Some of the young men are ceasing to apologize for this. They feel that the foreign Catholic priests do the country much more harm than Voodoo does. They are eager for the day when they shall expel the French and Belgian priests whom they say foster and propagate "war between the skins." They mean by that, that they encourage differences among the mulattoes and the blacks, besides impoverishing the country by the great sums that they collect and send to Rome and France. Also they say that the priests, in order to crush a powerful rival, place all the evils of politics and what not upon the shoulders of Voodoo.

The politicians, to cover up their mistakes, have also seized

91

upon this device. As someone in America said of whiskey, Voodoo has more enemies in public and more friends in private than anything else in Haiti. None of the sons of Voodoo who sit in high places have yet had the courage to defend it publicly, though they know quite well and acknowledge privately that Voodoo is a harmless pagan cult that sacrifices domestic animals at its worst. The very same animals that are killed and eaten every day in most of the civilized countries of the world. So since Voodoo is openly acknowledged by the humble only, it is safe to blame all the ill of Haiti on Voodoo. I predict that this state of affairs will not last forever. A feeling of nationalism is growing in Haiti among the young. They admire France less and less, and their own native patterns more. They are contending that Voodoo is not what is wrong with Haiti. The thing fettering the country is its politics and those foreign priests.

Well, anyway, there is Haiti as it is, and there is this class of new and thinking young Haitians who are on the side lines for the most part at the moment, becoming more and more world-and-progress conscious all the time. And always there is the dynamic and forceful Trujillo, the Ever-Ready, gazing across the frontier with a steely eye. Whither Haiti?

CHAPTER 8

✦

THE BLACK JOAN OF ARC

Haiti, the black daughter of France, also has its Joan of Arc. Celestina Simon stands over against The Maid of Orleans. Both of these young women sprung alike from the soil. Both led armies and came to unbelievable power by no other right than communion with mysterious voices and spirits. Both of these women stood behind weak ruling chairs, and both departed their glory for ignominy. The Duke of Burgundy burned Joan at the stake. The conquering hordes of Michel Cincinnatus Leconte drove Celestina Simon from the Haitian palace and doomed her to a dark and dishonored old age. But if Celestina and her father were driven out of power and public life, they have not lost their places in the minds of the people. More legends surround the name of Simon than any other character in the history of Haiti.

History says that General François Antoine Simon became President of Haiti in 1908, but practically the whole country agrees that he never should have been. There are countless tales of this crude soldier peasant's stumbling and blunders in the palace where he had no right to be. His not knowing what to do in matters of state; what to say to foreign diplomats; and how to behave amid the luxuries of the palace, all are told and told again. But these possibilities have never been considered by the men who made him president in a desperate effort to cut short the reforms instituted by the noble Nord Alexis. It was near the end of the presidential term of Nord Alexis and he was full of years. He did not wish to run for office again, but he was favoring a man who was pledged to continue his policies of honesty in government and the development of Haiti. This seemed a waste of money and opportunity to certain politicians. They had enough of the stringent honesty of President Alexis and wanted no more of the like. So they engineered General Simon into the palace. They knew he was too ignorant and boorish to make much of a president. But they did not shove him into the palace to do any governing. He was put there as a device. His "advisors" knew perfectly well what to do about matters of state. At least they knew what they *wanted* to do about such things. And the great benefits to be derived from having the perfect tool in office as a facade were too great to be lost on account of the tool's bad social form. What the "advisors" had not reckoned with was Celestina Simon and Simalo, the goat.

It was not that no one had ever heard of Celestina's powers as a Mambo. That was no secret. Everybody around Aux Cayes and the Department of the South generally knew that General François Antoine Simon was a great follower of the loa, and that his daughter Celestina was his trusted priestess. No one was surprised at this, for while Simon was the military governor of the Department of the South, it was well known that he had come up the military ladder from the most humble beginnings. Also, practically everyone had heard of his pet goat Simalo. It was claimed by the soldiers of Simon's army that they were invincible because of the presence of the priestess Celestina and her consort, Simalo, in the front ranks of the force. Their combined powers utterly routed the government forces at Ansa-à-veau, so they said.

General Simon, it is recalled, had taken the field because he had been removed from office by Nord Alexis. He had been removed because he let it be known that he had presidential ambitions and President Alexis had his own ideas as to who should follow him in office. So he determined to squelch Simon by demoting him. But as Nord Alexis well knew, Simon was being prompted by others with more intelligence but less courage. And Simon won the battle of Ansa-à-veau and won his way into the national palace only because the government was betrayed and because others had uses for a man like Simon. But Simon brought along with his usefulness, himself, his daughter Celestina, and Simalo, the goat. There are tales and tales of the services to the loa on that march from Aux Cayes to Port-au-Prince, especially the services that Celestina made to Ogoun Feraille, the god of war, to make the men of her army impervious to bullet and blade. The army came marching into the capital carrying their coco macaque sticks to which had been tied a red handkerchief. This was a sign that Ogoun was protecting them. The stories of Celestina's part in the battles, of her marching in advance of the men and firing them by her own ferocious attack upon the enemy had all preceded the army to the capital. The populace therefore made a great clamor as she entered the city at the head of the men of arms and called her the black Joan of Arc.

When her father became president, her prestige increased, and the flattery about her became almost hysterical when it was discovered that President Simon did and granted whatever Celestina approved. She was not only loved as a daughter, she was revered and respected as a great houngan. Nevertheless there was a great deal of laughter behind sophisticated hands in Port-au-Prince at the antics of the attachments of the president to his daughter and his goat.

But the laughter died very quickly. In the first place Simon was not as manageable as anticipated. He took flattery seriously and it bloated him. It was impossible to ignore the fact that the saying of Celestina and the behavior of Simalo were of greater importance to him than any other national affairs, for indeed, the woman and the goat had come to be affairs of the nation.

The disgust and the fear of the upper class Haitians grew with their astonishment. For instance, when it was common knowledge that Voodoo services and the ceremonies were being held in the national palace, many of them decided to keep as far away as possible and to have nothing at all to do with such persons, but President Simon thought differently. He gave great dinners and other state functions and the aristocrats dared not refuse his invitations. They knew the temper of the man too well for that. So they came at his thinly veiled command, ate, drank, and danced. Before his face they laughed loudly at all of his jokes and made the appearance of happiness. The moment his back was turned they looked at each other fearfully. They also looked with dread suspicion at the food and the wine. "Are we drinking wine or dirty *blood* and wine?" they asked each other in quick whispers. Dare they leave the potage untasted? Is this roast really beef or is it————? But just then the face of the president was turned toward them and they chewed and swallowed with fear and made out somehow to smile and flatter. Often it was said that a Voodoo ceremony was going on in the basement chambers while the state function was glittering its farcical way in the salon.

The Mountain House, the summer palace of President Simon, was the scene of the greatest ceremonies, however. It was rumored that there took place the celebrations of the dread Secte Rouge and that years later the blood stains on the walls and floor of one room were so ghastly that they were difficult to cover with paint. There Simon, and all those in the high places who believed with him, gathered for these services under the priestess Celestina and Simalo.

The most dramatic story of all tells about the breaking of Simalo's heart. Rumor had it that years before there had been a "marriage" between Celestina and Simalo. A houngan had mysteriously tied them together for many causes and the power of each depended upon the other. All had gone happily until they were elevated to the palace. Then the flattery of many men gave Simon hope that his black daughter might capture a man of position and wealth. His and her ears heard only the flattery. They heard none of the fear and loathing that was increasing about them. Simon and Celestina saw nothing to prevent an advantageous marriage, so they began to plan for it. So far as they could see, the only barrier was the previous betrothal to Simalo. So they set about getting a divorce.

A powerful houngan whom Simon had brought from the South with him was said to have officiated at this ceremony. At the same time an elaborate function was going on in the salon of the palace. It was to be a celebration of the freeing of Celestina from her vows to the goat so that she might marry a man. Celestina herself was kept in her own bedroom until the ceremony was over. It was said to be a terrible wrench to her and she supported the sorrow with difficulty. It was only the prospect of a brilliant marriage, now that she was the daughter of the president, that sustained her in grief.

President Simon himself went from salon to basement several times watching the progress in his impatience to report the "liberation" of Celestina, feeling of course that several men of wealth and education were ready to prostrate themselves before his daughter. And each time that he left the room, the uneasy crowd above stairs exchanged hurried looks and whispers about the ceremony going on beneath them. It was one of those secrets that everyone had gotten hold of.

Finally, as he started below again, an attendant met him in the corridor and whispered that the ceremony was over and "Celestina est libre." The President sought his daughter and led her into the great salon, announcing, "Celestina is free. She may marry anyone she chooses now."

The news was received in great embarrassment. There was a polite show of joy, but no man rushed forward to take the widow of Simalo. One young deputy who escorted her on several occasions was fired on from ambush and killed; it was never made clear just why. At any rate, she has never married a man.

As for Simalo, it is said that his grief over the divorce was so great that he did not linger long after that. Some say, of course, that he was killed by the houngan that same day. A few days later there were as many whispers about the manner of his death as there would have been about the archbishop. It was certain that he was dead and both Simon and Celestina were sodden with grief. It is said that they could not bear the thought of Simalo being dumped in a hole and buried like any other dead animal. He must be buried like a man who had obligations to a god and hopes of eternity. So a priest and the Catholic church were tricked into giving him a Christian burial. The body of Simalo in a closed coffin was borne to the Cathedral in great pomp and glory. It was represented to the priest that a close relative of the president had passed away. There were great bouquets of flowers, smoking censora, the chanted mass for the dead and great weeping. A most impressive funeral, all in all. It was only when the services were completely over that the priest became suspicious and discovered that all this holy service had been performed over a goat. He was furious and the scandal spread over all Haiti. Some contend that the ill luck that attended Simon after was because of his treatment of Simalo. Perhaps this elaborate funeral was an act of atonement. Perhaps Simon was hiding his heartbreak in the rites. It might have been the first flinching from the price of ambition. After all these years educated folk of Port-au-Prince are still laughing at the clown who occupied their palace for two years. But there is pathos too in the story.

It is the story of a peasant who gained the palace but lost his goat. He sacrificed his best friend to ambition which turned upon him and mocked his happiness to death. In the fog of flattery, he lost sight of the fact that goats and peasants are seldom the helms of empire.

Of this triumvirate, Celestina, Simon and Simalo who had come up from the south to the capitol of Haiti, perhaps Simalo, by his early death, came off best. There was President Simon in the palace, there by the grace of corrupt politicians who planned to use him to their own advantage, believing that he was there by the magic powers of his daughter and his goat. Here he was making every social, diplomatic and political blunder conceivable, and thinking that he was cutting a great figure. And all the while, his make-believe paradise was dissolving before harsh reality. His simple faith like the priests of Baal was in his daughter and in his gods and they failed him.

It must have been disheartening to the peasant-General-Governor-President Simon when, confident of victory on account of the powers of Ogoun, he took the field against Leconte, to find that the most numerous and best directed bullets always win battles in spite of the gods. But it is said that he never lost faith in the powers of Celestina and the loa. He firmly believed, but for her he never would have become governor of the South.

There are many to agree with him in this. It is said that Celestina was possessed of the greatest courage and urged her father to fight at every challenge. It was because of this prompt and strong action that he pulled himself up by his boot straps. Of course, they say his way of explanation that Celestina had this great courage was because she had such power from the loa. They never failed her until she broke her vows. But, anyway, it is a matter of history that she not only had great personal bravery, she was able to inspire others with the same, her father and his soldiers being the first to feel her personality.

The people laugh and laugh at the capers of President Simon in the palace. They do not laugh at Celestina. She is today an elderly woman living in poverty in the South and she is still to the thinking Haitian a sinister figure. The glory of the days when she had a special military attaché of her own (General André Chevalier) and wielded power absolute from the palace are gone. She is a surly figure of the past. Some say that she pronounced a terrible curse against the man whose victorious army drove Simon from power. So that when the palace was blown up and Leconte killed, they said it was the power of Celestina still at work.

There are numerous accounts of Simon's grief at the loss of his goat. He used to weary his listeners with his memories of the feats of Simalo in military campaigns. It was plain that he considered the goat more than beast, more than man, more than just a friend. There was something of worship there.

It is said that one Sunday after the death of Simalo, Simon had the cabinet members and several other persons of importance assembled at the palace. He delivered one of the orations that he delighted to make and having embarrassed himself by making a faux pas, dismissed them. But a few intimates were allowed to remain and wander about informally. The President was moving towards his private apartments when he ran into the Minister of War, General Septimus Marius. He stopped suddenly as if he had seen a ghost and then broke into tears and said, "My dear Marius, as soon as I see your long beard, I think of my dear Simalo." And he wept so hard that the other guests felt that they had better weep with him.

There seems to be no doubt that Celestina and Simon enjoyed their places of power in the palace. Also that the young Amazon stirred something heroic in the hearts of Haiti for a time. She brought a whiff of the battle field with her as she came and made virile men think again of Christophe and Dessalines.

But soon the tales of the "services" in the palace, the sacrifices at Mountain House, the cruelty of Celestina and the affairs of the goat filled Haiti's cup of disgust to the brim. Insurrections began. Simon and Celestina confident in their loa marched out to conquer as before. Simon beat down one uprising only to be met by others. He was living over the life of Macbeth and his lady, both betrayed by their mysteries. After many harried months, he bowed before that which he could no longer oppose with conviction. So Simon like many other presidents of Haiti sailed for Jamaica.

In his exile the peasant who had become a soldier, then a general, then a governor, then a president must have thought about his march from himself into the capital, into other men's hopes and schemes. In a foreign land there he had no army, no importance, no daughter, no goat. He had nothing but time for weapons and friends and the chances are he had never learned how to use time in bulk. Probably he used what he could of it in remembering, and no doubt he remembered the days when he was governor of Aux Cayes, when he, his priestess daughter and his goat were happy rulers, before ambition tricked them into the palace.

"Oh, well," they conclude, "what can you expect? One cannot expect to prosper who breaks his vows to the loa. If President Simon had not killed Simalo—"

Ah Bo Bo!

CHAPTER 9

∵

DEATH OF LECONTE

T his is the story of the death of President Leconte the way
the people tell it. The history books all say Cincinnatus
Leconte died in the explosion that destroyed the palace,
but the people do not tell it that way. Not one person, high
or low, ever told me that Leconte was killed by the explosion.
It is generally accepted that the destruction of the palace was
to cover up the fact that the President was already dead by
violence.

There are many reasons given for the alleged assassination,
and each one of these motives has its own cast of characters
in the tragedy. But the main actors always remain the same.
These men were ambitious and stood to gain political power
and what goes with it in Haiti by the death of President
Leconte.

For example, some tell a story of the little son of Leconte
who was said to be a love child. He loved the boy with a great
love, but that seemed not to be reason enough to cause him
to marry the mother of his child. She belonged to a high caste
family and there was said to be a great deal of hard feeling
between the family of the young woman and the President.

Those who contend that this friction was behind the assassination point out that the child was not in the palace when the explosion took place. He was at the home of his mother's people.

All the other reasons given for his alleged assassination were political. The only differences in the accounts were, whose political aspirations were being choked off by Leconte's actions.

It is not to be inferred from this that Leconte was a tyrant. On the contrary he is credited with beginning numerous reforms and generally taking progressive steps. He was merely in the way of other men's ambition by virtue of the office he held.

The first person who told me about it said that he was not even killed in the executive mansion. He said that a message came to the president to visit his little son who was with his mother at the time. He disguised himself and entered the bus driven by the aged coachman of the palace called Edmond, whose loyalty to Leconte was doubtful. Rumor says that they left the palace by the gate called Port Salnave, and that Leconte left the conveyance at the house of the father of his child's mother, whose father was one of his Ministers, and never came out again. That is, he never came out alive. The family whose honor had been outraged by the refusal of Leconte to marry the daughter of the house had secretly joined forces with the president's political enemies. Some of them were in the house when Leconte arrived. The arrangements for the body to be carried out on the Plain-Cul-de-Sac to be buried had already been made. It is said that he was killed after a short altercation. The body was wrapped up, placed in the bus and driven out to the estate of one of the conspirators to be buried. The old coachman was rewarded and the palace blown up. The very next person that I told this version to, agreed that Leconte did get into the bus and he did leave the palace by the gate Salnave. But they maintained that he was lured out by the coachman whom he trusted. This Edmond came to the President with a tale of his cabinet gathered at a certain place on the Plain-Cul-de-Sac and plotting the downfall of the president at that very moment. President Leconte must come and see this infamy with his own eyes. The President slightly disguised entered the bus and was driven off. Out on the Plain, the bus was surrounded and he was killed and buried out there on the estate of a powerful man who himself had presidential ambitions.

But I kept on talking to people and asking questions about Leconte and they kept on telling me things. So I came to hear from many people a story that was the same in all the essential points. Minor details differed of course. But the happenings that follow were repeated to me by numerous persons.

Sansarique, Leconte's Minister of the Interior, was most faithful to his chief and loved him like a brother. He got wind of a conspiracy against the life of Leconte and warned him time and again to be careful. But the President was not inclined to take these warnings too seriously. He knew that he was very popular with the people and went to work building Casernes and planning other improvements. But the conspirators grew bold by seeming immunity. They began to move with more assurance. Rumors of plots and conspiracies increased. Definite plans seemed to have been made and the Minister of the Interior began to be really alarmed and rushed to the President and mentioned names. He accused Tancred Auguste, Volcius Nerette, Chef de Sûreté, and La Roche, Minister of Agriculture, of plotting to overthrow the regime of Leconte and to make Auguste president in his stead. He urged the President to lose no time in arresting Auguste and Nerette. But such was the confidence of Leconte in his well-being that he refused to believe this advice. He put it down to over anxiety on the part of a friend. This was the state of affairs for some time before the night of the explosion.

One man told me what he saw on the night of August 7, 1912. It was the habit of many men of the upper class to gather at Thibeaut's Café on the Champ-de-Mars to eat, sip drinks, and play dice, practically every night. This night of August 7th, the crowd who loved a game of chance for moderate stakes gathered as usual. Because, he explained "when the tambour sounds, the hounsi come." Meaning those who love a thing will follow it.

But this particular evening, there was to be no dice. Thibeaut served the many social and political lights their coffee and some one called for the dice. Thibeaut's face went very stern. "Gentlemen, no dice tonight. You will please leave early as I wish to close the Café and get to bed at a good hour. Good evening, gentlemen."

The men were naturally surprised at this unusual announcement. They left the Café reluctantly in little groups and went elsewhere. My informant says that from the Champ-de-Mars, he and three associates looked towards the palace and saw the President standing alone on the balcony of the Palace. "Look at Conte Conte," somebody said, using the familiar name of affection that the people had made for him. The President was just standing there outlined by the Palace lights as if in deep thought. Across from the Palace and watching it closely was Tancred Auguste mounted on his grey horse.

The young men balked of their dice game and social evening soon left the Champ-de-Mars and the pensive President behind and went on their way seeking other amusements.

This is what they say was going on inside the Palace. Some time during the night the Chef de Sûreté came to the Palace accompanied by several men. He sent word to Leconte that he must see him on a matter of vital importance and thus persuaded the President to receive him at such an unusual hour. He said it was a matter which necessitated the greatest secrecy and Leconte hearing this took the party to the telegraph room where Nerette knew he always went when he wished to receive secret reports. This room was not only built sound proof, but it was detached from the Palace building proper for greater secrecy.

Inside the locked room Nerette began a recital of having discovered a plot against the President's regime. He began a rambling narrative that not only lacked any evidence of a plot, but the jumble of words was lacking in sense. Leconte asked

106

the Chef to tell him what he meant by these disconnected statements and began to pace up and down, no doubt trying to figure out for himself why he had been disturbed to listen to such a senseless tale. He knew there was something behind it. There were several minutes of silence while Leconte paced up and down, puzzled and annoyed. Nerette and his men huddled at one end of the room, the president pacing up and down. One time when Leconte had reached the end farthest away from Nerette, that plotter whispered to the men, "Qu'est ce que vous attendez?" (What are you waiting for?) The frightened men still huddled where they were and Nerette grew angry, "Eh, bien, Messieurs, Ca n ap'tan?" The armed butchers were lashed into action so that when the President's back was again turned to them they drew their knives and did what they had come there to do. They did in desperation that which they were afraid not to do. They butchered Leconte.

When the hacking and slashing was over, the body was removed through the Salnave door and carried to the house of one of the assassins. The work was done. Leconte was dead and his body actually removed from the palace without the faithful guard suspecting that he was not safely in bed. The conspirators most concerned were sent for and came hurriedly to the house to verify the information. The body was carefully examined. There was no mistake. The late President of Haiti was there at the feet of the men who toasted the success of the coup in rum. Then plans for the coming "elections" were rehearsed again. That settled, the final details that would dispose of the body and cover the evidence of the assassination were gone over for the last time. The body was left in the care and in the house of the same man where it now was. He was loyal to the conspirators and they had his assurance that the body would be disposed of as planned. The higher ups might go on and look to the matter of "elections." He knew they would remember him when making the new appointments. They could rest assured the body would never be seen again. Most certainly it would not be seen by anyone who favored

Leconte in his life time. So some of the conspirators hurried away to attend to matters of state while others remained there in the house with the body of Leconte, waiting. It was kept there until a man was found to take it away on a donkey. At first the body was wrapped and thrown across the donkey's back. But it was too bloody—too apt to attract attention in that way. So the peasant cut it up with his machete and loaded it in a sac paille (straw bag with two huge pockets. A sort of pannier for carrying loads on a donkey) and he was then ordered to dispose of it on an estate on the Plain-Cul-de-Sac. This peasant was paid, sworn to secrecy and dismissed. But soon he was bragging about his part in the crime. He would display his machete and explain proudly, "This is the knife that cut up the body of Leconte." During the administration that followed Leconte, it is said that he was ordered killed by a strychnine injection. But the President himself died of poisoning before it happened.

The conspirator to whose house the body of Leconte was taken before it was finally disposed of, from a nothing and a nobody, was given a government position immediately after the next administration came to power. Even his grandmother was given a pension. Indeed, the man is said to hold a government position at this moment. He seems to have fared better than anyone else who figured in the murder plot. For the candidate alleged to be at the bottom of the whole matter was himself assassinated by poisoning less than a year after taking office. Volcius Nerette was one of the 167 who were butchered in the prison by Sam and Etienne in 1915. The eight men with knives who did the actual killing of Leconte were arrested on a trumped-up charge and taken out side of the harbor in a boat and killed and their bodies thrown overboard. The man who cut up the body and hauled it away became an idiot. He still goes about the city laughing his laugh and showing the machete and gloating. But nobody listens.

When the word came back to the conspirators waiting in the house that the body had been disposed of, the brains of the plot hurried forth to find the man to carry out the final detail to cover up the murder of Leconte. He called on a young electrician named Faine (no relation to the well-known writer Jules Faine) and dragged him from his bed. Faine was told nothing about what had gone on before. He was ordered to blow up the palace at once or die. It is to be remembered that great stores of ammunition were hoarded in the palace. He was forced to rig up a device to set off this immense hoard of explosives. It is said that only fear of certain death persuaded the young man to do the work.

Thus early in the morning of August 8, 1912, the city of Port-au-Prince was rocked by an explosion that completely wrecked the palace. Other buildings near by were also injured. People were thrown out of their beds in Belair and even in Pétionville, approximately six miles away. Nearly three hundred soldiers, the palace guard, were belched out of the eruption, headless, legless, armless, eyes burnt out by the powder and just bodies and parts of bodies, mangled and mingled.

The people of Port-au-Prince awakened like that out of their sleep all rushed out doors because everybody thought it was an earthquake. When they got outside they saw it was the palace and came running, putting their cries of surprise and terror with the hurt and harmed who were crawling off from the wreckage. Sansarique rushed into the ruins seeking his friend Leconte, who was not there and would not have been able to answer him if he had been. Nobody could stop the Minister of the Interior. He tore off the hands that held him. He rushed about through the smoking ruins calling Leconte, hoping he could save him. He kept crying out that he had warned him against his enemies. Finding no way to help Leconte, finding nothing in the likeness of his friend, he wept for him bitterly. He was like old David at the gates when they brought home Absalom. They say that the friendship between Sansarique and Leconte was a beautiful thing. Here was another Damon and Pythias, another David and Jonathan. He alone of all those near to Leconte was not concerned with his political future. He had rushed into the ruins to do those things which become a man and a friend. No matter who tells the story and how, they dwell on the nobility of Sansarique. And indeed, it is a thing to make songs about.

When the daylight came they picked up something that nobody could say with any certainty was President Leconte and held a funeral. But then the way things were nobody could say the formless matter was not the late president either. So they held a state funeral and buried it.

All that being settled, right away, Tancred Auguste, with the help of his friends, was elected President of Haiti. Perhaps he could feel that divinity had pointed him to power. One day there had been Leconte occupying the palace, popular with the people, and going on about building things like Solomon. Seemingly this man was to occupy the national palace for many years to come. The people willed it to be that way. They had elected him and turned their thoughts towards peace.

But evidently God did not agree with the Haitian people, for behold God repudiated their candidate by belching him out of the palace. The poor taste of the people was corrected, and Tancred Auguste became their ruler. The sight of the explosion must have affected him deeply if rumor is true that he took to talking to himself. Also, they say he disliked to pass the ruins and avoided doing so until one day he attended a wedding and the carriages were passing the ruins before he realized it. The sight of the tragic spot must have touched his compassion too deeply, for he began to mutter aloud and almost left the carriage. At any rate, the palace food proved too rich for him, for less than a year after he had taken office he died of a digestive disturbance that his enemies called poison. So God must have changed His mind about him also. And while he was being buried, even before his body left the Cathedral for the cemetery, the mourners heard shots being fired from different parts of the City of Port-au-Prince. The successor to Tancred Auguste was being "elected."

This is what they say in Port-au-Prince about the death of President Leconte, who built the great Casernes.

Ah Bo Bo!

110

PART III

VOODOO
IN HAITI

CHAPTER 10

✺

VOODOO AND
VOODOO GODS

Dr. Holly says that in the beginning God and His woman went into the bedroom together to commence creation. That was the beginning of everything and Voodoo is just as old as that. It is the old, old mysticism of the world in African terms. Voodoo is a religion of creation and life. It is the worship of the sun, the water and other natural forces, but the symbolism is no better understood than that of other religions and consequently is taken too literally.

Thus the uplifted forefinger in greeting in Voodoo is really phallic and that means the male attributes of the Creator. The handclasp that ends in the fingers of one hand encircling the thumb of the other signifies the vulva encircling the penis, denoting the female aspect of deity. "What is the truth?" Dr. Holly asked me, and knowing that I could not answer him he answered himself through a Voodoo ceremony in which the Mambo, that is the priestess, richly dressed is asked this question ritualistically. She replies by throwing back her veil and revealing her sex organs. The ceremony means that this is the infinite, the ultimate truth. There is no mystery beyond the mysterious source of life. The ceremony continues on another phase after this. It is a dance analogous to the nuptial flight of the queen bee. The Mambo discards six veils in this dance and falls at last naked, and spiritually intoxicated, to the ground. It is considered the highest honor for all males participating to kiss her organ of creation, for Damballa, the god of gods, has permitted them to come face to face with truth.

Some of the other men of education in Haiti who have given time to the study of Voodoo esoterics do not see such deep meanings in Voodoo practices. They see only a pagan religion with an African pantheon. And right here, let it be said that the Haitian gods, mysteres, or loa are not the Catholic calendar of saints done over in black as has been stated by casual observers. This has been said over and over in print because the adepts have been seen buying the lithographs of saints, but this is done because they wish some visual representation of the invisible ones, and as yet no Haitian artist has given them an interpretation or concept of the loa. But even the most illiterate peasant knows that the picture of the saint is only an approximation of the loa. In proof of this, most of the houngans require those who place themselves under their tutelage in order to become hounci to bring a composition book for notes, and in this they must copy the houngan's concept of the loa. I have seen several of these books with the drawings, and none of them even pretend to look like the catholic saints. Neither are their attributes the same.

Who are the loa, then? I would not pretend to call the name of every mystere in Haiti. *No one* knows the name of every loa because every major section of Haiti has its own local variation. It has gods and goddesses of places and forces that are unknown fifty miles away. The heads of "families" of gods are known all over the country, but there are endless variations of the demigods even in the same localities. It is easy to see the unlettered meeting some unknown natural phenomenon and not knowing how to explain it, and a new local demigod is named. It is always added to the "family," to which it seems, by the circumstances, to belong. Hence, the long list of Ogouns, Erzulies, Cimbys, Legbas, and the like. All over

114

Rex Hardy, Jr.

The Voodoo altar, piled with sacred objects and food

Haiti, however, it is agreed that there are two *classes* of deities, the Rada or Arada and the Petro. The Rada gods are the "good" gods and are said to have originated in Dahomey. The Petro gods are the ones who do evil work and are said to have been brought over from the Congo, some say Guinea and the Congo have provided the two sets of gods but place names of Dahomey are included in the names of the Rada deities. Perhaps there is a mingling of several African localities and spirits under the one head in Haiti. Damballah or Dambala Ouedo Freda Tocan Dahomey, to give him his full name, heads the Rada gods. Baron Samedi (Lord of Saturday) Baron Cimeterre (Lord of the Cemetery) and Baron Crois (Lord of the cross), one spirit with three names is the head of the Petro loa. Let us first meet the Rada designations.

DAMBALA, OF DAMBALLAH OUEDO
(PRONOUNCED WAY-DOE)

Damballah Ouedo is the supreme Mystere and his signature is the serpent. Though the picture that is bought of him is that of St. Patrick, he in no way resembles that Irish saint. The picture of St. Patrick is used because it has the snakes in it which no other saint has. All over Haiti it is well established that Damballah is identified as Moses, whose symbol was the serpent. This worship of Moses recalls the hard-to-explain fact that wherever the Negro is found, there are traditional tales of Moses and his supernatural powers that are not in the Bible, nor can they be found in any written life of Moses. The rod of Moses is said to have been a subtle serpent and hence came his great powers. All over the Southern United States, the British West Indies and Haiti there are reverent tales of Moses and his magic. It is hardly possible that all of them sprang up spontaneously in these widely separated areas on the blacks coming in contact with Christianity after coming to the Americas. It is more probable that there is a tradition of Moses as the great father of magic scattered over Africa and Asia. Perhaps some of his feats recorded in the Pentateuch are the folk

116

Door of the room to Erzulie

beliefs of such a character grouped about a man for it is well established that if a memory is great enough, other memories will cluster about it, and those in turn will bring their suites of memories to gather about this focal point, because perhaps, they are all scattered parts of the one thing like Plato's concept of the perfect thing. At any rate, concerning Moses' rod and the serpent, they say that many witch doctors in Africa can so hypnotize a snake that it can be made rigid and seemingly lifeless and carried as a cane and brought to life again at the will of the witch doctor. They contend that that was why the rod of Aaron, which was none other than the rod of Moses, was such a cane thrust into the hand of Aaron at the right moment. Such were the "rods" of the magicians of the Pharaoh. But Moses knew that his "rod" fed on the variety that the king's men of magic used, so he knew what would happen the moment that the magicians turned their "rods" into snakes.

This serpent signature of Damballah, also spelt Damballa and Dambala, is responsible for the belief by the casual observer that the snake is worshipped in Haiti. This is not accurate. There is no actual worship of the snake as such in Haiti. It is treated with reverence because it is considered the servant of Damballah. Everywhere I found an altar to Damballah, I found either an iron representation of the snake beside the pool, or an actual green snake which lived in a special place upon the altar. And in each instance I asked about the divinity of the snake and they told me that the snake was not a god but the "bonne" (maid servant) of Damballah and was therefore protected and honored.

Damballah is the highest and most powerful of all the gods, but never is he referred to as the father of the gods as was Jupiter, Odin and great Zeus, and while he is not spoken of as the father of the gods, whenever any of the other gods meet him they bow themselves and sing, "Ohe', Ohe'! Ce Papa nous qui pe' passe'!" (It is our papa who passes.) He is the father of all that is powerful and good. The others are under him in power, that is all. He never does "bad" work. If you make a ceremony to any of the other gods and ask favors, they must come to Damballah to get the permission and the power to do it. Papa Damballah is the *great source.*

Around Damballah is grouped the worship of the beautiful in nature. One must offer him flowers, the best perfumes, a pair of white chickens; his "mange" sec (dry food) consisting of corn meal and an egg which must be placed on the altar on a white plate. He is offered cakes, french melons, watermelons, pineapples, rice, bananas, grapes, oranges, apples and the like. There must be a porcelain pot with a cover on the altar, desserts and sweet liquors, and olive oil. There must be a representation of Damballah within the oratory, a small crucifix, a bouquet, a bottle of liquor, a glass of oil to keep his lamps burning on his day. He brings good luck to those who make offerings to him regularly and faithfully. "It is possible for you to have a grand situation and it is even possible to become a minister or the president if you serve Papa Damballah faithfully. But yes!" His day is Wednesday in the afternoon of every week and his sacrifice is a pair of white chickens, hen and cock. The average houngan says that he is given the white cock and hen because he guards domestic happiness. Dr. Holly says it is another acknowledgment of the bi-sexual concept of the Creator, and that Damballah with the subtle wisdom and powers represented by the snake is to the Africans something of a creator, if not actively, certainly The Source. His color is white. His woman is Aida Ouedo. His signature is the ascending snakes on a rod or a crucifix. He is the fourth in the order of the service, being preceded by (1) Papa Legba, opener of gates (opportunities), (2) Loco Attison, Mystere of work and knowledge, (3) Mah-lah-sah, the guardian of the doorsill. None of these are so important as Damballah. But the order has been established to have things ready when he arrives through possession of some of the persons taking part in the ceremony. There is a definite behavior for the possession of each of the gods. The houngan (Voodoo priest) or the mambo or priestess can say at once what god possesses a person present. Perhaps the wrong impression is conveyed by the expression that the other gods precede Damballah in the services.

119

Actually, they are his suite and surround him and go before or after him in order to more quickly serve his commands. In the Voodoo temple or peristyle, the place of Damballah, there must also be the places of Legba, Ogoun, Loco, the cross of Guedé who is the messenger of the gods, of Erzulie, Mademoiselle Brigitte and brave Guedé. Damballah resides within the snake on the altar in the midst of all these objects. The construction must face the rising sun and there must be a door which looks toward the west.

SONGS TO DAMBALLAH

NO. 1

Me roi e' Damballah Ouedo, ou ce gran moun, ho, ho, ho, me roi e'.
Damballah Ouedo ou ce' gran moun la k'lle ou.
(My king is Damballah Ouedo. You are a great man, ho, ho, ho, my king is.)

NO. 2

Ah Damballah, bon jour, bon jour, bon jour, Damballah Ouedo!
Apres Manday, Damballah ou mah ou yeah, oh, oh, oh oui may lah, Damballah,
Ouido, moin, ah may Vinant lauh yo.

There is in Voodoo worship a reverent remoteness where Damballah is concerned. There are not the numerous personal anecdotes about him as about some of the lesser and more familiar gods. I asked why they did not ask more things of him, and I was told that when they make "services" to the other gods they are making them to Damballah indirectly for none of the others can do anything unless he gives them the power. There is the feeling of awe. One approaches the lesser gods and they in turn approach the great one. The others must listen and take sides in the neighborhood disputes, jealousies and feuds. One comes to Damballah for advancement and he is approached through beauty. Give Damballah his sweet wine and feed his wisdom with white pigeons.

120

Nobody in Haiti ever really told me who Erzulie Freida was, but they told me what she was like and what she did. From all of that it is plain that she is the pagan goddess of love. In Greece and Rome the goddesses of love had husbands and bore children, Erzulie has no children and her husband is all the men of Haiti. That is, anyone of them that she chooses for herself. But so far, no one in Haiti has formulated her. As the perfect female she must be loved and obeyed. She whose love is so strong and binding that it cannot tolerate a rival. She is the female counterpart of Damballah. But high and low they serve her, dream of her, have visions of her as of the Holy Grail. Every Thursday and every Saturday millions of candles are lighted in her honor. Thousands of beds, pure in their snowy whiteness and perfumed are spread for her. Desserts, sweet drinks, perfumes and flowers are offered to her and hundreds of thousands of men of all ages and classes enter those pagan bowers to devote themselves to this spirit. On that day, no mortal woman may lay possessive hands upon these men claimed by Erzulie. They will not permit themselves to be caressed or fondled even in the slightest manner, even if they are married. No woman may enter the chamber set aside for her worship except to clean it and prepare it for the "service." For Erzulie Freida is a most jealous female spirit. Hundreds of wives have been forced to step aside entirely by her demands.

She has been identified as the Blessed Virgin, but this is far from true. Here again the use of the pictures of the Catholic saints have confused observers who do not listen long enough. Erzulie is not the passive queen of heaven and mother of anybody. She is the ideal of the love bed. She is so perfect that all other women are a distortion as compared to her. The Virgin Mary and all of the female saints of the Church have been elevated, and celebrated for their abstinence. Erzulie is worshipped for her perfection in giving herself to mortal man. To be chosen by a goddess is an exaltation for men to live for.

The most popular Voodoo song in all Haiti, outside of the invocation to Legba, is the love song to Erzulie.

Erzulie is said to be a beautiful young woman of lush appearance. She is a mulatto and so when she is impersonated by the blacks, they powder their faces with talcum. She is represented as having firm, full breasts and other perfect female attributes. She is a rich young woman and wears a gold ring on her finger with a stone in it. She also wears a gold chain about her neck, attires herself in beautiful, expensive raiment and sheds intoxicating odors from her person. To men she is gorgeous, gracious and beneficent. She promotes the advancement of her devotees and looks after their welfare generally. She comes to them in radiant ecstasy every Thursday and Saturday night and claims them.

Toward womankind, Erzulie is implacable. It is said that no girl will gain a husband if an altar to Erzulie is in the house. Her jealousy delights in frustrating all the plans and hopes of the young woman in love. Women do not "give her food" unless they tend toward the hermaphrodite or are elderly women who are widows or have already abandoned the hope of mating. To women and their desires, she is all but maliciously cruel, for not only does she choose and set aside for herself young and handsome men and thus bar them from marriage, she frequently chooses married men and thrusts herself between the woman and her happiness. From the time that the man concludes that he has been called by her, there is a room in her house that the wife may not enter except to prepare it for her spiritual rival. There is a bed that she must make spotless, but may never rest upon. It is said that the most terrible consequences would follow such an act of sacrilege and no woman could escape the vengeance of the enraged Erzulie should she be bold enough to do it. But it is almost certain that no male devotee of the goddess would allow it to occur.

How does a man know that he has been called? It usually begins in troubled dreams. At first his dreams are vague. He is visited by a strange being which he cannot identify. He cannot make out at first what is wanted of him. He touches rich fabrics momentarily but they flit away from his grasp. Strange perfumes wisp across his face, but he cannot know where they came from nor find a name out of his memory for them. The dream visitations become more frequent and definite and sometimes Erzulie identifies herself definitely. But more often, the matter is more elusive. He falls ill, other unhappy things befall him. Finally his friends urge him to visit a houngan for a consultation. Quickly then, the visitor is identified as the goddess of love and the young man is told that he has been having bad luck because the goddess is angry at his neglect. She behaves like any other female when she is spurned. A baptism is advised and a "service" is instituted for the offended loa and she is placated and the young man's ill fortune ceases.

But things are not always so simply arranged. Sometimes the man chosen is in love with a mortal woman and it is a terrible renunciation he is called upon to make. There are tales of men who have fought against it valiantly as long as they could. They fought until ill luck and ill health finally broke their wills before they bowed to the inexorable goddess. Death would have ensued had they not finally given in, and terrible misfortune for his earthly inamorata also. However, numerous men in Haiti do not wait to be called. They attach themselves to the cult voluntarily. It is more or less a vow of chastity certainly binding for specified times, and if the man is not married then he can never do so. If he is married his life with his wife will become so difficult that separation and divorce follows. So there are two ways of becoming an adept of Erzulie Freida—as a "réclamé" meaning, one called by her, and the other way of voluntary attachment through inclination. Besides this merely amorous goddess, there is another Erzulie, or perhaps another aspect of the same deity. She is the terrible Erzulie, ge-rouge (Erzulie, the red-eyed) but she does not belong to the Rada. She belongs to the dreaded Petro phalanx. She is described as an older woman and terrible to look upon. Her name has been mentioned in connection with

123

the demon worship of the Bocors and the Secte Rouge.

The "baptism" or initiation into the cult of Erzulie is perhaps the most simple of all the voodoo rites. All gods and goddesses must be fed, of course, and so the first thing that the supplicant must do it to "give food" to Erzulie. There must be prepared a special bread and Madeira wine, rice-flour, eggs, a liqueur, a pair of white pigeons, a pair of chickens. There must be a white pot with a cover to it. This food is needed at the ceremony, during which the applicant's head is "washed."

This washing of the head is necessary in most of their ceremonies. In this case the candidate must have made a natte (mat made of banana leaf-stems) or a couch made of fragrant branches of trees. He must dress himself in a long white night shirt. The houngan places him upon the leafy couch and recites three Ave Marias, three Credos and the Confiteor three times. Then he sprinkles the couch with flour and a little syrup. The houngan then takes some leafy branches and dips them in the water in the white pot which has been provided for washing the head of the candidate. While the priest is sprinkling the head with this, the hounci and the Çanzos are singing:

"Erzulie Tocan Freida Dahomey, Ce ou qui faut ce' ou
  qui bon
Erzulie Freida Tocan Maitresse m'ap mouter
Ce'ou min qui Maitresse."

The hounci and the adepts continue to sing all during the consecration of the candidate unassisted by the drums. The drums play *after* a ceremony to Erzulie, *never during* the service. While the attendants are chanting, the houngan very carefully parts the hair of the candidate, who is stretched upon the couch. After the parted hair is perfumed, an egg is broken on the head, some Madeira wine, cooked rice placed thereon, and then the head is wrapped in a white handkerchief large enough to hold everything that has been heaped upon the head. The singing keeps up all the while. A chicken is then

124

killed on the candidate's head and some of the blood is allowed to mingle with the other symbols already there. The candidate is now commanded to rise. This is the last act of the initiation. Sometimes a spirit enters the head of the new-made adept immediately. He is "mounted" by the spirit of Erzulie, who sometimes talks at great length, giving advice and making recommendations. While this is going on a quantity of plain white rice is cooked—a portion sufficient for one person only—and he eats some of it. What he does not eat is buried before the door of his house.

The candidate now produces the ring of silver, because silver is a metal that has wisdom in it, and hands it to the houngan, who takes it and blesses it and places it upon the young man's finger as in a marriage ceremony. Now, for the first time since the beginning of the ceremony, the priest makes the libation. The five wines are elevated and offered to the spirits at the four cardinal points and finally poured in three places on the earth for the dead, for in this as in everything else in Haiti, the thirst of the dead must be relieved. The financial condition of the applicant gauges the amount and the variety of the wines served on this occasion. It is the wish of all concerned to make it a resplendent occasion and there is no limit to the amount of money spent if it can be obtained by the applicant. Enormous sums have been spent on these initiations into the cult of Erzulie Freida. It is such a moment in the life of a man! More care and talent have gone into the songs for this occasion than any other music in Haiti. Haiti's greatest musician, Ludovic Lamotte, has worked upon these folk songs. From the evidence, the services to Erzulie are the most idealistic occasions in Haiti. It is a beautiful thing. Visualize a large group of upper class Haitians all in white, their singing voices muted by exaltation doing service to man's eternal quest, a pure life, the perfect woman, and all in a setting as beautiful and idyllic as money and imagination available can make it. "Erzulie, Nin Nin, Oh!" is Haiti's favorite folk song.

Rex Hardy, Jr.

Drums and drummers

"Erzulie ninnin, oh! hey! Erzulie ninnim oh, hey!
Moin senti ma pe' monte', ce moin minn yagaza.

2.

"General Jean—Baptiste, oh ti parrain
Ou t'entre' lan caille la, oui parrain
Toutes mesdames yo a genoux, chapelette you
Lan main yo, yo pe' roule' mise' yo
Ti mouns yo a' genoux, chapelette you
Erzulie ninninm oh, Hey gran Erzulie Freida
Dague, Tocan, Mirorize, nan nan ninnin oh, hey
Movin senti ma pe' monte' ce' moin minn yagaza."

3.

(Spoken in "Langage" recitative)
"Oh Aziblo, qui dit qui dit ce' bo yo
Ba houn bloco ita ona yo, Damballah Ouedo
Tocan, Syhrinise o Agoue', Ouedo, Pap Ogoun oh,
Dambala, O Legba Hypolite, Oh
Ah Brozacaine, Azaca, Neque, nago, nago pique cocur yo
Oh Loco, co loco, bel loco Ouedo, Loco guinea
Ta Manibo, Docu, Doca, D agoue' moinminn
Negue, candilica calicassague, ata, couine des
Oh mogue', Clemezie, Clemeille, papa mare' yo.

4.

"Erzulie, Ninninm oh, hey grann' Erzulie
Freida dague, Tocan Miroize, maman, ninninm oh, hey!
Moun senti ma pe' mouti', ce moin mimm yagaza, Hey!"

More upper class Haitians "make food" for Erzulie Freida
than for any other loa in Haiti. Forever after the consecration,
they wear a gold chain about their necks under their shirts and
a ring on the finger with the initials E. F. cut inside of it. I have
examined several of these rings. I know one man who has
combined the two things. He has a ring made of a bit of gold
chain. And there is a whole library of tales of how this man

and that was "réclamé" by the goddess Erzulie, or how that one came to attach himself to the Cult. I have stood in one of the bedrooms, decorated and furnished for a visit from the invisible perfection. I looked at the little government employee standing there amid the cut flowers, the cakes, the perfumes and the lace covered bed and with the spur of imagination, saw his common clay glow with some borrowed light and his earthiness transfigured as he mated with a goddess that night—with Erzulie, the lady upon the rock whose toes are pretty and flowery.

PAPA LEGBA ATTIBON

Legba Attibon is the god of the gate. He rules the gate of the hounfort, the entrance to the cemetery and he is also Baron Carrefour, Lord of the crossroads. The way to all things is in his hands. Therefore he is the first god in all Haiti in point of service. Every service to whatever loa for whatever purpose must be preceded by a service to Legba. The peasants say he is an old man that moves about with a sac paille (large pouch woven of straw) and therefore the houngan must take everything to be used in his service in the Sac paille called Macout. They say he has a brother, however, who eats his food from a kwee, which is a bowl made from half a calabash.

The picture of John the Baptist is used to represent Papa Legba. The rooster offered to him must be Zinga, what we would call a speckled black and white rooster. All of his food must be roasted. He eats roasted corn, peanuts, bananas, sweet potatoes, chicken, a tobacco pipe for smoking, some tobacco, some soft drinks. All these things must be put in the Macoute and tied to the limb of a tree that has been baptized in the name of Papa Legba.

Of all the Haitian gods, Legba is probably best known to the foreigners for no one can exist in Haiti very long without hearing the drums and the chanting to Papa Legba asking him to open the gate.

"Papa Legba, ouvirier barriere pour moi agoe
Papa Legba, ouvirier barriere pour moi
Attibon Legba, ouvirier barriere pour moi passer
Passer Vrai, loa moi passer m' a remerci loa moin."

There are several variations of this prayer-chant. In fact at
every different place that I heard the ceremony I heard another version, but always it is that prayer song to the god of
the gates to permit them and the loa to pass. The other loa
cannot enter to serve them unless Legba permits them to do
so. Hence the fervent invocation to him. Another often sung
invocation is:

"Legba cli-yan, cli-yan Zandor, Zandor, Attibon Legba,
Zander immole'
Legba cli-yan, cli-yan Zand-Zandor Attibon Legba
Zander immole'."

Legba's altar is a tree near the hounfort, preferably with the
branches touching the hounfort. His offering is made in the
branches and his repository is at the foot of the tree. Legba is
a spirit of the fields, the woods and the general outdoors.
There is one important distinction between offering a chicken
to Legba and offering it to the other loa. With the others his
head is bent back and his throat is cut, but for Legba his neck
must be wrung.
Papa Legba has no special day. All of the days are his, since
he must go before all of the ceremonies. Loco Atisou follows
Legba in the service, and is in fact "saluted" in the Legba
ceremony. This is absolutely necessary. If it is not done Loco
will be offended and the gods called in the invocation will not
come.
Loco Atisou gives knowledge and wisdom to the houngan
and indicates to them what should be done. In case clients
come to them Loco shows the houngan what leaves and medic-
aments to use for treating the ailments. Either in the hounfort
or anywhere else, the houngan can take his Ascon and call

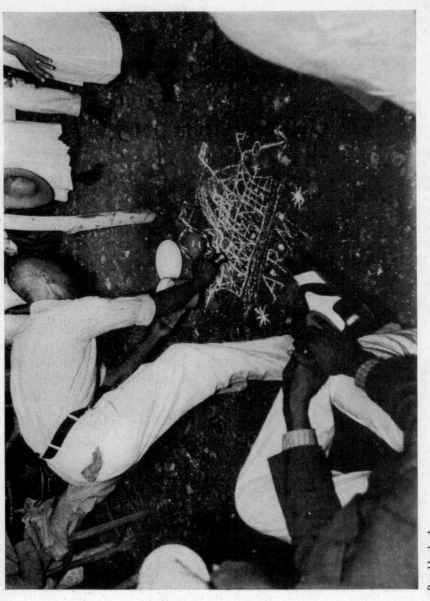

Rex Hardy, Jr.　　　　　*The signature of a god—Agone'ta-Royo—Master of Waters*

Papa Loco and he will indicate the malady of the patient if the sickness is natural. If it is unnatural, he will advise the houngan.

Loco is the god of medicine and wisdom, but at the same time a great drinker of rum. Sacrifice to him a gray cock. His day is Wednesday. The image of St. Joseph is used for Loco Atisou.

SONG OF LOCO ATISOU

Va, Loco, Loco Valadi', Va, Loco, Loco Valadi
Va, Loco, Loco Valadi', Va, Loco, Loco Valadi
Man, Jean Valou Loco, Loco Valadi.

Most of the other gods of national importance will be briefly explained as they occur in ceremonies. This work does not pretend to give a full account of either Voodoo or Voodoo gods. It would require several volumes to attempt to cover completely the gods and Voodoo practices of one vicinity alone. Voodoo in Haiti has gathered about itself more detail of gods and rites than the Catholic church has in Rome.

A study of the Marassas and the Dossou or Dossa, the twin gods represented by the little joined plates, is worthy of a volume in itself. The same could be said of the Ogouns, the Cimbys, and the ramifications of Agoue'ta-Royo, the Master of Waters, the Erzulies, the Damballas and the Locos. I am merely attempting to give an effect of the whole in the round. It is unfortunate for the social sciences that an intelligent man like Dr. Dorsainville has not seen fit to do something with Haitian mysticism comparable to Frazer's *The Golden Bough*. The history of the Ascon would be a most interesting thing in itself. The layman as well as the scientist would like to know how this gourd sheathed in beads and snake vertebrae, and sometimes containing a human bone, came to be the fixed and honored object that it is. It has its commandments as the voice of the gods and certainly it is hallowed. How did it get that way? Who began it? Where exactly?

CHAPTER 11

❖

ISLE DE LA GONAVE

Everybody knows that La Gonave is a whale that lingered so long in Haitian waters that he became an island. He bears a sleeping woman on his back. Any late afternoon anyone in Port-au-Prince who looks out to sea can see her lying there on her back with her hands folded across her middle sleeping peacefully. It is said that the Haitians prayed to Damballa for peace and prosperity. Damballa was away on a journey accompanied by his suite, including two wives, Aida and Cilla. When the invocations reached Damballa where he was travelling in the sky, he sent his woman Cilla with a message to his beloved Haitians. He commanded Agoue'ta-Royo to provide a boat for his wife and to transport her safely to Port-au-Prince so that she could give the people the formula for peace. Papa Agoue' sent a great whale to bear Cilla and instructed him to transport the woman of Damballa with safety and speed and comfort. The whale performed everything that the Master of Waters commanded him. He rode Madame Cilla so quickly and so gently that she fell asleep, and did not know that she arrived at her destination. The whale dared not wake her to tell her that she was in Haiti. So every day he swims far out to sea and visits with his friends. But at sundown he creeps back into the harbor so that Madame Cilla may land if she should awake. She has the formula of peace in her sleeping hand. When she wakes up, she will give it to the people.

From the house of George de Lespinasse high in Pacot I watched the island of La Gonave float out of the harbor with the sun each day and return at sundown. And I wanted to go out there where it was. William Seabrook in his *Magic Island* had fired my imagination with his account of The White King of La Gonave. I wanted to see the Kingdom of Faustin Wirkus. Then two weeks before Christmas of 1936 a friend of mine, Frank Crumbie, Jr., of Nyack, New York, suggested that we go over together and do some investigation. He knew people and Creole and I knew methods. So we made preparations to go.

Frank Crumbie, or Junior, as he was known among his intimates, knew where to find a boat. He engaged a small sailing boat known as a shallop to take us across the eighteen miles of bay water to La Gonave. The captain told us to be ready to sail between eight and nine at night because the wind would be right then. Then is the only time a sailing vessel can put out from Port-au-Prince for La Gonave. Mr. and Mrs. Scott drove us down to the waterfront with our army cots and other paraphernalia and saw us off. The captain and his crew of one other man poled the boat out into deep water and we began our all night voyage to the island of the sleeping woman.

The wind did not catch the sails at once. The men rowed and rowed. I looked at the big stars blazing so near overhead sunk in a sky that was itself luminous. Junior was already getting sea sick and trying to get comfortable. The men began a song and I asked Junior what it was they were singing so earnestly. He said, "A song to Papa Agoue', the Master of the Waters. They are asking him for a wind." The wind rose and soon we swept past the Bissotone Navy Yard and on our way. The stars soon lost themselves in clouds and down came a heavy shower of rain. I put on my rain coat and big straw hat.

134

Junior took refuge in his sleeping bag, but we got dampish just the same. The men took no notice of the downpour. The lights of Port-au-Prince had faded when the sky cleared. Then we saw the luminous sea! It glowed like one vast jewel. It glittered like bushels and bushels of gems poured into the casket that God keeps right behind His throne for beauty. The moving fish put on their gilding. It was a privilege to move upon this liquid radiance. Junior was sick by this time but the men who were used to Haitian night seas did not pay attention. I had the feeling of being adrift in a boat alone.

All night the captain and the crew talked, smoked cigarettes we gave them and sailed and talked so that daylight found us off the coast of La Gonave. We saw two or three little thatched houses. The captain told the crew to announce our arrival. He took a conk shell and stood up on the prow and blew several mingled rhythms and tones, "Tell them two ti blancs (unimportant whites or mulattoes) are coming." The crew blew again and sat down as the sun was rising. At 11:00 o'clock we landed at Ansa-a-galets.

La Gonave's well advertised mosquitoes met us at the landing. That same landing that Faustin Wirkus had built during his reign. But away from the mangrove swamps the town rose high and dry and the mosquitoes ceased to be important.

The days went by and we made acquaintances. The chief of police there and his subordinates were very kind and entertaining. I saw Haitian folk games played and began to hear the folk tales about Ti Malice and Bouke'. For the first time I heard about the sacred stones of Voodoo. I found on this remote island a peace I have never known anywhere else on earth. La Gonave is the mother of peace. Its outlines which from Port-au-Prince look like a sleeping woman are prophetic. And the moonlight tasted like wine.

One of the Lieutenants of the Garde d'Haiti was collecting sacred stones for Faustin Wirkus. He was telling Junior about it in my presence so I asked questions. The Haitian peasants come upon the stone implements of the dead and gone aborigines and think that they are stones inhabited by the loa. In

135

Africa they have a god of thunder called Shango or Shangor. He hurls his bolts and makes stones that are full of power. They think that these stones in Haiti were made by their god Shango and that the various gods of Voodoo reside in them. The moment that they see a stone of a certain shape and color they say that it belongs to a certain god because they have come to be associated that way. This one is Damballa. That one is Agoue'. Another is Ogoun. And so on. When one finds one of these stones it is considered very lucky. It is said, "You have found a loa." When the finder acquires enough money to pay for the ceremony, the stone is baptized in the rites of the god to whom it is dedicated and placed upon the little shrine in the home upon a white plate and treated with the greatest respect. At stated times it is bathed in oil and little things are offered to it. Some of these stones have been in certain families for generations. No amount of money could buy them. The way to tell whether a stone has a loa or not is to cup it in the hand and breathe upon it. If it sweats then it has a spirit in it. If not, then it is useless.

We heard about one famous stone that had so much power that it urinated. It was identified as Papa Guedé, who had ordered it to be clothed, so it wore a dress. It attracted so many people and caused so much disturbance indoors that the owner had it chained outside the door. One of the American officers of the Occupation named Whitney saw it and finally got it for himself. It was a curious idol and he wanted it for his desk. The Haitian guard attached to Whitney's station told him that it would urinate and not to put it on his desk but he did so in spite of warning and on several occasions he found his desk wet and then he removed it to the outdoors again. They said he took it away to the United States with him when he left.

At Ansa-a-galets I met the black marine. A sergeant of the Garde d'Haiti lived in the house beside mine and I kept hearing "Jesus Christ!" and "God Damn!" mixed up with whatever he was saying in Creole. When we became friendly enough to converse, I told him that I had heard him and said that it was remarkable to hear the ejaculations from him.

"Oh," he said, "I served with the Marines when they were here."

"I see," I replied facetiously, "then you are a black Marine."

"But yes," he replied proudly, "I am a black Marine. I speak like one always. Perhaps you would like me to kill something for you. I kill that dog for you." It was a half-starved dog that had taken to hanging around me.

"No, no, don't kill it. Poor thing!" He put his pistol back into its holster. "Jesus Christ! God Damn! I kill something," he swaggered. I learned afterwards that he had told all his friends and associates that he must be just like an American Marine because the femme American had recognized the likeness at once. Perhaps by this time he has promoted himself to Colonel Little.

I met Madame Lamissier Mille from Archahaie, that rich alluvial plain going north from Port-au-Prince which is called the granary of Haiti. There are so many wealthy and productive plantations of bananas, coconuts and garden produce that the whole place is swathed in rich green foliage. From this Lamissier I heard the name Vixama, which is hard to hear even in Haiti. You hear much about the mythical man in the mountain near St. Marc, but few know and breathe the name Vixama. What was more important than the secret name of a legendary figure, was the invitation to visit a real Bocor who has his hounfort at Archahaie whom she said was a "parent" of hers which means in Creole that they were related. This was the opening I had wished for, so I eagerly accepted. We passed Christmas day in Ansa-a-galets, and I had stewed goat with the Chief of Police. The next night our party of five marched single file down the stony path to the sea in the white light of a gross old moon and embarked for Port-au-Prince. When the sun arose the next morning it was pleasant to stretch myself along the gunwale and look far down into the water and see the animal life down there. I saw a huge shark point his nose up and lazily follow it to the surface; I saw a great ray swimming about and numerous parrot fish. It rained on us twice, but that night around nine o'clock, we landed in Port-au-Prince, and the next day Lamissier went off to Archahaie to find out when her cousin, the Bocor, would receive me. I was very eager for him to admit me, because Archahaie is the greatest place known in Haiti for Voodoo.

CHAPTER 12

✦

ARCHAHAIE AND
WHAT IT MEANS

Early in January I went to Archahaie to the hounfort of Dieu Donnez St. Leger. He has a large following and owns large plantations himself. He lives in a compound like an African chief with the various family connections in smaller houses within the enclosure. About one hundred people are under him as head of the family or clan. He is very intelligent, reads and writes well and sees to it that all of the children in his compound go to school. The arch above the door to the hounfort and peristyle were both painted in stripes alternating green, white, blue and orange. The walls were green and red.

He was extremely kind in allowing me to attend all of their ceremonies and in making explanations. He had his Mambo, Madame Isabel Etienne, take great pains with me to conduct me through the rites step by step and to teach me the songs of the services. I was in a fortunate position, for his place has such a large following that there were ceremonies nearly every day. Sometimes two or three in the same day. Red cocks were tied before the door of the mysteries awaiting the hour of sacrifice. I was learning many things and

139

The Jean Valou about the sacred center pole

Rex Hardy, Jr.

being astonished at the elaborate rituals that Voodoo has developed in Haiti. After the ceremonies the drums played for Congo dances and men and women helped to teach me the steps. First, of course, was the Jean Valou, the Congo and then the Mascaron. Other steps were introduced as the occasion demanded until I could follow whatever they did in the dance and singing.

One night something very interesting and very terrifying came to pass. A houngan had died and Dieu Donnez was to officiate at the Wete' loa non tete yum mort (Taking the spirit from the head of the dead). This ceremony is also called the Manger des morts (The food or feast of the dead) or the Courir Zinc (To run the Zinc fish hook of the dead). This ceremony is not always in honor of a houngan. It is also celebrated for a dead hounci or canzo.

That day a pair of white pigeons were obtained, some olive oil, flour, more than thirty pieces of fat pine wood, a pair of chickens, some coarse corn meal, and a saddle blanket, and a large white plate. Two chairs were placed under the peristyle and the dead body of the houngan was placed on them and covered with the saddle blanket.

The chickens and the pigeons were killed and cooked without seasoning. They were very careful that no salt whatever should touch anything. This reminded me of my experiences in Jamaica and how it was felt that salt was offensive to the dead. The coarse corn meal was put in a pan and parched or roasted as one would roast peanuts or coffee. Every minute or two the assistant would pick up the pan and shake it to make it roast evenly. When it was finished, it was placed in the white plate. Then slivers of pine wood were lighted and placed for illumination instead of candles.

Dieu Donnez himself made a sparkling fire under the peristyle and when it burned hot and fierce, he took the white plate with the corn meal in one hand and the white pot with the chickens in the other and approached the fire chanting:

141

"Har'au Va Erique Dan, Sobo Dis Vou qui nan
Ce'bon Die qui maitre, Afrique Guinin, tous les morts
Hai' 'an Va erique dan."

The body of the dead man sat up with its staring eyes,
bowed its head and fell back again and then a stone fell at the
feet of Dieu Donnez, and it was so unexpected that I could not
discover how it was done. There it was, and its presence
excited the hounci, the canzo and the visitors tremendously.
But its presence meant that the loa or mystere which had lived
in the dead man and controlled him was separated from him.
He could go peacefully to rest and the loa would be employed
by someone else. If the spirit were not taken away from the
head of the dead, then it would have to go and dwell at the
bottom of the water until this ceremony is performed. Some
say that the spirit of the houngan must pass one year at the
bottom of the water anyway. When the ceremony is finished,
after the man has been buried, the two chairs are dressed with
the saddle cover, but are otherwise unoccupied except in a
spiritual way, if you want to look at it like that.

Dieu Donnez then addressed the dead spirit in the African
jargon called "langage." That is a private matter with each
houngan and it varies with each time he employs it because
different loa dictate different things to him. So that is always
new. But the opening prayer which is taken from the Catholic
church remains fixed. No one knows what was said to the dead
man to get him to relinquish the mystere but he had sat up,
bowed his head with its unchanging eyes and laid back down
and the stone had fallen at the feet of Dieu Donnez St. Leger.
Now he produced a fish hook made of zinc and passed it
through the flames three times. This is the "Zinc" of the dead
that is his no longer. The power it held will pass on to his
successor, which in this case was his son.

Then all of the assistants began to march around the two
dressed-up chairs, each with a flaming pine torch in his or her
hands, and it was a most impressive sight. Mambo Etienne
rattled her ascon and began the singing. The whole crowd

142

Mambo Etienne, Archahaie

sang lustily and well. The two Petro drums began their rhythmic march from Guinea across the seas and the three Rada drums answered them in exultation.

The chickens cooked in olive oil without salt were placed on a white plate and Dieu Donnez offered them to the dead with tremendous earnestness and dignity. After that the plates were paraded around the two chairs and buried with the food on them.

It was then the thing of terror happened. There were some odd noises from a human throat somewhere in the crowd behind me. Instantly the triumphant feeling left the place and was succeeded by one of fear. A man was possessed, it seemed, and began crashing things and people as he cavorted toward the center of things. There was a whisper that an evil spirit had materialized, and from appearances, this might well have been true, for the face of the man had lost itself in a horrible mask. It was unbelievable in its frightfulness. But that was not all. A feeling had entered the place. It was a feeling of unspeakable evil. A menace that could not be recognized by ordinary human fears, and the remarkable thing was that everybody seemed to feel it simultaneously and recoiled from the bearer of it like a wheat field before a wind.

Instantly Dieu Donnez faced this one with his ascon and other signs of office to drive it away from there, but it did not submit at once. He uttered many prayers and the terror of the crowd grew as the struggle dragged out. The fear was so humid you could smell it and feel it on your tongue. But the amazing thing was that the people did not take refuge in flight. They pressed nearer Dieu Donnez and at last he prevailed. The man fell. His body relaxed and his features untangled themselves and became a face again. They wiped his face and head with a red handkerchief and put him on a natte where he went to sleep soundly and woke up after a long while with a weary look in his eyes.

They poured libations for the dead and the ceremony ended.

It was explained to me later that the Courir Zinc is not a

144

difficult ceremony to perform, but that it is dangerous for any except a full fledged and experienced houngan to try it for fear that evil spirits may appear and do great harm before the good loa can be summoned to drive them off. The happening confirmed the belief of the people that Dieu Donnez St. Leger is a great and a powerful houngan. It is said that he is also a powerful Bocor when he serves in that capacity.

Life had plenty of flip for me at Archahaie. I could put my army cot under the peristyle during the day and lie there in the cool and rest and watch the people come to Dieu Donnez for various things. Several sick persons were there at all times. The sick men sat around under the trees or laid on their nattes in long shirts without any trousers. Sometimes I visited among them and practised up on Creole. But usually I was wherever Madame Etienne was. Not because she was next to Dieu Donnez himself in importance but because she is a kindly person, very entertaining and an amazing dancer for all of her bulk. She has charge of running the establishment and no one dares disobey her. All of the food for the hundred or more people in the compound is prepared at a common point. The work is divided up by Madame Etienne and supervised by her. She works as hard as anybody.

Leaving the professional aspect of the place aside it is one of those patriarchal communities so numerous in Haiti. It is the African compound where the male head of the family rules over all of the ramifications of the family and looks after them. It is a clan. Dieu Donnez has a little house all to himself where he can retire and rest after tiresome and strenuous work. He would send for me to come there so that he could instruct me. There is nothing primitive about the man away from his profession. He is gentle but intelligent and business-like. All of his lectures had to be written. He took ashes and drew the signatures of the loa on the ground and I had to copy them until he was satisfied. Sometimes abruptly he would leave the hounfort and go on a tour of inspection of his extensive banana and coconut plantations. I have a suspicion that he is a person who likes solitude and that it was a way he had of escaping from the nig-nagging of crowds. He inherited his office of priest from his father, who many say was a greater houngan than Dieu Donnez is. Anyway, Dieu Donnez is a hereditary houngan and that is considered the real and the true way in Haiti. One day I said that I must go to Port-au-Prince to see about my mail and he let me go, saying that nothing important was in prospect for the time being anyway. So I rode one of those bone-racking, liver-shaking camions back to the capitol and Lucille, who was always so anxious about my safety whenever I was out of her sight.

But I was not in Port-au-Prince many days before the Master sent for me by a young man who is part of the clan and is also of the palace guard. Dieu Donnez said for me to be there within three days to bring a bottle of toilet water, a fountain pen for him and a bottle of ink. I went with portable stove, army cot and the things that Dieu Donnez wanted. And I am very glad that I went. He was going to set up a hounfort and make a houngan and these things would call for many ceremonies. I was very glad about it all. My Creole was getting pretty good by now.

The next day after my arrival at Archahaie, we set out for the place where the new hounfort was to be established. Dieu Donnez said that I could wait until next morning and come by camion but I said I'd rather walk with the rest. We set out gaily near sundown with great quantities of everything including the spirit of laughter. We sang as the dusk closed in on us plodding down the dusty road. We joked and frolicked. Madame De Grasse Celestin was riding her donkey amid two great sacs paille full of good things for the trip. After a while I rode some too and Mambo Etienne's son walked alongside and joked and sang and kept the little animal moving. So we went on like this for hours into the night. It was a dark night but nobody cared. We were like a happy army stealing a march.

We came to a point of huge mango trees where a man was standing beside the road. It was the place to leave the highway and go down a twining path across running water that chuckled among the greenery. Now and then houses hid behind the trees. We walked two miles perhaps and the straggling army halted again. We had reached our destination, the compound of Annee' La Cour, who is a cousin of Dieu Donnez and for whom the Master was going to set up the hounfort. We had halted because there were formalities that required it.

A canzo came out with a torch light and brought corn meal and water and a houngan made the signature of a loa upon the ground, and threw the water three times upon the ground for the dead. Mambo Etienne did the same. They went through a ritual proper to the occasion, but brief. The other canzo came after and threw water ceremonially. Then the hounci. After that we all went inside.

We found great piles of palm fronds piled under the peristyle and a quantity of gay colored paper. The women were waiting to be told what to do and Mambo Etienne put us all to work stripping the palm fronds into strips so fine that when it was done, it looked like a great, cream and green ostrich plume. Mambo Etienne and Annee' La Cour cut the fringe away from the central stalks and draped the "plumes" over the back of a chair. These were going to be cut into smaller pieces and used to decorate the peristyle and the various repositories of the gods. More work was going on out under the great elm tree that was to be dedicated to Loco and late in the night I went out there and spread up my bed to sleep. The next morning Dieu Donnez himself arrived with the rest of the clan in tow, and there was a great ceremony at the entrance for him. We were given some delicious hot tea called channelle before breakfast and it was a most refreshing and surprising thing. Channelle tea is a lovely habit for anybody to have. I was put to work cutting up the colored paper to be strung across the peristyle to decorate it and spent the entire morning at it. By that time a crowd was beginning to collect. When the peristyle was all decorated, I went out to the cooking place where the women were cooking great quantities of food. I noticed that Madame Etienne found the rocks herself to support the large cooking pots, and that she marked each rock with a cross mark in charcoal. She answered me that this was done to keep them from breaking when they were heated.

Soon Dieu Donnez sent for me to come to him under the peristyle. He was breaking up the Ascon. That must be done to remake it for a new Canzo or a houngan. He wanted me to see how it was done. I was allowed to help him restring the beads and snake-bones that surround the gourd that becomes the most sacred object in Haiti outside of the stones which contain loa. Each important god has a bead of a different color dedicated to him or her and these are represented in the arrangement of the beads on the Ascon and in the grand necklace that is worn by all the grades from a hounci to a houngan. The Collier hounci is neither as long nor as elaborate as the Collier Canzo or houngan. The necklace of the houngan is a splendid affair that is looped about his shoulders in a specific manner. It must be very long for that.

That afternoon the ceremonies began. The drums and the hounfort were dedicated. But of course, the very first ceremony was to Papa Legba. I ought to explain that while the people always say and sing "legba," the scholars tell me that the African word is Lecbah or Letbah. Perhaps the people are in error. All I know is they sing "Papa Legba, ouvrier barriere por moi passer." Anyway out in the courtyard of the hounfort of Annee' La Cour, the great preparation was going on. The drapeaux done in blue and white with the symbols in blue and red on it was flying from a pole high on the hounfort with its roasted ear of corn for the god who loves it. I saw the red rooster tied out in front of the house of ceremony. I saw the great tree well decorated with lacified palm fronds. Pieces of this stripped palm fronds were everywhere. In the hounfort were niches for the different gods. The pole with an iron serpent beside it for Damballa, "Li qui retti en ciel" (He who lives in the sky) and whose symbol on earth is the serpent. In the second room were the things dedicated to the congos with their resplendent colors. The congo and the Rada should not occupy the same room but they should be under the same roof.

Soon now, we were summoned to the hounfort to begin,

148

Houngan in full ceremonials with drapeaux (flags)

Rex Hardy, Jr.   *Enter the sabre and the drapeaux (the sword and the ceremonial flags)*

and Mambo Etienne tied my red and yellow handkerchief on my head in the proper loose knot at the back of my head. We removed our shoes and went into the hounfort, where Dieu Donnez, Annee' La Cour were already. The altar was set. Dieu Donnez was seated in a very low chair facing the altar. When we were all in that the place could hold, he covered his head with his ceremonial handkerchief and began the monotonous Litany:

> Dieu Donnez: Ela Grand-Pere Eternel,
> Us: Ela Grand-Pere, Eternal, sin dior e'
>   Ela Grand-Pere Eternel, Sin dior docor Ague'
>   Ela Grand-Pere Eternal Sime nan-min bon O
>   sain'en.
> Dieu Donnez: Ela Saint Michel.
> Us: Ela Saint Michel, sin dior e' . . ."

and so on as before.

This continued until Saint Gabriel Raphael, Nicolas, Joseph, John the Baptist, Saint Peter, Paul, Andre', Jacques, Jean, Phillipe', Come et Damien, Luc, Marc, Louis, Augustine, Vincent, Thomas, Laurent, Sainte Marie, Mere De Dieu, Saint Vierge Marie (A distinction between Virgin Mary and the mother of God), Sainte Catherine, Saintes Lucie, Cecile, Agnes and Agatha. These were all on the Christian side and the same response was sung for each name. Now the houngan began to chant the names of the Voodoo gods, and we responded as before, including the pagan deities in our chants.

"Ela Lecba Atibon, Sin Dior e', Ela Lecba Atibon, Sin dior docor Ague', Ela Lecba Atibon si' m nan min bon Dieu O Sain 'en."

We were led on to chant to Loco Atisson, Ela Aizan Velequiete, Ela Sobo, Ela Badere, Ela Agassou, Ela Ague' Ta-Royo, Ela Bosou, Ela Agaron, Ela Azacca, Ela Erzulie, Freda, Ela Ogoun Bodagris, Ela Ogoun Feraille, Ela Ogoun Shango, Ela Ogoun Taus Sam, Ela Ogoun Achade', Ela Ogoun Palama, Ela Ossage, Ela Baron Carrefour, Ela Baron La Croix, Ela

Baron Cimeterre, Ela Guede' Nibo, Ela Papa Cimby, Ela Nanchon Congo, Ela Nanchon Sine'gal, Ela Nanchon Ibo, Ela Nanchon Caplarou, Ela Nanchon Annine, Ela Papa Brise', Ela Contes Loas Petros, Ela Contes Boccos, Ela Contes Houngenicons, Ela Contes Laplaces, Ela Contes Port-Drapeaux, Ela Contes Ounci Canzos, Ela Ounci Des-sounins, Ela Contes Ounci Bossales, Ela Contes Hounfort, Ela Contes Oganiers.

Now inside a room of the hounfort, decorated for the occasion, we found a large table on which was placed food and drinks of all the gods to be honored along with the food of Legba, for Legba is never honored alone. He opens the gate so that the other gods come to their worshippers. All over the table there were plates, couis (pronounced Kwee) bottles and flacons. Under the table were the terrines, that is the baked clay containers like crude plates, cruches (little baked clay water-jugs), the chickens dedicated to the different gods, the perfumes and aromatics and leaves which would be used in the ceremonies. All of these were grouped about a watch light whose fuel is olive oil.

Here there was an interruption. Three women entered all dressed in black. They looked like a mother and her two daughters. The service was promptly stopped and the Mambo sent them away almost harshly. The older woman tried to argue, but they were hustled on out. I asked in a whisper why this was done and they said, "They have on black for mourning and so they cannot come in here. This is for the living. Baron Samedi must not be present."

I asked, "But suppose he manifests himself in some of the adepts? There must be some here consecrated to him."

"In that case, we would make a ceremony to drive him away. This is not the day of the dead. This is for the living. All the work would go wrong if he were here."

Dieu Donnez sprinkled the water in the direction of the four quarters of the world. The Canzos and the houncis followed his example. They all faced the door which looks toward the north and chanted, "Afrique-Guinin Atibon Legba, ouvrir barriere pour nous." Dieu Donnez then took the coui of corn meal and drew a design on the ground in the center of which he poured a little of each of the drinks dedicated to Legba. He took a piece of the baked banana, herring, a few grains of corn, a bit of watermelon, a bit of cake and placed them all in a single little heap within the design. Until then Dieu Donnez had done all these things seated in a very low chair. Now he arose and took two "poule Zinga" (speckled chickens), one in each hand. These he elevated to the east, the west, the north and the south in turn, saying: "Au nom du Grand Maitre, Tocan Frieda Dahomey, Marassas, Dossou, Dossa, toute l'Esprits, Atibon, Ogoun, Locos, Negue, fait, Negue Defait." The assistants knelt down. The houngan passed the two chickens over the heads of the kneeling Canzos and houncis. Then he turned to a niche dedicated to Legba and saluted it. Returning then to that north-facing door, he took the two chickens in one hand and a firebrand in the other, and set fire to the three heaps of gunpowder placed around the design or signature of Legba while the adepts were chanting:

"Ce Letbah, qui ap vini, ce papa Legba laissez barriere l'our."

The moment had come to consecrate the chickens to Legba. Dieu Donnez knelt and kissed the earth. He kissed three times the signature of Legba. The whole crowd followed his example. The drums woke up. First the tenor boulatier, then the sirgonh and last the thundering hountah, which controls the mood and the movement of the dancers. Some of the hounci began the Jean Valou. Dieu Donnez broke the wings of one of the chickens, then its legs, holding the throat of the fowl in such a way that it did not cry out as the sickening sound of cracking bones broke through the singing. Then he wrung its neck. In every other ceremony the throat is cut. The supposedly dead bird was placed upon the signature, but after what seemed like a full minute, even with its broken thighs, it leaped in its death agony and crashed into me. My heart flinched and my flesh drew up like tripe. With averted eyes I heard the next song begin with the rattle of the Ascon:

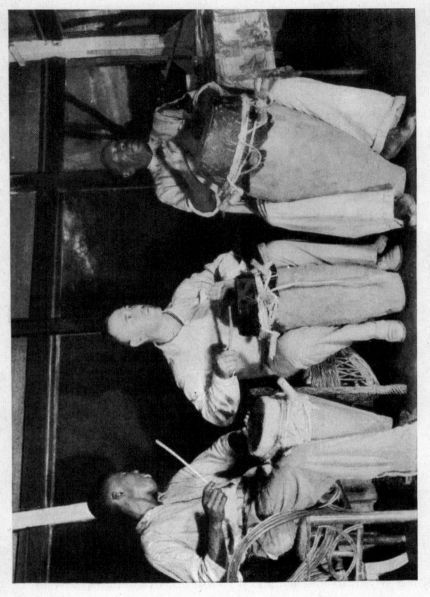

The drums woke up

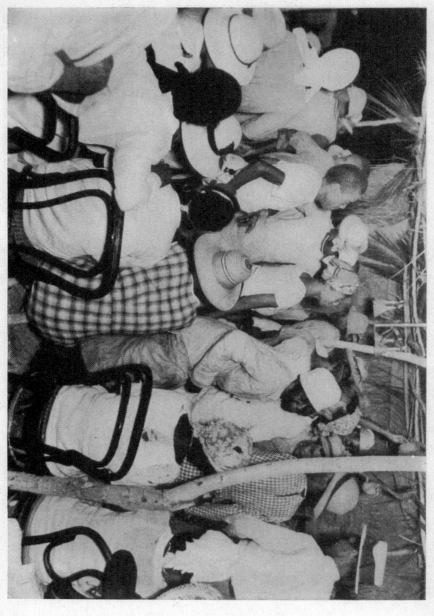

Jean Valou dance—voodoo ceremony

Rex Hardy, Jr. *In full ritual the Houngan kisses the sword*

"Ouanga te' papa Legba, Legba Touton, Legba Atibon—"
they began with a list and ended, "Toute hounci fait Croix."

The order of the ceremonies to the gods continued according to the rhythm of the offerings. The next god honored was Aisan who walks with the Marassas, Yumeaux ad Trumeaux and the child who follows the twins which is called the Dossou. They are the gods of the little joined plates that one finds displayed all over Haiti. The full name is Marassas Cinigal (black twins) Dahomey.

Mambo Etienne shook her Ascon and sang:

"Aisan, hey! Onape' laisse' coule'
Aisan, hey! Oua te' Corone' Gis."

We were now in full ceremony. Dieu Donnez bowed himself twice toward the altar. He took a white pigeon and lifted it to the four quarters of the earth before he killed it. Then all of the good angels and twins were supposed to enter the hounfort. This ceremony to the twins is observed by all who have or have had twins in the family. It is believed that twins have some special power to harm if they are not appeased. It seems that everyone in Haiti has been involved with twins in one way or another, so that the ceremony is universal. The food was all on white plates and divided into two parts. One part for the Marassas and the other for the adepts.

Mambo Mabo Aizan, who walks with the Marassas, the twins, is the wife of Papa Loco, whose full name is Loco Atison Goue' Azambloguide', Loa Atinoque', and he is always accompanied by a Nanchon-Aan-Hizo-Yan-go. In the ceremonies of the days of Grand Fete, when all of the mysteries are honored and saluted, the ceremony to Loco comes immediately after the Marassas. So Dieu Donnez took a grayish cock in his two hands and lifted it toward the altar at the same time that he bowed himself. Then he turned toward the east, toward the south and toward the west. He poured the libation of rum and clairin on the ground and chanted:

157

"Loco Anbe'! Ce Loco Azambloguidi
Loca Anhe'! Loco Atinogue' Apoyoci
Loco, Loco Atinis do guidi, Loco
Azamblonguidi Atinogue', Loco he'!"

The houngan saluted the white pot on the altar that was
dedicated to Loco. The Mambo and several servitors became
possessed and the crowd became excited because they were
glad that the god was manifesting himself so freely. In this
exalted condition these "horses" of Loco dressed an altar to
him. They placed a table and placed on it the sacred stone
dedicated to Loco, his white pot, chapilets, images of St. Joseph and his drinks. A visiting houngan became possessed and
the cry went up that "Papa Loco 'Amarre les points' "—that
is, he was "tying the points." That means that the loa was
personally taking a hand in execution of the things asked of
him by his followers. For instance, a man came to Dieu
Donnez to make good in a business venture. He had come to
the houngan to find out what he must do to insure success. He
wanted the houngan to invoke the "Master of his head," to
give him the information and assistance needed. The houngan
summoned his loa and he came and it was Papa Loco. He
demanded certain articles and indicated to Dieu Donnez
which ceremony to observe and how to conduct it. The loa
then left the houngan and he informed the man who had asked
the favor what the loa had demanded. The man gave the
houngan the money to buy the things and to celebrate the
ceremony. The supplicant, of course, would not be present at
this. But when Dieu Donnez went to perform the rites, Loco
took possession of the body of the houngan and performed the
ceremony himself. Then he was "tying the points." The reason it was known that Loco was there himself, was because he
said with the lips of the houngan, "Vivant yo pas rainmin loa,
yo rabi voodoo ce' ouanga yo rainmin."

But Loco can be terrible sometimes. He refuses to answer
when he pleases. He refused to answer the very next applicant. The man was very eager for an answer but the houngan

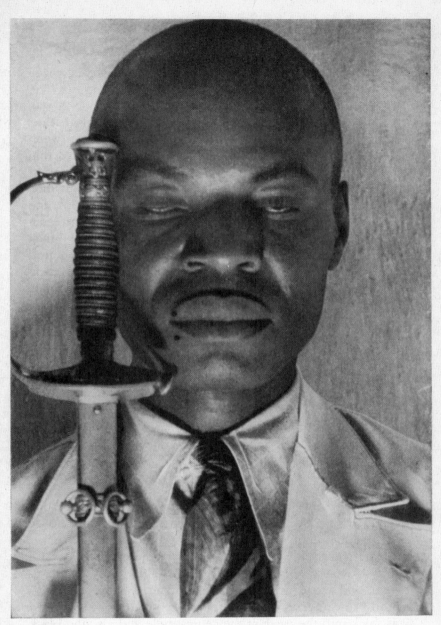

Rex Hardy, Jr.

The loa "mounts" the houngan

told him to wait until another time. But for two women who had asked health favors of Loco Papa Loco indicated a ceremony out under the tree that was his repository. So we took our chairs and went out under the tree. We marched three times around the tree carrying the chairs and singing. The little baskets with the offerings were hanging from the limbs. The houngans intoned the ceremony and we answered. Two live chickens were passed all about the heads and the shoulders of the two kneeling women. Dieu Donnez made a cross on top of the heads of both women with the corn meal. Both women were made to stand and were faced both ways as they danced around the tree. When they had danced so far, the priest faced them the other way. Finally the chicken of each woman was surrendered to the priest and killed with a knife—their heads bent far back to expose their throats. More singing with four women marching around the tree picking the chickens as they went. The loose feathers in the lamp light made a pattern of a loose tumbling circle in the air like playful little clouds or like suntracks in the sky. Some of the cooked chicken was returned and the two women executed a wild dance about the tree and the signature of Loco on the ground. Then some of the food was put in the hollow of the tree for the god.

There was a new note on the Rada drums. We went into the hounfort to the altar of Ogoun. There are many Ogouns. Ogoun Badagris, Ogoun Ferraille, Ogoun Shango or Chango, Ogoun Balingio. But this ceremony was to Ogoun Badagris. Before his altar there were eggs and corn meal, the signs of fertility. There were sweets, and parched corn and peanuts. Of course, the water dedicated to the dead and the liqueurs, cognac, red wine, rum clairin and a red cock. The same one that I had seen tied all day by one leg before the bath house of ceremony. I felt I knew that rooster because another had attacked him while he was tethered there and while he showed plenty of courage, being tied by the leg hindered his movements, and I had driven off his assailant. I looked into his round brown eye in the hounfort and looked away. A sword was stuck into the earth at the central pole and a round black

Altar to Ogoun Feraille, God of War (old iron and other metals are offered to him)

hat something like a Turkish fez was hung on the handle of it. Joswee, the sabreur (sword-bearer) who belonged to the compound of Dieu Donnez, engaged Pierre Charles the sabreur of Annee' La Cour in mock combat. It was a very lively encounter and brought wild cheering. As Pierre Charles was forced to give away before Joswee, a figure leaped into the door. It was all in blazing red from head to foot. The skirts of the robes were very full and trimmed in white lace. This figure rushed forward, put on the fez, seized the sword and challenged Joswee fiercely. The crowd went mad as the clever dance went on. Neither really conquered the other. It was not done to prove strength and courage. It was done as a symbol of Ogoun's power to help warriors and for the magnificent and spirited grotesque.

The Man in red dress was Ogoun. At a point, both lowered their blades and Ogoun planted a ceremonial kiss on the brow of Joswee. The drums commenced to walk with the songs and Dieu Donnez took the red rooster from Joswee. He surprised the fowl by setting off a little heap of gunpowder near him and the rooster leaped high. The crowd called that "foula poule." The servitors following Mambo Etienne knelt and kissed the earth. One female hounci, when she knelt before Madame Etienne received a good kick in the behind for not behaving properly. The second prayer was chanted and the tongue of the red rooster is torn out before it is killed with a sharp knife. Some of its blood is smeared on the wall with a cluster of feathers from the throat. The body of the rooster was placed before the altar. The drums changed their tempo and Dieu Donnez left the hounfort and crossed the peristyle followed by everybody because he was going to salute all the repositories in the place. Several servitors became possessed during this part of the ceremony. There was a great deal of spirited dancing under the peristyle after the repositories had been honored. The figure of Ogoun dominated the movement. Dieu Donnez was beating the hountah, the greatest Rada drum, women wishing children prostrated themselves before Ogoun and when he danced with them in a way to symbolize

Rex Hardy, Jr.

The sabreur before the gods

sex and procreation there was joy and even ecstasy in their faces. He did not always approach them from the front. He sometimes approached them from the rear as they danced face to face with someone else and made his motions of promise.

We then honored Damballa, the great and the pure. He was given the sweet soft drinks and white chickens. He it is who looks after peace and love in the home so that a pair of white chickens, a hen and a rooster, are offered him. They must be bought a month in advance and dedicated to his intention. When they have been sacrificed, they are laid side by side before the altar.

The last deity to be honored was Brave Guedé, who is a sort of messenger of all the gods. Then we danced for the rest of the night. We knew that the next day a Petro ceremony, "A day of promise," was in store for us but we danced the sun out of bed just the same. After daylight, the nattes or sleeping mats were full of people that looked like dead bodies getting some sleep before the ceremonies of the day should begin. Lamissier woke me up to hand me a cup of chanelle tea and to tell me that Dieu Donnez wanted me.

I had about two hours of instruction in the nature of the gods and something about their origins. I had some practise in drawing with corn meal the verver or signatures of various loa. Then he let me see him work on the Paquettes de Congo. They are those figures which must be present at a baptism and the new drapeaux (flags) and the new sabre were to be baptized on Sunday.

Before we go into the description of the outdoor altar to Petro, let me give you some idea of the differences between a Rada god and a Petro divinity.

As has been said before, Damballa and his suite are high and pure. They do only good things for people, but they are slow and lacking in power. The Petro gods on the other hand are terrible and wicked, but they are more powerful and quick. They can be made to do good things, however, as well as evil. They give big doses of medicine and effect quick cures. So these Petro gods are resorted to by a vast number of people

The mambo offers to Damballa

"Horse" mounted by Papa Guedé

who wish to gain something but fear them at the same time. The Rada spirits demand nothing more than chickens and pigeons, and there are no consequences or hereafter to what they do for you, while the Petros demand hogs, goats, sheep, cows, dogs and in some instances they have been known to take dead bodies from the tombs. The Petros work for you only if you make a promise of service to them. You can promise a service to be fulfilled as far away as thirty years, but at the end of that time, the promise *must* be kept or the spirits begin to take revenge. It seems that they actually do collect on the debt owed to them, for first the domestic animals of the family begin to die and when all these are gone, the children fall ill and die if the service is still not done and finally the head of the house. If you make a promise to the Petros *it is going to be kept.*

The Petros and the Congos, who sometimes unite, are the cults who make use of charms, ouangas (pronounced wanga). The Petro Quita Sec have the power to take human life. There is a long list of these spirits who have the same names as the Rada gods except that the second name distinguishes them from the rada. "Ge-rouge" after a name places that god in the Petros or the Congos. For instance we find Damballa Ge-rouge, which means "red-eyed," Erzulle, ge-rouge, Ogoun ge-rouge, Damballa-la-flambeau. The list included the Congos Savanne, that is, Congos of the open field or woods, such as Congo Mazambi, Congo Zandor, Marinette-pied-seche (dry foot), Erzulie Mapiangue, Bacca loup-gerow, Petit Jean Petro. They are recognized as evil, but one must feed them to have better luck than others. Louis Romin says, "All these mysteres make big cures and do heavy work. When you have a big sickness case about which Rada mysteres are too helpless to bring recovery Petro will undertake the treatment and *cure* the party. They give you luck to find a job or to start any kind of trading. They lend you big support or give you something to protect you in order that nothing will happen to you and that no one will cause you to be sick, and the demons or the devil will be unable to do you anything at night."

Offering to Congo Savanne

Therefore, since these evil mysteres are so useful, it is necessary for the houngan to have them under his control. Many, many families have their day of promise to the Petros for health, wealth or advancement in life.

The Petros make great use of fire. When a Petro ceremony is going on, there is always a big fire close by the hounfort with a bar of iron stuck into the middle of the flames.

Every Christmas, the Petros fix baths for all of those for whom they have worked during the year. They also give them "guards." Sometimes they dose their followers with machettas. Sometimes they cut a piece out of your body and put something in the hole and close it up. Two minutes afterwards, you feel nothing and know nothing about the wound. Neither can anyone see it again.

No Petro ceremony is held in the hounfort where the niche or repository of Damballa is. Even the door to the hounfort must be kept closed while the Petro service is going on. Neither can the two services be held in the same day.

The Petro *ceremony of promise* or of service to Petro is held in the open air.

Two large draperies or curtains are joined together at one end by a large hoop or circle of some kind and suspended from a limb of a tree. Beside this is a partition built to that end formed by the two sides of the niche. The loose ends opposite fall about a table which is covered by the curtains. A picture representing Maitresse Erzulie, St. Joseph and Loco is hung at the bottom of the niche which is decorated by a knot of red ribbon. A white plate is on the table with a knife, fork and spoon. As many different kinds of perfume as the supplicant can afford are on the table also with bouquets of flowers. At a little distance from the draped niche is the tonnelle, a palm thatched shed open on all sides which contains the two Petro drums. It must be ten metres from the niche. That distance is fixed.

The animals consecrated to Petro Quita Moudong are the pig, the goat, male and female; and the dog.

During the afternoon we saw the niche, the tonnelle being

Rex Hardy, Jr.

The priest opens the ceremony with a chant

built and three holes being dug not far from the niche. Everything was ready by night time. The houngan went into the court to see that everything was ready and it was. The fire, the niche, the tonnelle, the animals, the family who wished to make the promise to Petro and the Canzos and houncis. Seeing all this, he had the animals led up to the holes and began the services.

First came the Litany to Saint Joseph, then the Pater-Noster. These being intoned and finished, he demanded to know as a matter of form if the animals had been bought for the ceremony. A Canzo answered that they had been bought and they were now present. He then asked if they had been bathed. He was told that they had been bathed. He next asked if they had been perfumed. He was told that all of the animals present had been perfumed also. Since these things had been attended to, he said that they must be dressed. Then a sort of cape, or tunic was thrown over the back of each animal and tied with a ribbon about the neck and another under its tail. The heads of the animals were wrapped in a white cloth.

The officiating houngan gave the word after the Voodoo prayers had been said, and the procession with the animals began. It circled the niche, the tonnelle, the three holes and a house of ceremony. The three holes were illuminated by a dozen white candles. Here before the holes Dieu Donnez drew his sabre from its scabbard and cut off the testicles of the pig, which he first elevated for the edification of the crowd, then placed on a white plate prepared to receive this sacred burden. The houngan turned again to the groaning animal and stuck him in the throat and caught the blood, or part of it in the white soup plate. Then he drank some blood from the wound himself. Then the family who was making the promise was brought forward and placed money, gold money, in the plate with the blood. It could not be less than five dollars, somebody told me.

The family drank some of the blood from the plate and crossing themselves dipped their fingers in the blood and drew a cross on their foreheads and on napes of their necks in the hot blood of the pig. They put a cruche with wine in it in one of the end holes and a cruche with liquor in the other. The middle hole received the blood and the testicles of the hog. At that moment an adept knelt, kissed the earth three times and stated the demands of the family upon the gods.

The pig is always sacrificed the first day of the ceremony. The next day was the day of Quita, and in a ceremony essentially the same, the male and female goat were sacrificed. The male goat was brought under the tonnelle in its little flowered cape, but he was most unwilling. We chanted, we sang, and effort was made to lead the goat gaily about the center pole but he balked and had to be pushed every step of the way in the procession. The red-clad Ogoun bestrode him and the crowd yelled and pushed and pulled but the goat was emphatic in his desire to have nothing to do with the affair. The crowd sang and shouted exultantly but I could hear the pathetic, frightened bleat of the goat beneath it all, as he was buffeted and dragged to make a grand spectacle of his death.

The next day was spent in the chants and dances to Petro Quita and on which day a bull was sacrificed. Dressed in the ruffled cape tied upon its back, it was led about and the world ran behind it chanting:

"Wah, wah, wah, wah, wah O bay
Wah, wah, wah, wah, wah O bay
Wah, wah, wah, wah, wah O bay
Pas Tombé."

During the procession with the bull I heard the most beautiful song that I heard in all Haiti. The air was exquisite and I promised myself to keep it in mind. The sound of the words stayed with me long enough to write them down, but to my great regret the tune that I intended to bring home in my mouth to Harry T. Burleigh escaped me like the angels out of the Devil's mouth. The words they chanted as they followed the bull, which was unwilling, like the goat, to go, were:

Bah day, bah day, oh man jah ee!
Bah day, bah day, oh man jah ee!
Bah day, bah day, oh man jah ee!
Oh bah day, oh way, oh man jah ee.

The thing that the adepts seemed to enjoy most was the drink of Petro. That is a mixture of pig blood, fresh from the wound, white wine, red wine, a pinch of flour, cannelle and nutmeg. All of this is put in a bowl and whipped well. It was most agreeable to the participants, and eagerly quaffed. In fact it seemed extremely good and even a small sip was jealously sought.

The next morning, I received a message from my good friend Louis Romain to come to Port-au-Prince to witness a Canzo ceremony, so I got the first camion and did not see the end of the Petro at Archahaie. However I did see a Petro Moudong ceremony in which they sacrificed a dog.

That ceremony was the same except that the dog was not killed so soon in this instance. Only part of one of his ears was cut off by the priest. Then an assistant pulled the teeth of the dog and finally he was buried alive. The god had indicated that he desired his food thus.

I was under the wing of Louis Romain and his wife, who is herself a Mambo and they were extremely kind and considerate of me. Louis has the gift of making you understand in one sentence more than most people can with a page. I found every word he ever told me to be true. Never once did he attempt to mislead me. He saw to it that I went places and saw things. He was preparing me to "go Canzo" myself. That is the second degree of initiation in the department of the West. It is the second step towards the priesthood.

The usual routine is this:

The spirit enters the head of a person. He is possessed of this spirit and sometimes he or she is troubled by it because the possession comes at times and places that are, perhaps, embarrassing. On advice, he goes to a houngan and the spirit is identified and the "horse" is advised to make food for the

Mme. Romain, a mambo

loa who is the master of his head. As soon as the person is financially able, he or she goes through the ceremony of baptism known as "getting the head washed." Three days before the reception of the degree, the candidate presents himself to the houngan, who receives him and makes certain libations to the spirit who has claimed the candidate. The libation varies according to the god. It is a sweet liquor if it is Damballa, rum for Ogoun, Loco or Legba. The candidate is dressed in a long white shirt with sleeves to the wrists. The head of the applicant is wrapped in a large white handkerchief and he is put to bed on a natte where he must remain for seventy-two hours. The last day, which is the day of consecration, his head is washed, and he is given something to eat and drink. He usually rises possessed of his loa, who continues the service in place of the houngan. Then he is a hounci bossal, the first step of the way to the priesthood. This does not mean that all houncis become houngans. Far from it. Only a small proportion ever take the second step, which is the Canzo.

The Canzo is a hounci who "brule son zinc" (burns his zinc fish hook). The second degree renders the hounci invulnerable to fire. Like the candidate for the first degree, the hounci who wishes to be Canzo presents himself at the hounfort of the houngan seven days before the service is to be finished. He carries with him a long white night gown, He is put to bed in the first room of the hounfort on a bed of mimbon leaves. But an odd number of candidates cannot take the degree at the same time. It must be an even number, or one must wait, because the hounci are put to bed in pairs. The two men who sleep together thus are called brothers-in-law. If it is a pair of women, they are sisters-in-law. They are given nothing to eat except fresh fruits, milk and the like. The Mambo or the priest lies down occasionally to instruct the candidates, and they are cautioned to relax and to permit the spirit to dominate them.

When the seventh day, which is the day of consecration arrives, a great fire is built and a large kettle of water put on it and allowed to boil. A small stone or a piece of money is thrown in the pot by the houngan. The houngan, after saluting

175

the gods of the candidates, sounds the Ascon and pronounces the sacred words: "Ce grand Maitre qui passe avant nous, tous les saints, les morts, Marassas, Afrique Guinin, Ce yo qui fait, quit defait." (This Grand Master, that is Lord of Lords, who passes before us, all the saints, the dead, the twins, African gods, that which they do, they are able to undo.) The adepts, the houncis, the Canzos already consecrated salute with the drums the newly elected.

The houngan pours the libations, some into the flames. He places a small amount of gunpowder near the small kettle; he approaches it with a fire brand in his hand, and sets it off. He sets off a small amount of gunpowder in the hand of each candidate. Then he himself, to the great astonishment of the crowd, puts both hands into the boiling pot and takes out the stone or the money there without burning himself.

Then the brule zinc begins. The four little clay pots are put on three iron pegs for each pot. The pine wood is set and a blazing fire under each pot is kept up. Two small chickens are torn to death and some of the features dipped in their blood are stuck to each pot. The drums are beating and the Canzo who has been assigned to each candidate conducts him or her in line. A huge sheet or cloth is spread over the Canzos and candidates. They dance around the blazing pots from one to the other. The boiling chickens have been removed from the water and cornmeal added. One servitor takes the boiling corn meal from a pot, rolls it into balls with his hands and passes them quickly to a candidate, who passes it along. They are instructed to anoint their hands from the white plate of olive oil so that they will not burn themselves from the hot corn meal mush. They proceed from pot to pot. The left foot and the left hand of each candidate is thrust into the fire, but they are not burned. It is to prove to them that they are impervious to fire that the food and the hand are exposed to flame. All this time the drums are beating furiously and the crowd of servitors and hounci are dancing round in the circle behind the Canzos with their candidates. When the fiery ordeal is over, the corn meal balls, the knife, fork and white plate, with a piece of white calico, the iron bars called "pieds-zin," are all tied up together with the calico and some leaves, and they are buried in a large hole. Pieces of the pine wood (bois pins) and some of all the food, a glass, one of the ounzin, some money, rum and clairin all are buried. The houngan orders the houncis to cover the hole. They toss in the dirt and stamp it down with the left foot. The next day, the houngan invests the new Canzo, who are all dressed in new white things, with grand colliers (necklaces) and the Ascons. Now they may hold consultations and serve the houngans most directly. It is a very joyful time for everybody. The peristyle of the hounfort fairly glitters with the crowds all dressed in new white for the final details.

The next step is to become a priest, but that is for the few. The way most acceptable to become a priest is by inheritance. But many are "claimed" by the gods. There are still others who just take up the trade.

The most famous houngans in Haiti are:

Do-See-Mah (sound spelling) of Cotes De Fer, a horse back ride up in the hills from the Sea. Port-de-Paix is the nearest large town. Do-See-Mah is the houngan of the upper classes. He is said to be so independent that he will not see anyone about his profession on Sunday no matter how urgent the case.

Ti Cousin (Little Cousin) of Leogane. Said to be the richest houngan in all Haiti. He has applied business methods to his profession and certainly has prospered. He is overlord of great stretches of land and many people. Some say that he is more often a Bocor than a houngan.

Dieu Donnez St. Leger of Archahaie. He is not a rich man, but he is not a poor one either. Every young person under his care must attend school.

Di Di, a little beyond Archahaie on the north.

Archahaie is the most famous and the most dreaded spot in all Haiti for Voodoo work. It is supposed to be the great center of the Zombie trade. But Kenscoff and many other localities have their names in the mouths of the people.

Ah Bo Bo!

177

CHAPTER 13

✦

ZOMBIES

What is the whole truth and nothing else but the truth about Zombies? I do not know, but I know that I saw the broken remnant, relic, or refuse of Felicia Felix-Mentor in a hospital yard.

Here in the shadow of the Empire State Building, death and the graveyard are final. It is such a positive end that we use it as a measure of nothingness and eternity. We have the quick and the dead. But in Haiti there is the quick, the dead, and then there are Zombies.

This is the way Zombies are spoken of: They are the bodies without souls. The living dead. Once they were dead, and after that they were called back to life again.

No one can stay in Haiti long without hearing Zombies mentioned in one way or another, and the fear of this thing and all that it means seeps over the country like a ground current of cold air. This fear is real and deep. It is more like a group of fears. For there is the outspoken fear among the peasants of the work of Zombies. Sit in the market place and pass a day with the market woman and notice how often some vendeuse cries out that a Zombie with its invisible hand has

Felicia Felix-Mentor, the Zombie

filched her money, or her goods. Or the accusation is made that a Zombie has been set upon her or some one of her family to work a piece of evil. Big Zombies who come in the night to do malice are talked about. Also the little girl Zombies who are sent out by their owners in the dark dawn to sell little packets of roasted coffee. Before sun up their cries of "Cafe grille" can be heard from dark places in the streets and one can only see them if one calls out for the seller to come with her goods. Then the little dead one makes herself visible and mounts the steps.

The upper class Haitians fear too, but they do not talk about it so openly as do the poor. But to them also it is a horrible possibility. Think of the fiendishness of the thing. It is not good for a person who has lived all his life surrounded by a degree of fastidious culture, loved to his last breath by family and friends, to contemplate the probability of his resurrected body being dragged from the vault—the best that love and means could provide, and set to toiling ceaselessly in the banana fields, working like a beast, unclothed like a beast, and like a brute crouching in some foul den in the few hours allowed for rest and food. From an educated, intelligent being to an unthinking, unknowing beast. Then there is the helplessness of the situation. Family and friends cannot rescue the victim because they do not know. They think the loved one is sleeping peacefully in his grave. They may motor past the plantation where the Zombie who was once dear to them is held captive often and again and its soulless eyes may have fallen upon them without thought or recognition. It is not to be wondered at that now and then when the rumor spreads that a Zombie has been found and recognized, that angry crowds gather and threaten violence to the persons alleged to be responsible for the crime.

Yet in spite of this obvious fear and the preparations that I found being made to safeguard the bodies of the dead against this possibility, I was told by numerous upper class Haitians that the whole thing was a myth. They pointed out that the common people were superstitious, and that the talk of Zombies had no more basis in fact than the European belief in the Werewolf.

But I had the good fortune to learn of several celebrated cases in the past and then in addition, I had the rare opportunity to see and touch an authentic case. I listened to the broken noises in its throat, and then, I did what no one else had ever done, I photographed it. If I had not experienced all of this in the strong sunlight of a hospital yard, I might have come away from Haiti interested but doubtful. But I saw this case of Felicia Felix-Mentor, which was vouched for by the highest authority. So I know that there are Zombies in Haiti. People have been called back from the dead.

Now, why have these dead folk not been allowed to remain in their graves? There are several answers to this question, according to the case.

A was awakened because somebody required his body as a beast of burden. In his natural state he could never have been hired to work with his hands, so he was made into a Zombie because they wanted his services as a laborer. B was summoned to labor also but he is reduced to the level of a beast as an act of revenge. C was the culmination of "ba' Moun" ceremony and pledge. That is, he was given as a sacrifice to pay off a debt to a spirit for benefits received.

I asked how the victims were chosen and many told me that any corpse not too old to work would do. The Bocor watched the cemetery and went back and took suitable bodies. Others said no, that the Bocor and his associates knew exactly who was going to be resurrected even before they died. They knew this because they themselves brought about the "death."

Maybe a plantation owner has come to the Bocor to "buy" some laborers, or perhaps an enemy wants the utmost in revenge. He makes an agreement with the Bocor to do the work. After the proper ceremony, the Bocor in his most powerful and dreaded aspect mounts a horse with his face toward the horse's tail and rides after dark to the house of the victim. There he places his lips to the crack of the door and sucks out the soul of the victim and rides off in all speed. Soon the victim falls ill, usually beginning with a headache, and in a few hours is dead. The Bocor, not being a member of the family, is naturally not invited to the funeral. But he is there in the cemetery. He has spied on everything from a distance. He is in the cemetery but does not approach the party. He never even faces it directly, but takes in everything out of the corner of his eye. At midnight he will return for his victim.

Everybody agrees that the Bocor is there at the tomb at midnight with the soul of the dead one. But some contend that he has it in a bottle all labelled. Others say no, that he has it in his bare hand. That is the only disagreement. The tomb is opened by the associates and the Bocor enters the tomb, calls the name of the victim. He *must* answer because the Bocor has the soul there in his hand. The dead man answers by lifting his head and the moment he does this, the Bocor passes the soul under his nose for a brief second and chains his wrists. Then he beats the victim on the head to awaken him further. Then he leads him forth and the tomb is closed again as if it never had been disturbed.

The victim is surrounded by the associates and the march to the hounfort (Voodoo temple and its surroundings) begins. He is hustled along in the middle of the crowd. Thus he is screened from prying eyes to a great degree and also in his half-waking state he is unable to orientate himself. But the victim is not carried directly to the hounfort. First he is carried past the house where he lived. *This* is always done. *Must* be. If the victim were not taken past his former house, later on he would recognize it and return. But once he is taken past, it is gone from his consciousness forever. It is as if it never existed for him. He is then taken to the hounfort and given a drop of a liquid, the formula for which is most secret. After that the victim is a Zombie. He will work ferociously and tirelessly without consciousness of his surroundings and conditions and without memory of his former state. He can never speak again, unless he is given salt. "We have examples of a man who gave salt to a demon by mistake and he come man again and can write the name of the man who gave him to the loa,"

183

Jean Nichols told me and added that of course the family of the victim went straight to a Bocor and "gave" the man who had "given" their son.

Now this "Ba Moun" (give man) ceremony is a thing much talked about in Haiti. It is the old European belief in selling one's self to the devil but with Haitian variations. In Europe the man gives himself at the end of a certain period. Over in Haiti he gives others and only gives himself when no more acceptable victims can be found. But he cannot give strangers. It must be a real sacrifice. He must give members of his own family or most intimate friends. Each year the sacrifice must be renewed and there is no avoiding the payments. There are tales of men giving every member of the family, even his wife after nieces, nephews, sons and daughters were gone. Then at last he must go himself. There are lurid tales of the last days of men who have gained wealth and power thru "give man."

The wife of one man found him sitting apart from the family weeping. When she demanded to know the trouble, he told her that he had been called to go, but she was not to worry because he had put everything in order. He was crying because he had loved her very much and it was hard to leave her. She pointed out that he was not sick and of course it was ridiculous for him to talk of death. Then with his head in her lap he told her about the "services" he had made to obtain the advantages he had had in order to surround her with increasing comforts. Finally she was the only person left that he could offer but he would gladly die himself rather than offer her as a sacrifice. He told her of watching the day of the vow come and go while his heart grew heavier with every passing hour. The second night of the contract lapsed and he heard the beasts stirring in their little box. The third night which was the one just past, a huge and a terrible beast had emerged in the room. If he could go to the Bocor that same day with a victim, he still could go another year at least. But he had no one to offer except his wife and he had no desire to live without her. He took an affectionate farewell of her, shut

184

himself in his own room and continued to weep. Two days later he was dead.

Another man received the summons late one night. Bosu Tricorne, the terrible three-horned god, had appeared in his room and made him know that he must go. Bosu Tricorne bore a summons from Baron Cimiterre, the lord of the cemetery. He sprang from his bed in terror and woke up his family by his fear noises. He had to be restrained from hurling himself out of the window. And all the time he was shouting of the things he had done to gain success. Naming the people he had given. The family in great embarrassment dragged him away from the window and tried to confine him in a room where his shouts could not be heard by the neighbors. That failing, they sent him off to a private room in a hospital where he spent two days confessing before he died. There are many, many tales like that in the mouths of the people.

There is the story of one man of great courage who, coming to the end of his sacrifices, feeling that he had received what he bargained for, went two days ahead and gave himself up to the spirit to die. But the spirit so admired his courage that he gave him back all of the years he had bargained to take.

Why do men allegedly make such bargains with the spirits who have such terrible power to reward and punish?

When a man is ambitious and sees no way to get there, he becomes desperate. When he has nothing and wants prosperity he goes to a houngan and says, "I have nothing and I am disposed to do anything to have money."

The houngan replies, "He who does not search, does not find."

"I have come to you because I wish to search," the man replies.

"Well, then," the houngan says, "we are going to make a ceremony, and the loa are going to talk with you."

The houngan and the man go into the hounfort. He goes to a small altar and makes the symbol with ashes and gunpowder (indicating that it is a Petro invocation), pours the libation and begins to sing with the Ascon and then asks the seeker,

185

Altar to Baron Cimeterre

"What loa you want me to call for you?"

The man makes his choice. Then the houngan begins in earnest to summon the loa wanted. No one knows what he says because he is talking "langage" that is, language, a way of denoting the African patter used by all houngans for special occasions. The syllables are his very own, that is, something that cannot be taught. It must come to the priest from the loa. He calls many gods. Then the big jars under the table that contain spirits of houngans long dead begin to groan. These spirits in jars have been at the bottom of the water for a long time. The loa was not taken from their heads at death and so they did not go away from the earth but went to the bottom of the water to stay until they got tired and demanded to be taken out. All houngans have one more of these spirit jars in the hounfort. Some have many. The groaning of the jars gets louder as the houngan keeps calling. Finally one jar speaks distinctly, "Pourquoi ou derange' moi?" (Why do you disturb me?) The houngan signals the man to answer the loa. So he states his case.

"Papa, loa, ou mem, qui connais toute baggage ou mem qui chef te de l'eau, moi duange' on pour mande' ou servir moi." (Papa, loa, yourself, who knows all things, you yourself who is master of waters, I disturb you to ask you to serve me.)

The Voice: Ma connasis ca on besoin. Mais, on dispose pour servir moi aussi? (I know what you want, but are you disposed to serve me also?)

The Man: Yes, command me what you want.

Voice: I am going to give you all that you want, but you must make all things that I want. Write your name in your own blood and put the paper in the jar.

The houngan, still chanting, pricks the man's finger so sharply that he cries out. The blood flows and the supplicant dips a pen in it and writes his name and puts the paper in the jar. The houngan opens a bottle of rum and pours some in the jar. There is the gurgling sound of drinking.

The Voice: And now I am good (I do good) for you. Now I tell you what you must do. You must give me someone that

187

you love. Today you are going into your house and stay until tomorrow. On the eighth day you are returning here with something of the man that you are going to give me. Come also with some money in gold. The voice ceases. The houngan finishes presently, after repeating everything that the Voice from the jar has said, and dismisses the man. He goes away and returns on the day appointed and the houngan calls up the loa again.

The Voice: Are you prepared for me?

The Man: Yes.

The Voice: Have you done all that I told you?

The Man: Yes.

The Voice (to houngan): Go out. (to man) Give me the gold money.

(The man gives it.)

The Voice: Now, you belong to me and I can do with you as I wish. If I want you in the cemetery I can put you there.

The Man: Yes, I know you have all power with me. I put myself in your care because I want prosperity.

The Voice: That I will give you. Look under the table. You will find a little box. In this box there are little beasts. Take this little box and put it in your pocket. Every eighth day you must put in it five hosts (Communion wafers). *Never forget to give the hosts.* Now, go to your house and put the little box in a big box. Treat it as if it were your son. It is now your son. Every midnight open the box and let the beasts out. At four o'clock he will return and cry to come in and you will open for him and close the box again. And every time you give the beasts the communion, immediately after, you will receive large sums of money. Each year on this date you will come to me with another man that you wish to give me. Also you must bring the box with the beasts. If you do not come, the third night after the date, the beasts in the box will become great huge animals and execute my will upon you for your failure to keep your vow. If you are very sick on that day that the offering falls due say to your best friend that he must bring the offering box for you. Also you must send the name of the

188

person you intend to give me as pay for working for you and he must sign a new contract with me for you.

All is finished between the Voice and the man. The houngan re-enters and sends the man away with assurance that he will commence the work at once. Alone he makes ceremony to call the soul of the person who is to be sacrificed. No one would be permitted to see that. When the work in the hounfort is finished, then speeds the rider on the horse. The rider who faces backwards on the horse, who will soon place his lips to the crack of the victim's door and draw his soul away. Then will follow the funeral and after that the midnight awakening. And the march to the hounfort for the drop of liquid that will make him a Zombie, one of the living dead.

Some maintain that a real and true priest of Voodoo, the houngan, has nothing to do with such practices. That it is the bocor and priests of the devil—worshipping cults—who do these things. But it is not always easy to tell just who is a houngan and who is a bocor. Often the two offices occupy the same man at different times. There is no doubt that some houngans hold secret ceremonies which their usual following know nothing of. It would be necessary to investigate every houngan and bocor in Haiti rigidly over a period of years to determine who was purely houngan and who was purely bocor. There is certainly some overlapping in certain cases. A well known houngan of Leogane, who has become a very wealthy man by his profession is spoken of as a bocor more often than as a houngan. There are others in the same category that I could name. Soon after I arrived in Haiti a young woman who was on friendly terms with me said, "You know, you should not go around alone picking acquaintances with these houngans. You are liable to get involved in something that is not good. You must have someone to guide you." I laughed it off at the time, but months later I began to see what she was hinting at.

What is involved in the "give man" and making of Zombies is a question that cannot be answered anywhere with legal proof. Many names are called. Most frequently mentioned in this respect is the Man of Trou Forban. That legendary character who lives in the hole in the mountain near St. Marc. He who has enchanted caves full of coffee and sugar plantations. The entrance to this cave or this series of caves is said to be closed by a huge rock that is lifted by a glance from the master. The Marines are said to have blown up this great rock with dynamite at one time, but the next morning it was there whole and in place again. When the master of Trou Forban walks, the whole earth trembles. There are tales of the master and his wife, who is reputed to be a greater bocor than he. She does not live with him at Trou Forban. She is said to have a great hounfort of her own on the mountain called Tapion near Petit Gouave. She is such a great houngan that she is honored by Agoue' te Royo, Maitre l'eau, and walks the waters with the same ease that others walk the earth. But she rides in boats whenever it suits her fancy. One time she took a sailboat to go up the coast near St. Marc to visit her husband, Vixama. She appeared to be an ordinary peasant woman and the captain paid her no especial attention until they arrived on the coast below Trou Forban. Then she revealed herself and expressed her great satisfaction with the voyage. She felt that the captain had been extremely kind and courteous, so she went to call her husband to come down to the sea to meet him. Realizing now who she was, the captain was afraid and made ready to sail away before she could return from the long trip up the mountain. But she had mounted to the trou very quickly and returned with Vixama to find the captain and his crew poling the boat away from the shore in the wildest terror. The wind was against them and they could not sail away. Mme. Vixama smiled at their fright and hurled two grains of corn which she held in her hand on to the deck of the boat and they immediately turned into golden coin. The captain was more afraid and hastily brushed them into the sea. They sailed south all during the night, much relieved that they had broken all connections with Vixama and his wife. But at first light the next morning he found four gold coins of the same denomination as the two that he had refused the day before. Then he knew that the woman of Vixama had passed the night on board and had given them a good voyage as well—the four gold coins were worth twenty dollars each.

There are endless tales of the feats of the occupant of this hole high up on this inaccessible mountain. But in fact it has yet to be proved that anyone has ever laid eyes on him. He is like the goddess in the volcano of Hawaii, and Vulcan in Mt. Vesuvius. It is true that men, taking advantage of the legend and the credulous nature of the people, have set up business in the mountain to their profit. The name of this Man of Trou Forban is known by few and rarely spoken by those who know it. This whispered name is Vixama, which in itself means invisible spirit. He who sits with a hive of honey-bees in his long flowing beard. It is he who is reputed to be the greatest buyer of souls. His contact man is reputed to be Mardi Progres. But we hear too much about the practice around Archahaie and other places to credit Trou Forban as the head-quarters. Some much more accessible places than the mountain top is the answer. And some much more substantial being than the invisible Vixama.

If embalming were customary, it would remove the possibility of Zombies from the minds of the people. But since it is not done, many families take precautions against the body being disturbed.

Some set up a watch in the cemetery for thirty-six hours after the burial. There could be no revival after that. Some families have the bodies cut open, insuring real death. Many peasants put a knife in the right hand of the corpse and flex the arm in such a way that it will deal a blow with the knife to whoever disturbs it for the first day or so. But the most popular defense is to poison the body. Many of the doctors have especially long hypodermic needles for injecting a dose of poison into the heart, and sometimes into other parts of the body as well.

A case reported from Port du Paix proves the necessity of this. In Haiti if a person dies whose parents are still alive, the mother does not follow the body to the grave unless it is an only child. Neither does she wear mourning in the regular sense. She wears that coarse material known as "gris-blanc." The next day after the burial, however, she goes to the grave to say her private farewell.

In the following case everything had seemed irregular. The girl's sudden illness and quick death. Then, too, her body stayed warm. So the family was persuaded that her death was unnatural and that some further use was to be made of her body after burial. They were urged to have it secretly poisoned before it was interred. This was done and the funeral went off in routine manner.

The next day, like Mary going to the tomb of Jesus, the mother made her way to the cemetery to breathe those last syllables that mothers do over their dead, and like Mary she found the stones rolled away. The tomb was open and the body lifted out of the coffin. It had not been moved because it was so obviously poisoned. But the ghouls had not troubled themselves to rearrange things as they were.

Testimony regarding Zombies with names and dates come from all parts of Haiti. I shall cite a few without using actual names to avoid embarrassing the families of the victims.

In the year 1898 at Cap Haitian a woman had one son who was well educated but rather petted and spoiled. There was some trouble about a girl. He refused to accept responsibility and when his mother was approached by a member of the girl's family she refused to give any sort of satisfaction. Two weeks later the boy died rather suddenly and was buried. Several Sundays later the mother went to church and after she went wandering around the town—just walking aimlessly in her grief, she found herself walking along Bord Mer. She saw some laborers loading ox carts with bags of coffee and was astonished to see her son among these silent workers who were being driven to work with ever increasing speed by the foreman. She saw her son see her without any sign of recognition. She rushed up to him screaming out his name. He regarded her without recognition and without sound. By this time the foreman tore her loose from the boy and drove her away. She went to get help, but it was a long time and when she returned she could not find him. The foreman denied that there had ever been anyone of that description around. She never saw him again, though she haunted the water front and coffee warehouses until she died.

A white Protestant missionary minister told me that he had a young man convert to his flock who was a highly intelligent fellow and a clever musician. He went to a dance and fell dead on the floor. The missionary conducted the funeral and saw the young man placed in the tomb and the tomb closed. A few weeks later another white minister of another Protestant denomination came to him and said, "I had occasion to visit the jail and who do you suppose I saw there? It was C. R."

"But it is not possible. C. R. is dead. I saw him buried with my own eyes."

"Well, you just go down to the prison and see for yourself. He is there, for nobody knows I saw him. After I had talked with a prisoner I went there to see, I passed along the line of cells and saw him crouching like some wild beast in one of the cells. I hurried here to tell you about it."

The former pastor of C. R. hurried to the prison and made some excuse to visit in the cell block. And there was his late convert, just as he had been told. This happened in Port-au-Prince.

Then there was the case of P., also a young man. He died and was buried. The day of the funeral passed and the mother being so stricken some friends remained overnight in the house with her and her daughter. It seems that the sister of the dead boy was more wakeful than the rest. Late in the night she heard subdued chanting, the sound of blows in the street approaching the house and looked out of the window. At the moment she did so, she heard the voice of her brother crying out: "Mama! Mama! Sauvez moi!" (Save me!) She screamed and aroused the house and others of the inside looked out and saw the procession and heard the cry. But such is the terror inspired by these ghouls, that no one, not even the mother or sister, dared go out to attempt a rescue. The procession moved on out of sight. And in the morning the young girl was found to be insane.

But the most famous Zombie case of all Haiti is the case of Marie M. It was back in October 1909 that this beautiful young daughter of a prominent family died and was buried. Everything appeared normal and people generally forgot about the beautiful girl who had died in the very bloom of her youth. Five years passed.

Then one day a group of girls from the same school which Marie had attended went for a walk with one of the Sisters who conducted the school. As they passed a house one of the girls screamed and said that she had seen Marie M. The Sister tried to convince her she was mistaken. But others had seen her too. The news swept over Port-au-Prince like wild fire. The house was surrounded, but the owner refused to let anyone enter without the proper legal steps. The father of the supposedly dead girl was urged to take out a warrant and have the house searched. This he refused to do at once. Finally he was forced to do so by the pressure of public opinion. By that time the owner had left secretly. There was no one nor nothing in the house. The sullen action of the father caused many to accuse him of complicity in the case. Some accused her uncle and others her god father. And some accused all three. The public clamored for her grave to be opened for inspection. Finally this was done. A skeleton was in the coffin but it was too long for the box. Also the clothes that the girl had been buried in were not upon the corpse. They were neatly folded beside the skeleton that had strangely outgrown its coffin.

It is said that the reason she was in the house where she was seen was that the houngan who had held her had died. His wife wanted to be rid of the Zombies that he had collected. She went to a priest about it and he told her these people must be liberated. Restitution must be made as far as possible. So the widow of the houngan had turned over Marie M. among others to this officer of the church and it was while they were wondering what steps to take in the matter that she was seen by her school mates. Later dressed in the habit of a nun she was smuggled off to France where she was seen later in a convent by her brother. It was the most notorious case in all Haiti and people still talk about it whenever Zombies are mentioned.

In the course of a conversation on November 8, 1936, Dr. Rulx Léon, Director-General of the Service d' Hygiene, told me that a Zombie had been found on the road and was now at the hospital at Gonaives. I had his permission to make an investigation of the matter. He gave me letters to the officers of the hospital. On the following Sunday I went up to Gonaives and spent the day. The chief of staff of the hospital was very kind and helped me in every way that he could. We found the Zombie in the hospital yard. They had just set her dinner before her but she was not eating. She hovered against the fence in a sort of defensive position. The moment that she sensed our approach, she broke off a limb of a shrub and began to use it to dust and clean the ground and the fence and the table which bore her food. She huddled the cloth about her head more closely and showed every sign of fear and expectation of abuse and violence. The two doctors with me made kindly noises and tried to reassure her. She seemed to hear nothing. Just kept on trying to hide herself. The doctor uncovered her head for a moment but she promptly clapped her arms and hands over it to shut out the things she dreaded.

I said to the doctor that I had permission of Dr. Léon to take some pictures and he helped me to go about it. I took her first in the position that she assumed herself whenever left alone. That is, cringing against the wall with the cloth hiding her face and head. Then in other positions. Finally the doctor forcibly uncovered her and held her so that I could take her face. And the sight was dreadful. That blank face with the dead eyes. The eyelids were white all around the eyes as if they had been burned with acid. It was pronounced enough to come out in the picture. There was nothing that you could say to her or get from her except by looking at her, and the sight of this wreckage was too much to endure for long. We went to a more

195

cheerful part of the hospital and sat down to talk. We discussed at great length the theories of how Zombies come to be. It was concluded that it is not a case of awakening the dead, but a matter of the semblance of death induced by some drug known to a few. Some secret probably brought from Africa and handed down from generation to generation. These men know the effect of the drug and the antidote. It is evident that it destroys that part of the brain which governs speech and will power. The victims can move and act but cannot formulate thought. The two doctors expressed their desire to gain this secret, but they realize the impossibility of doing so. These secret societies are secret. They will die before they will tell. They cited instances. I said I was willing to try. Dr. Legros said that perhaps I would find myself involved in something so terrible, something from which I could not extricate myself alive, and that I would curse the day that I had entered upon my search. Then we came back to the case in hand, and Dr. Legros and Dr. Belfong told me her story.

Her name is Felicia Felix-Mentor. She was a native of En-nery and she and her husband kept a little grocery. She had one child, a boy. In 1907 she took suddenly ill and died and was buried. There were the records to show. The years passed. The husband married again and advanced himself in life. The little boy became a man. People had forgotten all about the wife and mother who had died so long ago.

Then one day in October 1936 someone saw a naked woman on the road and reported it to the Garde d'Haiti. Then this same woman turned up on a farm and said, "This is the farm of my father. I used to live here." The tenants tried to drive her away. Finally the boss was sent for and he came and recognized her as his sister who had died and been buried twenty-nine years before. She was in such wretched condition that the authorities were called in and she was sent to the hospital. Her husband was sent for to confirm the identification, but he refused. He was embarrassed by the matter as he was now a minor official and wanted nothing to do with the affair at all. But President Vincent and Dr. Léon were in the neighborhood at the time and he was forced to come. He did so and reluctantly made the identification of this woman as his former wife.

How did this woman, supposedly dead for twenty-nine years, come to be wandering naked on a road? Nobody will tell who knows. The secret is with some bocor dead or alive. Sometimes a missionary converts one of these bocors and he gives up all his paraphernalia to the church and frees his captives if he has any. They are not freed publicly, you understand, as that would bring down the vengeance of the community upon his head. These creatures, unable to tell anything —for almost always they have lost the power of speech forever—are found wandering about. Sometimes the bocor dies and his widow refuses their responsibility for various reasons. Then again they are set free. Neither of these happenings is common.

But Zombies are wanted for more uses besides field work. They are reputedly used as sneak thieves. The market women cry out continually that little Zombies are stealing their change and goods. Their invisible hands are believed to provide well for their owners. But I have heard of still another service performed by Zombies. It is in the story that follows:

A certain matron of Port-au-Prince had five daughters and her niece also living with her. Suddenly she began to marry them off one after the other in rapid succession. They were attractive girls but there were numerous girls who were more attractive whose parents could not find desirable husbands for. People began to marvel at the miracle. When madame was asked directly how she did it, she always answered by saying, "Filles ce'marchandies peressables" (Girls are perishable goods, it is necessary to get them off hand quickly). That told nobody anything, but they kept on wondering just the same.

Then one morning a woman well acquainted with the madame of the marrying daughters got up to go to the lazy people's mass. This is celebrated at 4:00 A.M. and is called the lazy people's mass because it is not necessary to dress properly to attend it. It is held mostly for the servants anyway. So people who want to go to mass and want no bother, get up and go and come back home and go to sleep again.

This woman's clock had stopped so she guessed at the hour and got up at 2:00 A.M. instead of 3:00 A.M. and hurried to St. Anne's to the mass. She hurried up the high steps expecting to find the service about to begin. Instead she found an empty church except for the vestibule. In the vestibule she found two little girls dressed for first communion and with lighted candles in their hands kneeling on the floor. The whole thing was too out of place and distorted and for a while the woman just stared. Then she found her tongue and asked, "What are you two little girls doing here at such an hour and why are you dressed for first communion?"

She got no answer as she asked again, "Who are you anyway? You must go home. You cannot remain here like this."

Then one of the little figures in white turned its dead eyes on her and said, "We are here at the orders of Madame M. P., and we shall not be able to depart until all of her daughters are married."

At this the woman screamed and fled.

It is told that before the year was out all of the girls in the family had married. But already four of them had been divorced. For it is said that nothing gotten through "give man" is permanent.

Ah Bo Bo!

CHAPTER 14

✥

SECTE ROUGE

I f you stay in Haiti long enough and really mingle with the
people, the time will come when you hear secret societies
mentioned. Nobody, of course, sits down and gives lectures on these dread gatherings. It is not in any open way that
you come to know. You hear a little thing here and see a little
thing there that seem to have no connection at first. It takes
a long time and a mass of incidents before it all links up and
gains significance. To bring it down to a personal thing, I came
at it backwards. I did not move from cause to effect. I saw the
effect and it aroused my curiosity to go seek the cause.

For instance, I kept meeting up with an unreasoning fear.
Repeated incidents thrust upon my notice a fear out of all
proportion to the danger. That is, to what seemed to be the
danger. Some of the things I heard and saw seemed crazy until
I realized that it was all too simple to be nothing more than
it showed from the outside. The first of these incidents came
after I had been in Haiti less than a month.

I had taken my little house in the suburbs of Port-au-Prince
with the excellent maid that Mme. Jules Faine had found for
me. One night I heard drums throbbing at a distance. They

199

came from the mountain that rose as a sort of backdrop behind the village. Immediately the sounds caught my attention, not just because they were drum tones. I had heard plenty drum music since I had been there. You cannot avoid hearing the drums in Haiti. Besides M. Clement Magliore, publisher of *Le Matin* and other friends had taken me to Saturday night bomboches and I had heard the rada drums. But the drum that I was hearing this night did not have the deep singing quality of the rada. This was a keen, high-pitched sound that was highly repetitious. I resolved to go and see this new kind of dance, or whatever it was.

I began to dress and woke up Lucille, the maid. I told her what I planned to do and told her to get dressed. She got up and dressed readily enough, but she refused to go. She refused to go outside the door. Lucille went even further than that. She went and stood guard and would not let me go outside of the door either. And all the explanation she would give was, "It is very bad to go there, Mademoiselle. Do not search for the drums. Anyway the drum is not near. It is far away. But such things are very bad."

Since I could not do anything to make her go with me, I had to stay home. This incident struck me as strange, the more I thought about it. It was not usual for Lucille not to want to do anything I wanted done because she loved to please. Already I was beginning to love her and to depend upon her. Later on I put her on the roster of my few earthly friends and gave her all my faith. Lucille with her great heart, her willingness to help, her sympathy under varying conditions and her great honesty. The treasury of the United States could be left in her hands with absolute safety. In addition she is extremely kind. Thinking the incident of the drum over for several days I asked Lucille what she meant. Why was it bad for me to go to the music-makers? She knew that I had been to other native gatherings. Why not this one also? She gave some sort of a general answer. I have asked her many times since, but to this day, she has never said anything more definite than "Some things are very dangerous to see, Mademoiselle. There are

200

many good things for you to learn. I am well content if you do not run to every drum that you hear." That was the first instance.

The second incident came shortly afterwards and was more pointed. After two months I grew tired of my landlord swindling me and moved to Pacot. There Joseph bestowed himself upon me as a yard-boy. Two days after I agreed to keep him, he moved his wife and infant child into his room that was in a sort of basement. All went well for a week or two. One night I was propped up in bed writing as usual, when I smelled an odor of something burning. It smelled awful. Like rubber and several other things equally disagreeable smouldering. I stood it as long as I could in bed, and then I got up and called Lucille, who slept in the room next to mine. We went about looking for the source. When we got to the salon which was directly over Joseph's room the smell was overwhelming, so I concluded he was responsible for it.

I called down to Joseph and demanded to know what on earth was going on. He told me he was burning something to drive off bad things. What bad things, I wanted to know. I was good and angry about the thing. He said not to be angry, please. But cochon gris (gray pigs) qui mange' moun (who eat people) were after his baby and he "was make a little ceremony to drive them away." I told him to come into the house and tell me about it, but he refused. He was not going to open his room door until daylight. The house was so arranged that he must come into the yard, round the corner of the house and mount a high flight of steps before he could enter the house. This he refused to do. He begged me not to be angry, but he could not come out until daylight.

When I came down to breakfast the next morning and looked down at the yard and saw Joseph's wife sitting there in the sunlight calmly nursing her child, Joseph's explanations of the night before seemed so ridiculous that I grew very peevish and I made myself a promise to give him a highly seasoned piece of my mind. But he did not wait for me to summon him. As soon as he saw me at the table he came of

201

his own accord. He told me that he had seen figures in white robes and hoods, no, some of them had red gowns and hoods, lurking in the paraseuse (hedge) the night before. He thought the cochons gris knew that he had a very young baby and they wanted to take it and eat it.

"Now Joseph," I objected, "you are trying to excuse yourself for disturbing me by telling a fantastic lie. In the first place I have never seen a grey pig and do not believe they exist. In the second place, hogs do not go about in robes of any sort and neither do they go about eating babies. Pas capab'."

"But yes, Mademoiselle, there are very bad thing that go about at night. I have great fear from what I see last night. I want you to take my baby in the house with you. Then nobody can steal him."

"No, Joseph, your baby is too young. He would cry all of the time and disturb me. I must have quiet to write a book."

"But he is very little, Mademoiselle. He cannot cry much. Take him to sleep at night, please, Mademoiselle. If you don't want baby in the house, then please give me seven gourds and I put my wife and baby on the boat and send them to Petit Gouave. My family will take care of them. Then I come back and I work for you very good because then I will not worry about my baby die. First they make him die, then they take him from the grave."

The discussion was broken off there because an upper class Haitian came at that moment for a morning visit. The Haitian peasant is very humble before his betters, so Joseph shut up quickly and went on back to cleaning up the yard. The gentleman and I went on the front gallery that commands such a magnificent view of Port-au-Prince and the sea, and sat down. I laughed and told him the fantastic explanation that Joseph had made. He laughed briefly, then he said he was thirsty. He would neither permit me to go for a glass of water for him, nor call Lucille to bring it. He would just go out to the kitchen and let Lucille give it to him there. After he went to the rear, I thought I'd join him and offer him a drink of rum. When I reached the end of the salon I saw that he was not asking

Lucille for water at all. He was on the back gallery speaking to Joseph in the yard. He was speaking in Creole and calling Joseph every kind of a stupid miscreant. He ended his tirade by saying that since Joseph had been so foolish as to tell a foreigner, who might go off and say bad things about Haiti, such things, he was going to see that the Garde d'Haiti gave him a good beating with a coco-macaque. Knowing that I would embarrass my friend by letting him know that I had heard, I went back to the porch as quietly as I could and waited until he returned before I mentioned the rum.

When he came back to where I sat he accepted the rum and then explained to me with all the charm that an upper class Haitian is so full of, that the peasants of Haiti were a poetical group. They loved the metaphor and the simile. They had various figures of speech that could easily be misunderstood by those who did not know their ways. For example: It was the habit of the peasant to say "mange' moun" (eat a man) when he really meant to kill. Had I never heard the Haitian threat "map mange' ou sans cel" (I'll eat you without salt)? It is of course the same exaggerated threat that is commonly used in the United States by white and black. "I'll eat you up! I'll eat you alive; I'll chew you up!"

I acknowledged that I had heard the expression in the market several times. I added that we Negroes of America also employed the figures of speech continuously. Very well then, he replied, I would understand, and not take the mode of speech of the peasants literally. He never referred directly to Joseph and neither did I. He sipped his rum, and I drank coconut water and we studied the magnificent panorama before us and spent a pleasant morning. But the thing left me quivering with curiosity and I wanted to call Joseph and ask questions. I did not do this because I knew that the time had passed for him to answer me truthfully. He was visibly cowed by that Gros Negre. I would have given most anything to know what it was Joseph had started to explain.

A little later I told a very intelligent young Haitian woman that I was going to the mountains shortly to study Voodoo practices. We had come to be very close to each other. We had gotten to the place where neither of us lied to each other about our respective countries. I freely admitted gangsters, corrupt political machines, race prejudice and lynchings. She as frankly deplored bad politics, overemphasized class distinctions, lack of public schools and transportation. We neither of us apologized for Voodoo. We both acknowledged it among us, but both of us saw it as a religion no more venal, no more impractical than any other.

So when I told her that I was going to Archahaie to live in the compound of a bocor in order to learn all I could about Voodoo, I did not expect her to take the attitude of the majority of the Haitian elite, who have become sensitive about any reference to Voodoo in Haiti. In a way they are justified in this because the people who have written about it, with one exception, that of Dr. Melville Herskovits, have not known the first thing about it. After I had spoken she sat very still for a while, and then she asked me if I knew the man well that I was going to study with. I said no, not very well, but I had reports from many directions that he was powerful. She was very slow about talking, but she said that I was not to go about trusting myself to people that I knew nothing about. Furthermore it was not possible for me to know whom to trust without advice. All was not gold that glittered. There were different kinds of priests. Some of them worked with two hands. Some things were good to know and some things were not. I must make no contacts nor must I go anywhere to stay unless I let my friends advise me. She was as solemn and specific about the warning as she was vague about what I was to fear. But she showed herself a friend in that she introduced me to an excellent mambo (priestess) whom I found sincere in all her dealings with me.

A physician of very high calibre said the same thing to me at Gonaives the day that I visited the Zombie there at the hospital and photographed her, or it. Over the coffee cups we discussed the possibility of a drug being used to produce this semblance of death. That is his theory of the matter. He said that he would give much to know the secret of it. It was his belief that many scientific truths were hidden in some of these primitive practices that have been brought from Africa. But the knowledge of the plants and formulae are secret. They are usually kept in certain families, and nothing will induce the guardians of these ancient mysteries to divulge them. He had met up with some startling things in primitive chemistry by reason of his position at the hospital, but never had he been able to break down the resistance of the holders of those secrets. One man was placed in prison and threatened with a long term unless he told. The prisoner produced a fever temperature much higher than any mortal man is supposed to be able to stand to force the prison authorities to release him. But this they refused to do. Then he sent another prisoner to get a little pouch of powdered leaves which he had hidden in his clothes. He refused to let either the doctors or the gendarmes get it for him. When he had it, he mixed a pinch of it with water, allowed it to stand for a few minutes and drank the mixture. In three hours his temperature was perfectly normal. Soon they released him without being able to gain one word of information out of him. He merely stated that what they asked was a family secret brought over from Guinea. He could not reveal it. That was final. He left the prison and the hospital as he had come.

Hearing this, I determined to get at the secret of Zombies. The doctor said that I would not only render a great service to Haiti, but to medicine in general if I could discover this secret. But it might cost me a great deal to learn. I said I was devoted to the project and willing to try no matter how difficult. He hesitated long and then said, "Perhaps it will cost you more than you are willing to pay, perhaps things will be required of you that you cannot stand. Suppose you were forced to—could you endure to see a human being killed? Perhaps nothing like that will ever happen, but no one on the outside could know what might be required. Perhaps one's humanity and decency might prevent one from penetrating very far. Many Haitian intellectuals have curiosity but they know if they go to dabble in such matters, they may disappear permanently.

But leaving possible danger aside, they have scruples."

Things like this kept on happening. Like Arius and Lucille having one of those quarrels over jurisdiction that all Haitian servants seem to be having eternally, and during which Arius saying that she had better be careful how she insulted him. She must know whom she was dealing with before she went too far. On hearing this, Lucille was as terrified as if he had pointed a gun at her heart. She came to me and wanted to leave. I persuaded her against it and chided Arius a little. But the next day when an old man entered the yard with his black head covered with a red handkerchief, Lucille fled the place and went down to the nearest police station for protection. Then at La Gonave I heard references to things done by some society in a village across the Morne from Ansa-a'-galets which the Garde d'Haiti was going to suppress. Then on one of those little sailboats that matches itself against wind and tide for eighteen miles between Ansa-a'-galets and Port-au-Prince, I heard some more puzzling talk. Things mentioned, not by name, but by insinuation, and only briefly at that. Then that quick hush of uneasiness. But in all this time, not one single individual had ever mentioned directly the existence of secret societies let alone put a name to one. What had been conveyed was a feeling of fear of something that nobody wanted to discuss.

Then one afternoon in the Tourist Bar, a man who is a Haitian and also not a Haitian said something that suddenly connected all of these happenings and gave them a meaning beside. So I began to see a great deal of him. From time to time he told me many things and, without knowing it, put me on the trail of what to look for. One N'gan (houngan) with whom I was particularly friendly answered my questions quite frankly and took me to a house in the Belair district where the cobblestones of the floor were polished like marble from the passage of so many feet and so many generations that they inspired awe in themselves. There first I saw and examined a paper, yellow with age, that bore the "mot de passage" (password) and discovered that Cochon Gris was a name of a society.

On the way back home I remarked that I had seen no altar and hounfort as I was accustomed to in Voodoo worship. There were a few things about, but I knew what to expect and the regular set-up was not there. There were a dozen bottles on a table, some crunches, or clay water jugs. The place of honor was given to an immense black stone that was attached to a heavy chain, which was itself held by an iron bar whose two ends were buried in the masonry of the wall. A well used cuvette was before the stone that had the same look of age and memory as an ancient gibbet. When we first entered, the bocor had touched the stone proudly and said, "This is for Petro. It has the power to do all things—the good and the evil." Certainly neither of us disputed the statement. But when we were clear of the place, I said I knew that the bocor had lied to us. The houngan was proud of me, then, as a pupil because I had noticed the difference. He said that it really was not a place of Voodoo. That the Cochon Gris was a secret society and a thing forbidden by law and detested by all except the members. That they used the name of Voodoo to cloak their gatherings and evade arrest and extinction.

Later on I introduced the subject in a conversation with a well-known physician of Port-au-Prince and he discussed the matter most intelligently.

"Our history has been unfortunate. First we were brought here to Haiti and enslaved. We suffered great cruelties under the French and even when they had been driven out, they left here certain traits of government that have been unfortunate for us. Thus having been a nation continually disturbed by revolution and other features not helpful to advancement we have not been able to develop economically and culturally as many of us have wished. These things being true, we have not been able to control certain bad elements because of a lack of a sufficient police force."

"But," I broke in, "with all the wealth of the United States and all the policing, we still have gangsters and the Ku Klux

Klan. Older European nations still have their problems of crime."

"Thank you for your understanding. We have a society that is detestable to all the people of Haiti. It is known as the Cochon Gris, Secte Rouge and the Vinbrindingue and all of these names mean one and the same thing. It is outside of, and has nothing to do with Voodoo worship. They are banded together to eat human flesh. Perhaps they are descended from the Mondongues and other cannibals who were brought to this Island in the Colonial days. These terrible people were kept under control during the French period by the very strictures of slavery. But in the disturbances of the Haitian period, they began their secret meetings and were well organized before they came to public notice. It is generally believed that the society spread widely during the administration of President Fabre Geffrard (1858–1867). Perhaps it began much earlier, we are not sure. But their evil practices had made them thoroughly hated and feared before the end of this administration. It is not difficult to understand why Haiti has not even yet thoroughly rid herself of these detestable creatures. It is because of their great secrecy of movement on the one hand and the fear that they inspire on the other. It is like your American gangsters. They intimidate the common people so that even when they could give the police actual proof of their depredations, they are afraid to appear in court against them.

"The cemeteries are the places where they display the most horrible aspects of their inclinations. Someone dies after a short illness, or a sudden indisposition. The night of the burial, the Vinbrindingues go to the cemetery, the chain around the tomb is broken and the grave profaned. The coffin is pulled out and opened and the body spirited away. And now, if you are friendly to Haiti as you say you are, you must speak the truth to the world. Many white writers who have passed a short time here have heard these things mentioned, and knowing nothing of the Voodoo religion except the Congo dances, they conclude that the two things are the same. That gives a

208

wrong impression to the world and makes Haiti a subject for slander."

Dr. Melville Herskovits heard this society mentioned at Mirablais as the "Bissage," and "Cochon sans poils" (*Life in a Haitian Valley,* page 243). He quotes Dr. Elsie Clewes Parsons as saying that the peasants around Jacmel told her "people *do* eat people at Aux Cayes. I *know* it." Her informant went on to tell of human finger nails being found on what had been sold as pigs' feet (pages 246, 247).

"But how can I say these things until I am very sure?" I asked him. I had participated in many ceremonies, and had never seen anything that even bordered on human sacrifice, but I knew that I did not know every Voodoo ceremony in Haiti. How could I say unless I eliminated the possibility of an occasional sacrifice? Later I found what he said to be true.

Then I found out about another secret society. It is composed of educated, upper class Haitians who are sworn to destroy the Red Sect in Haiti. They are now taking the first step of the program. That is, to drive the adepts of the organization out from under the cloak of Voodooism so that they may be recognized and crushed by the government. Naturally, there are laws against murder in Haiti, however committed. In addition the penal code contains provisions against magic practices which can be invoked when evil traits are discovered. Official Haiti knows of the Secte Rouge and frowns upon it, but one must have legal proof to gain a conviction. A high official of the Garde d'Haiti told me that he has every known member in the neighborhood of Port-au-Prince under surveillance. "But one cannot arrest a man for what he believes," he said, "one must have proof that the suspect has put his belief to action. And when we have that, ah, you shall see something." My attention was called to the trial and conviction of the sorceress in the affair of Jeanne Nelie, "That affair which gave place to a trial which echoed around the world." The effect of this conviction was to cause the adepts of Secte Rouge to take refuge under the greatest secrecy which has since been axiomatic. Now they give themselves names of the Petros, the Erzulies and the Locos, and perhaps many other Voodoo loas.

I witnessed one such fraudulent ceremony myself one night on the Plain Cul-de-Sac. In company with a man who knew all about Voodoo in that part of Haiti, I was returning from a Congo dance when we approached a small cluster of houses where a ceremony was in progress. I asked to stop and see it and we did. I got a very disagreeable surprise, because they sacrificed a dog. This must be some new cult of Voodoo, I concluded, so I asked. They told me it was a service to Mondongue, who always made his appearance in the form of a great dog, and when one beheld such a manifestation, it was certainly a time for fear. My friend and I soon left. When we were far away, he said to me, "They do not make a Voodoo service at all. Mondongue is not a loa of Voodoo. They do not always content themselves with dog, I am afraid." He showed the strongest feeling of revulsion to the whole matter and I was glad because then I did not need to hide my own distaste. I had not read St. Mery at that time and had never heard the name Mondongue pronounced in all Haiti:

"Never has there been a character more hideous than that of these last (The Mondongues), whose depravities have reached the execrable of excesses, that of to eat their fellows.. There were brought to Saint Dominique (Haiti) some of these butchers of human flesh (for at the houses of these butchers the flesh of humans has been sold as veal) and here (in Haiti) they caused, as in Africa, the horror of the other Negroes.— One is convinced that these people have kept up their odious inclinations. Notably in 1786 a Negress was confined in a hospital on a plantation in the vicinity of Jeremy. The proprietor having remarked that the greater part of the Negro babies perished in the first eight days after their birth, spied upon the midwife whom he surprised eating one of these infants who had recently been buried. She confessed that she caused them to die for this purpose."*

*Tome Premier, page 39, L. E. Moreau de St. Mery.

The most celebrated meeting place in the Department of the West used to be the bridge across the lake at Miragoane. An awful sight to the late traveller! The bridge covered with candles, the brilliantly costumed figures, themselves bearing multiple candles and the little coffin that is their object of worship, in the center of the floor of the bridge, the sharp piercing voice of the little drum and the wildly dancing horde.

This is how a meeting was held.

The two marked stones were struck together, the whispered word was sent secretly, but swiftly by word of mouth to all of the adepts. A full meeting was to be held in a town some miles south of Port-au-Prince. This distance is a bit tiresome even by automobile, considering the condition of the roads. But one of the remarkable things concerning the members of the Red Sect is their great mobility. They cover great distances with incredible speed.

The meeting is in a sort of court surrounded by several small cailles (thatched houses). There is a huge silk cotton tree in the open space, and behind the houses, fields and fields of cane.

The night was very dark but starry. Only a homemade lamp made simply and crudely from a condensed milk can fought against the blackness. Members came in like shadows from all directions. One came down a narrow path from the main road. Two more came into the opening from cane fields, parting the rustling leaves so skillfully that there was no sound. They kept coming like this and every member carried his sac paille which held his trappings. There was subdued talk but no whispers. The time had not come for expression, that was all. They kept coming until perhaps a hundred persons were gathered there. Looking around the court, they were just ordinary looking people. Might be anybody at all getting ready for a prayer meeting or a country dance.

All of the officers came at last and the word went around for everyone to robe themselves. This was quickly done and the drab crowd became a shining assembly in red and white with bared heads. Some began to leap and dance, imitating the

211

motions of various animals. The singing and dancing became general and the head coverings were put on. The adepts were now all transformed into demons with tails and horns, cows, hogs, dogs and goats. Some even became cocks, and all of a most terrifying aspect. Standing silently in that dimlit courtyard they were enough to strike terror into the breast of the most courageous. But now they began to dance and sing. The little, high pitched drum resounded and the Emperor, a most fearful sight, took the center of the group and began to sing and the President, the Minister, the Queen, the cuisineres, the officers, the servants, bourresouse, and all the grades joined in and the sound and the movement was like hell boiling over. Over and anew they sang to the drums.

> Carrefour tingindingue, mi haut, mi bas-e'
> Carrefour tingindingue, mi haut, mi bas-e'
> Oun prali' tingindingue, mi haut, mi bas, tingindingue
> Oun prali' tingindingue, mi haut, mi bas, tingindingue
> Oun prali' tingindingue, mi haut, mi bas, tingindingue

Now the whole body prepared to depart. Every member lighted a candle and, chanting to the drums, they struck a rhythmic half dance, half trot and marched forth to a certain cross-road not more than a mile away. The Secte Rouge was going to the cross-roads to do honor to the loa who rules there. What they wished for tonight would be in his realm. They were going there to give food and drink and money to Maitre Carrefour (Lord of the Cross Roads) and after that they were going to ask favors of him.

As the fearsome procession pranced on down the highway, it halted before several doors and danced furiously. The doors opened and other figures leaped out, red-robed like the rest. They had candles blazing on top of their heads, on the backs of their hands and planted on their feet. They joined the dancing and marched off with the band. These turned out to be honorary members, who partake in the dancing only until a further degree is conferred upon them. The honorary members are those who are in sympathy with the society, but for one reason or another are not yet fully initiated. The group moves on with the little coffin being carried in the very middle of the procession. It is brilliant with candles. This was the soul about which everything moved.

At the cross-roads, Maitre Carrefour was given food and drink and money. But only the copper one cent pieces of Haitian money known as "cob." The coffin was set down in the very center of the cross roads and the ceremony performed. After Maitre Carrefour had been well fed and his thirst slaked, he was asked for powers. He was asked to grant powers to find victims on the road and he was asked for powers to overtake and overpower these victims. Finally the Master of the Cross-roads gave a sign of assent by entering the head of one of the female adepts. She became possessed. The entire body of the society became jubilant of success and concluded the service and marched off to a cemetery not too far away.

They were going there to do honor to Baron Maitre Cimiterre and to ask him for powers similar to those already granted by Maitre Carrefour, that is, success in their maneuvers, fortune to find victims, and power to catch and to eat them.

They were singing again, but the song had changed. Now they were singing and whirling as they went.

"Sortie Nan Cimiterre, toute corps moin senti malingue'
Sortie Nan Cimiterre, toute corps moin senti malingue'
Sortie Nan Cimiterre, toute corps moin senti malingue,'
Sortie Nan Cimiterre, toute corps moin senti malingue'"

And so singing and dancing they arrived at the gate of the cemetery. The main body halted at the gate while the queen entered and went to a grave that had evidently been selected in advance and began to dance about it. This she did five times, but stopped at the head of the tomb to sing each time that she arrived there. After the fifth turn she took a bottle of clairin

213

and with it outlined a large cross upon the stone and placed a candle at the head and a kwee (bowl made by cutting a calabash in half lengthwise) with blood seasoned with condiments in it at the foot of the cross. The cross is the emblem of Baron Cimiterre, who is also called Baron Samedi, and Baron Croix. She danced some more and sang a song that began with

"Cote' toute moun" (where are all men, or everybody).

Then everybody entered the cemetery in single file, each person with his or her hand on the hip of the person before and with a lighted candle in the other. The youngest adept is selected and stretched upon the tomb and all the lighted candles are placed around him. The kwee, a bowl made of half a calabash, is set upon his navel. Everybody around the tomb place the palms of their hands together and sing, moving around the tomb until each person returns again to stand before their own candle. The invocation was made and when it was felt Baron Samedi had granted the request, the queen announced, "The powers are joined with the degrees!" All others bowed and covered their eyes so that nobody knew the exact moment that she left the cemetery. Nor which way she went. Then the youngest adept arose and went and none saw him go either. Then all the rest ran out in every direction as fast as they could because all feared that Baron Cimiterre would select him or her as a victim. But soon the whole convoy was joined together again not far from the cemetery. The last two men came out of the gate walking backwards, brandishing well sharpened machetes, defending the rear from an attack by the Lord of the Dead.

Now it was decided that the convoy should proceed to a certain bridge over a stream that crossed the highway near a sedgy lake. This it seems, had long been a favorite rendezvous. At the bridge, more candles were brought forth and every part of the structure was brilliantly illuminated, even to the rails at the sides. The little coffin was set down in the center of the floor of the bridge. It was an awful sight. This bridge lighted up by hundreds of flickering candles, peopled by a horde of fantastic creatures with the coffin, the symbol of their strange appetites and endeavors, in the midst.

A strong guard for defense was stationed along the road on either side of the bridge to prevent attacks from enemies. There had been trouble on other occasions. The Brave Guedé, servants of Baron Samedi, who are particularly numerous in that neighborhood, and who consider this bridge their particular place of worship, had fallen upon the Secte Rouge in the midst of their celebration in times past and inflicted serious injuries. So these guards, armed with machetes, were thrown out along the road to deal with these people without mercy in case they attempted to dislodge the Red Sect this night.

Now the members of the society went running and dancing along the routes hunting for victims. They had been granted all powers and everything else was arranged. The higher officers remained on the bridge relatively inactive. They would intercept any luckless person who tried to pass that point. Woe be to the wayfarer who had no "mot de passage" who approached that bridge that night.

The bourresouse, the advance guard, ran fast and hunted farther afield than all the rest. The success of the whole matter rests upon the courage, discretion, and efficiency of this advance guard. They are beautifully trained stealthy scouts. They faded off into the darkness swiftly like so many leopards with their cords in their hands. These cords are made from the dried and well cured intestines of human beings who have been the victims of other raids. They are light and have the tensile strength of cello strings. The gut of one victim drags to his death his successor. Except in special cases no particular person is hunted. The advance guard, cord in hand ready for instant use, stalks the quarry. And the amount of territory that these guards can cover in a short time is unbelievable. When a victim is located, he is surrounded and the cord is whipped about his throat to silence him first. Then he is bound and led before the main convoy.

The main convoy waited there on the bridge relatively inactive until the word came that someone was approaching from the west on horse back. At any moment the rider might have been dragged from his horse without giving him an opportunity for resistance, but knowing that he must cross that bridge the guards and the other servants allowed him to proceed. Just before he reached the brilliantly lighted bridge, he dismounted and hesitated a long time, evidently considering turning back. But finally he, a well dressed young man, approached with the utmost diffidence and was challenged. Dripping with terror, he first made the sign of the cross, before he thought to answer, "Si lili te' houmba, min dia, mi haut." It was a glorious thing that that handsome, well dressed young man knew that fantastic sentence. The Emperor was favorably impressed by him also. He was almost paternal in his manner as he bade the boy proceed.

Soon after, one detail of the bourresouse returned with game from the chase and led their victim before the Emperor, the Queen, the President, the minister and all of the other officers. Finally all of the guards returned, but that took hours. When all were in, the whole convoy moved back to the original meeting place. Then the ceremony began to change the three victims into beef. That is, one was "turned" into a "cow" and two into "pigs." And under these terms they were killed, and divided. Everyone received their share of the game except the honorary members. They serve without being allowed a taste.

By that time dawn is nigh. The animals and demons are "transformed" again into human beings who may walk anywhere without attracting the least attention. After the happenings of the night one might expect the sun to rise on Judgment Day. But no, it was just a common day outside in the court.

The identities of the Secte Rouge, Cochon Gris, Vinbrindingue are really secret, hence the difficulty for the Garde d'Haiti to cope with it. Like the American gangster and racket-

216

eer, their deeds are well-known. But the difficulty is to prove it in court. And like the American racketeer, the Secte Rouge takes care that its members do not talk. It is a thing most secret and it stays that way. The very lives of the members depend upon it. There is swift punishment for the adept who talks. When suspicion of being garrulous falls upon a member, he or she is thoroughly investigated, but with the utmost secrecy, without the suspect knowing that he is suspect. But he is followed and watched until he is either accounted innocent or found guilty. If he is found guilty, the executioners are sent to wait upon him. By hook or crook, he is gotten into a boat and carried out beyond aid and interference from the shore. After being told the why of the thing, if indeed that is necessary, his hands are seized by one man and held behind him, while another grips his head under his arm. A violent blow with a rock behind the ear stuns him and at the same time serves to abraise the skin. A deadly and quick-acting poison is then rubbed into the wound. There is no antidote for this poison and the victim knows it. However well he might know how to swim, when he is thrown overboard, he knows it would be useless. He would never be alive long enough to reach the shore. When his body strikes the water, the incident is closed.

Ah Bo Bo!

CHAPTER 15

✵

PARLAY CHEVAL OU
(TELL MY HORSE)

Gods always behave like the people who make them. One can see the hand of the Haitian peasant in that boisterous god, Guedé, because he does and says the things that the peasants would like to do and say. You can see him in the market women, in the domestic servant who now and then appears before her employer "mounted" by this god who takes occasion to say many stinging things to the boss. You can see him in the field hand, and certainly in the group of women about a public well or spring, chattering, gossiping and dragging out the shortcomings of their employers and the people like him. Nothing in Haiti is quite so obvious as that this loa is the deification of the common people of Haiti. The mulattoes give this spirit no food and pay it no attention at all. He belongs to the blacks and the uneducated blacks at that. He is a hilarious divinity and full of the stuff of burlesque. This manifestation comes as near a social criticism of the classes by the masses as anything in all Haiti. Guedé has another distinction. It is the one loa which is entirely Haitian. There is neither European nor African background for it. It sprang up or was called up by some local need and now is firmly established among the blacks.

This god of the common people has no hounfort. A cross at the head of a tomb inside the yard of the hounfort is his niche. If there is none there it is enough for the houngan to plant a cross dedicated to him.

The apparel of this god is in keeping with his people. He likes to dress himself in an old black overcoat, a torn old black hat with a high crown and worn-out black pants. He loves to smoke a cigar. He cavorts about, making coarse gestures, executing steps like the prancing of a horse, drinking and talking.

His drink is very special. This god likes clairin well seasoned with hot peppers, to which powdered nutmeg is added at times. The grated nutmeg should always be in this strong, raw rum infusion, but when it is not to be had, Guedé will content himself with the pepper in alcohol. He also drinks pure clairin, that raw white rum of Haiti. He eats roasted peanuts, and parched corn which is placed at the foot of the cross on a plate. No white cloth is used in this offering as in others.

There is no real service or ritual for Guedé. One places a circle of twenty white candles about the cross dedicated to him. Some adepts offer him an old redingote or an old pair of pants, but roasted peanuts and parched corn are customary. The people who created Guedé needed a god of derision. They needed a spirit which could burlesque the society that crushed him, so Guedé eats roasted peanuts and parched corn like his devotees. He delights in an old coat and pants and a torn old hat. So dressed and fed, he bites with sarcasm and slashes with ridicule the class that despises him.

But for all his simple requirements, Guedé is a powerful loa. He has charge of everyone within the regions of the dead, and he presides over all that is done there. He is a grave-digger and opens the tombs and when he wishes to do so he takes out the souls and uses them in his service.

Guedé is never visible. He manifests himself by "mounting" a subject as a rider mounts a horse, then he speaks and acts through his mount. The person mounted does nothing of his own accord. He is the horse of the loa until the spirit departs. Under the whip and guidance of the spirit-rider, the "horse" does and says many things that he or she would never have uttered un-ridden.

"Parlay Cheval Ou" (Tell My Horse), the loa begins to dictate through the lips of his mount and goes on and on. Sometimes Guedé dictates the most caustic and belittling statements concerning some pompous person who is present. A prominent official is made ridiculous before a crowd of peasants. It is useless to try to answer Guedé because the spirit merely becomes angry and may reprove the important person by speaking of some compromising event in the past in the coarsest language or predicting something of the sort in the near future to the great interest of the listening peasants who accept every word from the lips of the horse of Guedé as gospel truth. On several occasions, it was observed that Guedé seemed to enjoy humbling his betters. On one occasion Guedé reviled a well-dressed couple in a car that passed. Their names were called and the comments were truly devastating to say the least.

With such behavior one is forced to believe that some of the valuable commentators are "mounted" by the spirit and that others are feigning possession in order to express their resentment general and particular. That phrase "Parlay cheval ou" is in daily, hourly use in Haiti and no doubt it is used as a blind for self-expression. There are often many drunken people in the cemeteries who claim to be "mounted." The way to differentiate between the persons really "mounted" and the frauds is to require them to swallow some of the drink of Guedé and to wash their whole face in it. The faker will always draw back because he fears to get that raw rum and hot pepper in his eyes, while the subject really mounted will do it. They do it without being told and it never seems to injure them. So one is forced to the conclusion that a great deal of the Guedé "mounts" have something to say and lack the courage to say it except under the cover of Brave Guedé.

Down in the neighborhood of Port-au-Prince behind St. Joseph's I witnessed one of these simulated possessions. A man was crying, "Tell my horse," again and again and defaming many persons. A girl approached. He called her Erzulie and shouted, "Erzulie, don't you remember I have connections with you for a cake?" The girl was chagrined no end and looked pathetic. One of the men took a hand and cried, "Shoo!" as if he were shooing chickens. Immediately the faker started to run. He stopped after a step or two and looked about him and asked, "Who did that to me?" Everybody laughed. I asked why he seemed afraid. They explained that the majority of such characters are chicken thieves and they live in fear of the police. They knew the nasty accusation against the girl was inspired by malice at being refused, so they knew the way to stop it and did. The "mount" moved on away looking like a wet chicken.

A tragic case of a Guedé mount happened near Pont Beudet. A woman known to be a Lesbian was "mounted" one afternoon. The spirit announced through her mouth, "Tell my horse I have told this woman repeatedly to stop making love to women. It is a vile thing and I object to it. Tell my horse that this woman promised me twice that she would never do such a thing again, but each time she has broken her word to me as soon as she could find a woman suitable for her purpose. But she has made love to women for the last time. She has lied to Guedé for the last time. Tell my horse to tell that woman I am going to kill her today. She will not lie again." The woman pranced and galloped like a horse to a great mango tree, climbed it far up among the top limbs and dived off and broke her neck.

But the peasants believe that the things that "mounts" claim to see in the past and future are absolutely accurate. There are thousands of claims of great revelations. They are identical for the most part, however, with the claims that the believers in fortune-tellers make in the United States.

The spirit Guedé (pronounced geeday) originated at Miragoane and its originator's especial meeting place was the

222

bridge across the lake at Miragoane, where the Departments of the South and the West meet. These people who originated this cult were Bossals who were once huddled on the waterfront in Port-au-Prince in the neighborhood of the place where all of the slaves were disembarked from the ships. There came to be a great huddle of these people living on a very low social and economic level in the stretch flanking the bay. For some cause, these folk had gained the despisement of the city, and the contempt in which they were held caused a great body of them to migrate to the vicinity of Miragoane, and there the cult arose. It is too close to the cult of Baron Cimeterre not to be related. It is obvious that it is another twist given to the functions of that loa. The spirit of Guedé is Baron Cimeterre with social consciousness, plus a touch of burlesque and slapstick.

It is interesting to note that this cult does not exist in the North nor in the Artibonite. He belongs to the South and the West, and the people in the West and South who do not make food for Guedé are careful not to anger him or to offend in any way. It is dangerous to make his spirit angry. When a "mount" of this spirit is making devastating revelations the common comment is "Guedé pas drah." (Guedé is not a sheet), that is, Guedé covers up nothing. It seems to be his mission to expose and reveal. At any rate, Guedé is a whimsical deity, and his revelations are often most startlingly accurate and very cruel. Papa Guedé is almost identical with Baron Cimeterre, Baron Samedi and Baron Croix, who is one god with three epithets, and all of them mean the Lord of the dead. Perhaps that is natural for the god of the poor to be akin to the god of the dead, for there is something about poverty that smells of death.

One man stood out against all the rest and insisted that Baron Cimeterre and Baron Samedi were separate deities. Maybe so, but I do not blame the others who think that they are the same. The general belief is that both, if one could consider them separately, live in the cemetery. This physician, who says that he is an authority, maintains that Baron Cimeterre has his abode in an elm tree, lives always in the forest, and may be worshipped anywhere in the woods. Baron

Samedi lives in the cemetery or anywhere else he chooses. Baron Cimeterre speaks with authority like a great lord while Baron Samedi always announces his presence with "Ca ou vley?" (What do you want of me?) Both of them, like Guedé, can open tombs and command the dead to do their bidding. Baron Cimeterre is absolute ruler of the cemetery and Baron Samedi is also. This authority says that both of these gods are doctors and point out roots and herbs to be used, and that they give specific directions as to how they must be used. Sometimes he prescribes leaves and states that they must be powdered; at other times he might use those same leaves as a tea; at other times he might use the same leaves as a poultice. But Louis Romain, who is a great houngan, says that this god is not a doctor. Papa Loco is the god of medicine and knowledge.

Some say that you must talk to Baron Samedi or Cimeterre with a cow foot. That is necessary because you must place your hand in his while you make your request of him. When he leaves, he will take away with him whatever he is holding. So you get the foreleg of a cow with a foot attached and offer that as your hand. He holds to the foot and when he leaves you, merely let go of the other end and all is well. You do not lose your hand and arm as you would have done had you not taken care.

Baron Samedi delights in dressing his "horses" in shabby and fantastic clothes like Papa Guedé. Women dressed like men and men like women. Often the men, in addition to wearing female clothes, thrust a calabash up under their skirts to simulate pregnancy. Women put on men's coats and prance about with a stick between their legs to imitate the male sex organs. Baron Samedi is a very facetious god like Guedé. He is simple in his tastes also. Since he craves neither hounfort nor altar, when the houngan wishes to summon him to ask a service, he goes into the court and to the tree which is the repository of Baron Samedi and sprinkles the ground with clairin or rum and lights either three or thirteen white candles.

The people love Samedi because he knows the herbs and roots to make them well and because he is a loquacious god and gives them plenty of detail along with the medicine. Sometimes he sends the dead on a mission. Sometimes he will not permit a soul to leave the cemetery because he will not permit them to be used to do a mischief to a person he has chosen, nor to one who has placed himself under his protection. Baron Samedi has no especial offering. When the houngan wishes to summon him outside of the hounfort, as in the woods or the plains, a shot fired in the air will summon him and he will appear and ask, "Ca ou vley?" In certain parts of Haiti, however, they offer Baron Samedi a black goat or a black chicken. It is placed on a plate and placed beneath the tree for him. Beside the plate they place an ear of corn, a bottle of clairin and three bottles of Kola.

Baron Cimeterre is also very popular all over Haiti. He is also a doctor of medicine and prescribes a great number of healing baths for the sick people under his care. He is very powerful but also temperamental and full of whimsy.

The houngan who wishes to summon him goes to the elm tree consecrated to him and raps three times with the baguette of a Rada drum and recites the prayer common in all voodoo ceremonies. He then demands of Damballah the authority or permission to enter into communication with Baron Cimeterre. He says to Baron Cimeterre, "Ce ou minn, Baron moi vley. Chretiens besoin concones ou." (It is you that I call for or want. Living people need you.) Then he sings a song to Baron Cimeterre. Baron becomes incarnate in the houngan or in a canzo. Sometimes he employs the dead. It is Baron Cimeterre that one invokes to draw a dead man from his tomb. Without this formality, one could not leave the cemetery with the souls one had invoked.

One offers Baron Cimeterre a black goat or a black chicken, which is prepared and placed at the roots of the tree. At the moment of invocation one pours rum or clairin on the roots of the tree.

November first and second are great days of obligation to these spirits. The houngan and the Mambo go to the cemetery on the night of the first to begin the invocation for All Saints

Day which follows. The graveyard is blazing with lighted candles for this important celebration. It must have been a joyful thing to the Africans newly arrived in Saint Dominique to find their worship of the dead confirmed in the European All Saints Day, but the services to Baron Samedi or Cimeterre are more than just an expansion of Halloween. The Christian Church has merely given the cult an annual feast day. The rest of it has come out of Africa with adaptations on Haitian soil. This cult of the dead has so many ramifications that it touches in some way the majority of the Voodoo cults and services.

CEREMONY OF THE TETE L'EAU

In Haiti spirits inhabit the heads of streams, known as sources, the cascades, and the grottoes. Sometimes the spot has a master, or a mistress, and sometimes it has both. The loa most commonly found in possession of these nooks and grottoes are Papa Badere, Cimby Apaca, Papa Sobo, Papa Pierre, and the white woman, Mademoiselle Charlotte.

Spirits occupy all of the sources, cascades and grottoes, but certain places in Haiti are ruled by spirits who are known to reside there by everyone in the country. For instance, the grotto at Leogane is inhabited by Madam Anacaona. Papa Sobo rules the grotto at Turgean and Cimby-Apaca-endeux-eaux.

The ceremony Tete l'eau (Head of the water) is a thing to induce the belief in gods and spirits. It is held on a night when the moon is shining full and white—and in Haiti the moonlight is a white that the temperate zones never could believe possible. The ceremony is held from nine to ten o'clock at night; that is, the ceremony does not begin until that hour. About that time the adepts and the invited guests begin to arrive at the source. There is a large white table cloth and sometimes two. Dishes and silver sufficient to serve all of the company is provided.

The houngan opens the ceremony by invoking the Master of the source. As always he salutes first the superior spirits. He invokes The Master of All Things, then Jesus, Mary, Joseph and John the Baptist. He recites the Ava Maria, the credo, the Pater Noster. The adepts respond with the prayers. Then the houngan sprinkles the source, the cascade or the grotto, as the case might be, with flour, breaks three to thirteen eggs in the source or cascade. He turns himself towards the four cardinal points successively, and taking in his hands the sealed bottles of fine wines, he offers them with an air of majesty to the spirit. Opening then the bottles, he pours some from each on the ground all around the source. The different wines are poured separately and in turn. At this moment of making the libation the houngan approaches the source, strikes three blows upon the Rada drums, and the resonance rolls over the moonlit water and the towering rocks sheathed in verdure. He strikes three other notes from the Petro drums, which sing so humanly, and the rhythmic sound departs in pursuit of the other music fleeing over the hills. A gun is fired and all of the assistants bow themselves toward the source and remain with the head bowed while the houngan intones the liturgic song:

"Faitre, Maitre, L'Afrique Guinin ce' protection
Nous Ap Maide', ce d'lo qui poti mortel, protection
Maitre d'lo pour-toute petites li"

(Master, African Master of Guinea, we ask your protection. The water, which is able to hear mortals, we ask protection for all of us children.)

At this exhortation the crowd responds. Then the houngan commands the houncis and the canzos present to prepare a plate for the spirit who protects the place. They immediately spread the table cloth beside the source and lay the plates for all, but they are careful to reserve a particular plate for the god or goddess. This plate that the houngan carries himself to the source before anyone touches anything to eat, is thrown into the water with all that it contains. It must contain a piece of everything served at the feast for the main course and a piece of each of the cakes for the dessert. Only after this is done may the adepts and the guests approach the table to eat. And there is plenty to eat and to drink! There is roast turkey, chicken, beef, goat and white rice. Great plates of different kinds of bread and several kinds of cakes. To drink there is champagne, red wine, white wine, beer, clairin, tafia and various liqueurs. Nearly always, the spirit becomes embodied in the houngan and thus takes part in all of the eating and drinking. There is music and happiness. The feast usually continues until three or four o'clock in the morning.

This ceremony is a lovely and impressive affair when conducted by a member of the upper class. Like the ceremony to Erzulie, it loses in beauty and purpose when it is celebrated by people too poor to make the proper provisions. Many wealthy people who do not wish to make a public announcement that they make food for Voodoo gods, merely announce to their friends that "A repast is offered on the banks of such and such a river *very* near the source," or often the servants of the family organize the service if not too many outsiders are asked. In this case the food is merely served on a plate at the source and the drinks poured. This ceremony is so beautiful in setting and spirit that it is necessary to participate in it to fully appreciate it.

The most famous cascade in all Haiti is at Saut d'Eau, a triple waterfall just above Ville Bonheur. Every year, people make a pilgrimage from all over the country to this beautiful waterfall which translates into "leap of the water." Up until about three years ago there were two divisions of the falls, but since the flood in Haiti of 1933 there are now three beautiful torrents tumbling down from their great heights that men might see and worship.

My sister-in-law, Emma Williams, wife of Dr. Leonard Williams of Brooklyn, was visiting me in Haiti when the day in July came for everybody to go up to Haiti's holy place of miracles. Hermann Pape had offered to drive us in his car, and we so gladly accepted. It was a lively party in Hermann's sedan with plenty of food and things to drink. We bumped along the rocky road and passed people walking briskly with youth. Old people padded along and stepped aside to let us pass. Women and men rode bourriques and horses. They went any way they could, but they went. It is the great annual "going up" in Haiti. When it came time to ford a river with the car, we paused. The men went in for a swim and the women spread the table beside the stream and we ate, ascended spiritually a little on the beauty of the scenery and drove on to Ville Bonheur.

We got to Ville Bonheur after dark and found a great number of little booths selling candy, Kola and the things that people usually buy when they go off gala. There was music of different kinds. Hermann got into one of the many dice games that were going on. It was very strange to me because they played it with three dice in a cup instead of two in the hand the way I had been taught. We were all tired but the great crowds, the flambeaux and candle-lighted places kept us moving from one excitement to another. It was like a fair only less hard and brittle. There is a softness and gentleness of manner about the Haitian peasant that makes itself felt whenever and wherever you get near him. The ground was practically paved with mango seeds and everybody was looking for a place to sleep. The insides of the few houses of the town had already been taken, for many people had come the day before. The women who were selling candles were doing a great business. Many of them were pushing about through the crowd selling the new prayers to the miraculous virgin and the two others. These printed prayers to the three women of miracles were printed partly in Spanish and partly in French to accommodate both the Haitians and the Dominicans. We bought both prayers and candles.

Finally Hermann found us a place to sleep. It was under the porch of a little caille. The car was moved over there and we got out our folding cots. Hermann slept on the natte beside us. The other young man who had come along to help Hermann with the driving as well as to enjoy the trip finally wandered off and we simmered off to sleep at last.

We woke and found several peasants standing around us in utter silence and gazing down on us in our riding breeches and boots. As soon as we stirred, they were happy to help us find water to wash our faces and get ourselves fixed up. We were

229

going up to the spot where the miraculous virgin lit in a palm tree. At daylight throngs were pouring into the enclosure where the church stood and slowly trickling out again.

We had that small cup of coffee that all Haitians take in the morning. But first we must get all six of the persons in our party together. We found the two ladies easily but that other young man remained invisible until Hermann met Ti Jean and he told him that our missing companion had found a lady friend to sleep with and was late abed. Hermann led us all to the house and was all for us peeping in but we declined and waited until he came out of his own accord.

We had coffee and waded through the sellers of candles and amulets. These amulets were little heart-shaped affairs made of printed cotton with a string to wear about the neck. Some were selling colored cords to hang as an offering upon the sacred tree at the falls. We bought things and went into the enclosure where an unfinished church was standing. This is where the sacred palm tree once stood. On either side of the path were blackened stones, and each one of these stones was surrounded by an ecstastic crowd anointing themselves with the candle grease that sobbed down over the stones from the votive candles. They anointed their faces and their arms and their bare breasts. Some had ailing feet and legs and they anointed them. Several women were rubbing their buttocks and thighs without any self-consciousness at all. And thousands upon thousands poured into the place and up to the church and back again. The mass was celebrated at an early hour and when we entered the enclosure the people were pouring out of the church. There was Ti Cousin, the great houngan of Leogane, striding past all in snowy white linen; Dieu Donnez St. Leger, the great one of famed Archahaie, going toward the church. The scene was like a great place of flame in that no part of it was still at any time and it had so many different movements making up the whole. And it had its changing colors like fire too and one could feel the inner heat from the people.

This great shrine of Haiti got its first breath of life in 1884, they say. In that year a beautiful, luminous virgin lit in the fronds of a palm tree there and waved her gorgeous wings and blessed the people. She paused there a long time and the whole countryside saw her. Seeing the adoration of the people, the Catholic Priest of the parish came out to drive off the apparition. Finally she sang a beautiful song and left of her own volition. She had not been disturbed at all by the priest. People came to the palm tree and were miraculously cured and others were helped in various ways. The people began to worship the tree. The news spread all over Haiti and more and more people came. The Catholic Church was neglected. So the priest became so incensed that he ordered the palm tree to be chopped down, but he could find no one who would chop it. Finally he became so incensed at the adoration of the people for the tree that he seized a machete and ran to the tree to cut it down himself. But the first blow of the blade against the tree caused the machete to bounce back and strike the priest on the head and wound him so seriously that he was taken to the hospital in Port-au-Prince, where he soon died of his wound. Later on the tree was destroyed by the church and a church was built on the spot to take the place of the palm tree, but it is reported that several churches have burned on that site. One was destroyed by lightning. That is the story of the Virgin of Ville Bonheur.

The cascade at Saut d'Eau attracts as many people as the palm tree. From Ville Bonheur they mount on horseback to the falls. There the people drape their offerings of colored cotton cords on the sacred tree, undress and climb the misted rocks so that the sacred water may wet their bodies. Immediately many of them become possessed. The spirit Agoue' ta-Royo enters their heads and they stagger about as if they are drunk. Some of them talk in the unknown tongues. Louis Romain, the houngan of the Bolosse who was preparing me for initiation at the time begged me not to enter the water. He said, and others agreed with him that Agoue' ta-Royo, the Maitre L'Eau (Master of Waters) might enter my head and since I was not baptized he might just stay in my head for years and worry me.

The belief is widespread in Haiti that Agoue' ta-Royo carries off people whom he chooses to a land beneath the waters.

Saut d'Eau. Disrobing to ascend the falls

Saut d'Eau. After the touch of the sacred stream

One woman told me that she had lived there for seven years. There are thousands who say that they have been there. They say they have no memory of how they got there nor how they left. There is a great belief in a land beneath the waters. Some say it is not beneath the waters, but one must pass through the waters to get there. One man told me that there is a place in Haiti where a great cave has been hollowed out by a waterfall and that if one knows the way they may pass under the fall and enter this great cave. He says that there is an opening from the cave like a chimney that permits one to emerge again and that this is where people have been taken who speak of having been under the water for years. He promised several times to show me this place, but he never got around to it. Some day when I have a great deal of leisure, I shall visit Haiti for the express purpose of visiting the kingdom of Agoue' ta-Royo and see things for myself.

There was a fly in the ointment that day. The local priest who is a Haitian had used his influence to station a gendarme at the falls. Therefore there were few cases of possession. There was a lavish denunciation of the priest though. High and low were there and all felt that a police at the waterfall at Saut d'Eau was a desecration, but expressions of fervor were not to be suppressed entirely and the hundreds of people entering the eternal mists from the spray and ascending the sacred stones and assuming all possible postures of adoration made a picture that might have been painted by Doré. It was very beautiful and fitting. Whether they had the words to fit their feelings or not, it was a moving sight to see these people turning from sordid things once each year to go into an ecstasy of worship of the beautiful in water-forms. Perhaps the priest has some good reason for attempting to break up this annual celebration at the waterfalls. I only heard that the Church does not approve and so it must be stopped if possible.

I fail to see where it would have been more uplifting for them to have been inside a church listening to a man urging them to "contemplate the sufferings of our Lord," which is just another way of punishing one's self for nothing. It is very much better for them to climb the rocks in their bare clean feet and meet Him face to face in their search for the eternal in beauty.

MANGER YIAMM (FEAST OF THE YAMS)

Another simple and lovely ceremony that I had the pleasure of witnessing is the Feast of the Yams. It is celebrated in all parts of Haiti and is compulsory with all the cults of Voodoo. The Rada cult, the Congo, the Petro, the Ibo and Congo Petro, all must do honor to the Yam once each year. It is not an expensive feast, fortunately, so that everybody can look forward to it with pleasure. It falls on the day before the day of the great animal sacrifices.

We had to buy the yams for the feast on the last day in October. We must also buy a piece of salt fish to go along with the yams. Plenty of olive oil and white candles too. The olive oil to cook the yams and the fish with. The candles for illumination and because they are required in the rites.

The Feast of the Yams is a ceremony that must be done annually. If one is an adept of any Voodoo cult at all, then he must observe Manger Yiamm. I was glad that it had to be done while I was there.

The ceremony was celebrated this way. We gathered under the peristyle. The houngan invoked the mysteries beginning with that long formula in which a long list of the Christian saints are called first, and then a long list of the more important loa of Voodoo, the adepts responding behind each name. Each was saluted and the favorite drink of each loa was poured on the ground around the center post for the dead. Then the hounci gathered around and the houngan approached the repositories of all of the loa in the hounfort, whom he saluted with equal reverence. The houncis now gathered up all the yams that had been brought by the crowd and prepared to cook them. The service went on with prayers and the whole assembly chanting the Pater Noster, the Credo and the Confiteor. Then they began to sing the airs dedicated to the various loa. They sang songs to Papa Legba, Papa Loco, Papa Cimby, to some Congos, to Maitre Grand Bois, Papa Badere, Manchon Ibo, but the most beautiful ones it seemed to me were dedicated to Grand Erzulie.

All this time the yams and fish were being prepared. Some adepts were sent out to cut a great quantity of banana leaves. These were arranged into a sort of bed and the whole thing surrounded by candles. Then everybody assembled upon this couch of leaves to wait for the yams to be served. The candles were lighted and it was very agreeable to lie on the fresh cool leaves surrounded by light.

When the word came that the yams were ready, the houngan sprinkled flour all around the couch. Then he went into the hounfort and the food was carried in to him and he offered some of it to the loa. Then everyone was served and we passed the rest of the night singing and amusing ourselves. Several people were possessed during the singing and dancing. Three or four loa presented themselves at the same time through different people. A great many prophetic statements were made and some of those present were profoundly moved by the revelations. One spirit identified as Grande Libido entered one of his servants and forced him to chase away a guest whom he had especially invited. The loa said that the guest was a stranger to true Voodoo worship, but he was given to demon-worship. This revelation was most embarrassing to the guest, who tried to deny it. But his friend, possessed of his loa, began to announce dates, places and incidents of his practices and he ran out of the place in the greatest haste and confusion. Soon after, the loa left the friend who had driven him out and as soon as he came to himself, he asked for his friend and was much distressed at what had taken place. He left us singing and dancing and went off to seek him.

CHAPTER 16

✦

GRAVEYARD DIRT
AND OTHER POISONS

They take dirt from a graveyard to maim and kill. And the
principle behind this practice is more subtle than the
surface shows. It is hardly probable that more than one
per cent of the people who dig into an old grave to get a
handful of dirt to destroy an enemy, or the enemy of a client,
know what they do. To most of them it is a superstition connected in their minds with the idea of ghosts and the belief in
their power to harm. But soil from deep in an old grave has
prestige wherever the negro exists in the Western world. In
the United States it is called goofer dust and there is a great
deal of laughter among educated people over it. The idea of
some old witch doctor going to a cemetery at dead of night
to dig arm-length deep in a grave for dirt with which to harm
and kill does seem ridiculous. Now, wait just a moment before
you laugh too hard at this old hoodoo man or woman of
magic. Listen to some men of science on the same subject.

Sir Spencer Wells ("The Disposal of the Dead"), "Shane
found germs of scarlatina in the soil surrounding a grave after
thirty years."

Dr. Domingo Foriero of Rio de Janeiro, "If each corpse is

the bearer of millions of organisms specific of ill, imagine what a cemetery must be in which new foci are forming around each body! More than twenty years after the death of a body, Shane found the germs of yellow fever, scarlatina, typhoid and other infectious diseases."

Pasteur: "What outlooks are opened to the mind in regard to the possible influence of soil with the etiology of disease and the probable danger of the earth of cemeteries!"

So it appears that instead of being a harmless superstition of the ignorant, the African men of magic found out the deadly qualities of graveyard dirt. In some way they discovered that the earth surrounding a corpse that had sufficient time to thoroughly decay was impregnated with deadly power. It happened ages before the idea gained ground in the civilized areas. It might, in some accidental way, come out of the ancestor worship of West Africa. That is a mere shot in the dark, but what it illuminates is the great interest in subtle ways of providing death, and this brings up the whole matter of poisons and poisonings, not only in Haiti, but wherever the negro exists in the Western world.

Naturally, this cult of poisoning that has come in fragmentary form from Africa has built up an alertness and caution that is extreme in certain quarters. Naturally the accusations far out-number the actual cases. But who knows what the actual cases are? Even in countries with the most efficient crime detection agencies and with medical science, many, many cases of poisoning escape detection as has been proven by police records. There have been many instances where poisoners were detected only because they killed too many in the same way. In the United States great masses of young negro children are taught to eat and drink nowhere except at home. There is the gravest suspicion of unsolicited foods. In Jamaica, British West Indies, people carry bissy (Kola Nut) as an antidote. In Haiti there is extreme wariness and precaution. One educated man told me that he never orders the same drink at the same saloon on consecutive visits so that it is impossible to anticipate his order and prepare a bottle for him.

238

What is most interesting is that the use of poisons follows the African pattern rather than the European. It is rare that the poison is bought at a drug store. In most cases it is a vegetable poison, which makes them harder to detect than the mineral poisons so often used by the Europeans. And when the European poison is used it is seldom employed in the same fashion. Who has made all of these experiments and not only found out the poisonous plants in the New World, but found the most efficient use of them? It is a clear case of an African survival distorted by circumstances.

For example, let us look at death by hair. Kussula (Cudjoe Lewis), who was brought over from Africa in 1859 to be a slave, and who died in Mobile, Alabama, in 1934, told me that his King in Africa was a good man and did not like wicked things. So he allowed no man to keep the head of a leopard. I asked him what was wicked about possessing the head of a leopard. He said that men made bad medicine and killed people with it. Just how, he could not say, because, he explained, he was only a boy when he was brought away and he had not learned. But it was very bad for a man to keep the head of a leopard. If one killed a leopard and did not bring the head to the King, then everybody knew that he was a wicked man who meant to do evil, and so he was executed at once before he had a chance to do it. I met Chief Justice Johnson of Liberia and asked him for a leopard skin. He said that he would send me one, but that it was certain that he could not get me one with the head, because the native chiefs always kept the heads of all leopards killed in their territory. Duke, an African dancer in New York, told me that the head was important because of the whiskers. Duke is a Fanti from the Gold Coast and he said that there, also, it was a capital crime to keep the head of a leopard. And when the head was brought to the king, before the hunter was allowed to leave, the leopard's whiskers were counted and not one must be missing on pain of death. The assumption, that if the hunter has kept one, then he intends to kill someone with it and so he is a murderer already by intent, so they execute him at once. The whiskers, he stated most positively were deadly poison, not a quick violent death, but very sure. How and why, he could not, or would not tell me.

Now, there are no leopards in Jamaica or Haiti. But in both places, when I asked about poisons, I was told about *chopped hair from the tail of a horse.* Chop it up short and mix it in something like mush and give it to the one you wish to kill and their stomach and intestines will become full of sores and death is certain. The short bits of hair will penetrate the tissues like so many needles and each bit will first irritate, then puncture, the intestine. A clear adaptation of the African leopard whisker method of killing. There is a variation of this in Jamaica also. They curry a horse and clean off the curry comb in the food of the victim. He not only gets the hair, he gets all the germs from the skin and hair of the horse. A violent and fatal vomiting is said to follow this.

Kossula, who was a Takkoi, from a country in Nigeria, "three sleeps" from the Abomeh, capital city of Dahomey, Chief Justice Johnson of Liberia and Duke from the Gold Coast all report the same practise in their separate areas. And these areas are all inside the territory from which the greater part of the slaves were drawn for service in the Americas. Leopard whiskers not being available, those adept in the practise of killing by hair looked for a substitute and found the coarse, stiff hair of the horse's tail.

Duke also told me of the poison to be found in the rudimentary legs of a rock python and the gall-bladder of a crocodile. In Jamaica I heard of the poisonous qualities of the gall-bladder of the alligator. Dried and powered lizards in Africa and powered lizards in Jamaica, Haiti and Florida. And the numerous vegetable poisons that had been worked out as to application, dosage and deadliness in Africa had to find substitutes in the Western world. And the fact that so many have been found, the tremendous quantity of experimentation that has been done, again proves the inclination of the seekers.

There is no way of knowing how many other plants are used

240

as poisons, but the following were checked and rechecked in different areas of the West Indies!

1. Night Shade (Jamaica). Antidote—Bissy (Kola Nut).
2. Red Head (Jamaica). Antidote—Bissy (Kola Nut).
3. Bitter Cassava (Jamaica). Antidote—Mix clay and water and drink.
4. Dumb cane (Jamaica). Antidote—None known. (The juice from this plant attacks the throat first and so constricts the vocal cords that the victim cannot speak. A flood of saliva pours from the mouth and drenches the lower part of the face. Terrible skin eruptions occur wherever this poisoned saliva has touched.)
5. Rose Apple (root is black and very poisonous). Antidote—None known.
6. Dogwood root (Haiti, Jamaica, Bahamas). Antidote—None known.
7. Black sage (Haiti, Jamaica, Bahamas). Antidote—None known.
8. Dust of Bamboo (Haiti, Jamaica, Bahamas). Antidote—None known.

ANIMAL DERIVATIVES

1. Horse hair
2. Dried gallowass (a poisonous lizard).
3. Dried Mabolier (Haitian lizard).
4. Spiders, worms and insects.
5. The gleanings from a curry comb after currying a horse.

MINERAL DERIVATIVES

1. Ground bottle glass.
2. Calomel. (Applied externally. The drug is mixed with water and the under garments of the victim are soaked in the solution for an hour or two and dried without rinsing. It is absorbed through the skin when the wearer perspires and produces a dangerous swelling.)
3. Arsenic. (Dr. Rulx Léon in defending Haiti from the charge of primitive poisonings, estimated that most of the

poisoning done in Haiti is done by Arsenic. He says that during the last days of slavery a quantity of Arsenic was stolen by the slaves from some plantation owners and was later parcelled out. That was around 1793 and it is hardly probable that the original supply has lasted until the present. Anyway there is bountiful evidence of other poisons being used. In 1934, however, there was an attempt to assassinate President Stenio Vincent by Arsenic. It was established that thirty grains of Arsenic was bought in Santo Domingo for the purpose by the conspirators. It was bought outside Haiti to cover the trail, but it was traced to the purchaser nevertheless. It had been ordered in the name of a legislator who knew nothing of the matter. Names very big in the political life of Haiti were mentioned in connection with this attempt upon the life of the President. But the affair occurred just before the visit of President Roosevelt and so the matter was hushed up quickly. Eighteen grains of the thirty purchased are still unaccounted for. A grocery store on the Champ de Mars failed because it was rumored that a member of the family which owned the business had actual possession, or access to, the missing eighteen grains of Arsenic. No one but the family traded at *that* store. It goes without saying that few would be concerned very much about this particular eighteen grains if great quantities of the same thing were known to be loose in Haiti already. There is a poison which the Cacos use to treat the blades of their machetes before a battle.)

The subject of poisons and poisonings in the whole area of the Caribbean is too important to omit altogether, though a thorough study of the matter would require years of investigation. It has such an immense background and an infinite sinister future. There are the various reasons for poisoning and the accompanying temptation. There is the age-old inclination; there is the security of secrecy and the ease of gaining the weapon that exists in all countries. In addition to death by poisoning, in Haiti there is the necessity of poisoning the bodies of the dead against the ravages of the Zombie-makers and the Société ge Rouge (Red-eyed Society, another name for the Secte Rouge).

Ah Bo Bo!

CHAPTER 17

❖

DOCTOR RESER

A thing is mighty big when time and distance cannot shrink it. That is how vivid my memory is of the colorful Dr. Reser of Pont Beudet. I am breaking a promise by writing this, and maybe the cocks are crowing because of it, but all the cocks in creation can crow three times if they must. I am going to say something about Dr. Reser. A piece about Haiti without Dr. Reser would be lacking in flavor.

I heard many things about Dr. Reser before I met him. A great deal is said about the white man who is a houngan (Voodoo priest). All of the foreigners living in Port-au-Prince know him and like him. A great many Haitians admit that he is deep in the inner secrets of Voodoo, and startling legends have grown up about him. Some say that he belongs to the Société de Couleve (Snake Society) which is supposed to be headed by Dr. Arthur Holly. Its object is said to be the extermination of the Secte Rouge and the devil worshippers in Haiti. One young man assured me that they all wore a snake tattooed on their forearms. He had seen the snake on Dr. Reser's arm. It had life. He had seen Dr. Reser feed it eggs.

After I met Reser I asked to see this symbol. It turned out to be a dragon which he had had tattooed on his arm when he was in the navy. But to many Haitians it is a sacred snake that eats eggs and performs miracles of magic.

Therefore it was not long before I went out to Pont Beudet and found this much-talked-of man. But then everybody finds Dr. Reser as soon as they land in Port-au-Prince. He is one of the showpieces of Haiti, like the Citadel. This white American is better known than any other living character in Haiti.

As officer in charge of the state insane asylum at Pont Beudet, Dr. Reser has a comfortable house with a large well screened veranda. He has three sets of bed springs suspended by chains with comfortable mattresses on this screened porch. And these contraptions make good swings in the daytime and good beds at night. He is a gracious host and serves good native food at his table and tall, cool fruit drinks on his porch. He is a facile conversationalist on an amazing number of subjects. Philosophy, esoterics, erotica, travel, physics, psychology, chemistry, geology, religions, folk lore and many subjects I have heard him discuss in a single afternoon.

So I took to spending time on his porch when I was not busy otherwise. We would play cards and talk and swap tales and listen to the harmless lunatics who wandered about the grounds and occasionally came up to the screened porch to beg a cigarette or say something that seemed important to their crippled minds. It was very nice to lie sprawled on my back on one of those swing-beds and pass the day. His house boy, Telemarque, was sure to appear with lemonade or orange juice about once every hour. The insane patients would be depended upon to yell something startling ever so often, and then Dr. Reser talks well. He has been in Haiti eleven years by the calendar but in soul he came from Africa with the rest of the people.

Seeing how the Haitian people, high and low, far and near, love and trust him, I tackled him one day on the business of being a white king of Haiti.

"Doctor Reser," I called over from one swing-bed to the other.

"I am not a doctor, you know. I am a pharmacist's mate, first class, retired U.S.N. They began to call me doctor while I was in the Public Health service at Port-de-Paix and they have just kept it up."

"I stand corrected, but getting back to what I started to say, Doctor, the people all seem to love you so much. Now in all the adventure tales I have ever read, the natives, finding a white man among them, always assume that he is a god, and at *least* make him a king. Here you have been in Haiti for eleven years according to your own story. You are on the most friendly terms with the Haitians of any white man in Haiti and still no kingly crown. How is that?"

"Well, I tell you, Zora, if you show yourself sincere, the Haitians will make a good friend of a white man, but hardly a king. They just don't run to royalty."

"Not even a *white* man?"

"Not even a white man, and the Haitians who made themselves kings did not fare so well, either, if you will recall."

I sat bolt upright at that. He had his mouth open and he was making broad statements.

"But on the island of La Gonave they made a king out of a sergeant of Marines."

"Oh, no, they didn't."

"But King Faustin Wirkus—"

"All I have to say about Wirkus and that white king business is that he had a good collaborator. Let's have another round of orange juice."

"You mean to say he was no king at all?"

"I mean just that."

"May I quote you as saying that?"

"Certainly. Now, how about that orange juice?"

"With pleasure, Doctor. Can I change the subject and talk about you instead?"

"I suppose so."

"Why is it then that the Haitians and the Haitian peasants

247

particularly love *you* so much?"

"They are infinitely kind and gentle and all that I have ever done to earn their love is to return their unfailing courtesy."

One tall lanky patient of the asylum hung around the porch and kept reciting the tales of Fontaine. It was a steady monotonous flow of syllables with his eyes fixed on us. It was a curious thing to see his mouth so active and the upper part of his face so still. It was plain that the upper part of his face did not know what the lower part was doing. One Syrian, formerly a merchant in Port-au-Prince, kept standing with his face against the porch wishing Dr. Reser well.

"Doctor Reser! Doctor Reser!" he kept calling. "I like for you to eat a very good eating. The very best eating in the United States."

"Thank you very much," Dr. Reser answered each time.

"Dr. Reser, I was driving very fast to Port-au-Prince—about sixty meters an hour—and I make three times around a pork [pig]. I tell the man, 'You pay five dollars duty to American government every time you leave pork in the street.'"

"Yes, yes," Dr. Reser answered with feigned interest. "Perhaps you want to go and look after the chickens for me."

The man hurried off very happy in the thought of performing a service for Dr. Reser and the conversation took up again on the porch.

I was speaking of returning to Port-au-Prince but Dr. Reser would not hear of it. They were expecting Joseph White, the American Vice-Consul, and his little new wife; M. C. Love, of the West India Oil Company; Frank Crumbie, Jr., of Nyack, New York; Mr. and Mrs. Scott and John Lassiter, American fiscal agents to the Haitian government; all were coming out that night with some newly arrived officials of the Pan American Airways.

Dr. Reser was giving a Voodoo dance for them and he was asking me to stay. I was on very friendly terms with all of them and so I was grateful to Dr. Reser for asking me. Cicerone, the greatest drummer in all Haiti, performed upon the *Houn-*

tah, the great thundering rada drum, that night. Everyone who cannot go to Africa should go to Pont Beudet, Haiti, to hear Cicerone play. He is not much to look at. He is past middle life, and is small and black and sort of shaggy. The magic of him is in those hands. The sun-stuff that places him among the geniuses of the timpani is found in those fingers that have actually been modified by their association with the taut heads of drums. Ah, yes, one must hear Cicerone of Pont-Beudet!

It was all very glinty and strong, what went on that night. The white visitors, whether they would have had it different or not, were a sort of audience around the walls. Strong action in the center. Many of Dr. Reser's Haitian friends came in. Some were upper class, educated men who received the introduction with poise and charm. Some were the peasants who were going to participate in the dance. They were all so glad to see Dr. Reser and made extravagant expressions of pleasure. One dark brown man with aquiline feature told him, "It is *such* a pleasure to see you again. I would have been humpbacked if I had not met you!" All of this was spoken in Creole, of course.

The evening got under way. Cicerone and the other drummers paid many of the guests the compliment of playing a special salute for each, after which the guest paid the drummers the compliment of a round of drinks or the cash for the purpose. The evening rose in spirit—the drumming, the singing, the dancers and the dancing. I was taught the Jean Valou. Midnight dashed past us on the run. Finally the others left and I was put to bed in Dr. Reser's bedroom while he and the others who lived there slept in the swing-beds on the porch.

The crowing of roosters, the small waking noises of the world, and the little dawn wind, all acknowledging the receipt of the new day, got me up. It took shape out of a ropy white mist, but there it was, the very last day that God had made, and it went about the business of changing people the way days always do. I got up to go home at once.

But I did not go as I had planned. A young woman came

to bring a message to Dr. Reser. It was from Aux Cayes in the south. It had been passed along by word of mouth of market women until it came to the young woman in Port-au-Prince, and it was an invitation to attend a ceremony in the south. What kind of ceremony was it going to be? It was to be a ceremony where the food was to be cooked without fire. Real food? Yes, a great pot of real food—enough to feed all of the people attending the ceremony—would be cooked without fire. Was such a thing *possible?* The young woman asked for a cup and saucer, a piece of laundry blue, a cup of cold water and a fresh egg. No, she did not wish to acquire the egg herself for fear that we might believe that she had one prepared. Dr. Reser went out and got one himself and gave it to her. She placed it in the cup at once. Poured some of the cold water on it and covered the cup with the saucer and made a cross mark on the saucer with the bluing. Then she bowed her head and mumbled a prayer for a few minutes. None of us could catch the exact words of what she said in that prayer. When it was over, she lifted the saucer and offered the egg to Dr. Reser with a diffident smile and told him to break it. He refused on the grounds that he had on his best gray suit and did not wish to have it spattered with egg. She assured him time and time again that the egg would not spatter over his clothes. At last he broke the egg very carefully and found it done. That was startling enough. But the realest surprise came when the egg was found to be harder in the center than anywhere else. The young woman now begged him to eat the egg. He was so reluctant to do so that it was necessary for her to coax him a great deal, but she prevailed at last and he ate the egg. Then she assured him that he would never die of poisoning. He would always be warned in time to avoid eating poisoned food or touching poisoned surfaces. Would he now accept the invitation to the ceremony? He would with great unction and avidity. I asked to come along and so it was arranged. A few days later we jolted over the rocky road south to Aux Cayes. It was night when our party arrived. A guard stood beside the main highway to guide us to the hounfort.

After the proper little ceremonies of greeting an important
guest and the one of entering was over we were assigned
sleeping space and went to bed, on our nattes under a great
mimbon tree.

Their ceremony was held in the court of a great hounfort
and the members of the society all came bearing foodstuffs.
There were great heaps of peas, carrots, cabbage, string beans,
onions, corn meal, rice and egg-plant.

The next morning the women were up preparing the little
cups of coffee that everyone drinks in Haiti before breakfast.
Then there was breakfast. After that the women went about
dressing the food for the ceremony while the men amused
themselves with a game of dice that is played with three
"bones" instead of the two that we used in the United States.

Many, many things came to pass in a ceremonial way and
then the "cooking" of the food without fire began. All that I
could see, and afterwards when I talked it over with Dr. Reser,
he confirmed my impression, was that the people formed a
circle about the big iron pot that contained the mingled food.
The Mambo began to sing, with the Ascon of course, and then
the drums began to sound. At the first note of the boulatier,
the smallest of the Rada drums, the men took off their hats and
the women the colored handkerchiefs that every woman wears
to a ceremony and began to dance, circling the pot. As they
went they chanted and waved their hats and handkerchiefs at
the pot as if fanning an invisible flame. This went on and on.
When the houngan and the Mambo concluded the ritual, the
food was dipped up with a wooden spoon and served to all.
Everybody ate with their fingers for it is an unbreakable law
of this ceremony that no metal except the pot must touch this
food, so knives, forks and spoons are forbidden.

How was the food cooked? I do not know. Dr. Reser and
I tried bribery and everything else in our power to learn the
secret, but it belongs to that small group and nothing we could
devise would do any good. Dr. Reser knew the girl who had
boiled the egg in cold water very well indeed. I would say that
they are very intimate friends. He concentrated upon her

251

finally, but all she would say was that it was a family secret brought from Africa which could not be divulged. He kept at her and she yielded enough to say that she could not tell him until he had been baptised in a certain ceremony. He went to the trouble and expense to have the baptism. After that was over, she returned to her original position that it was an inherited secret which she could not divulge under pain of death. So that is as far as we got on the food-without-fire ceremony. This is an annual affair and some day I shall try again.

I visited Dr. Reser many more times and polished my shoulder in his bed-swings and listened and ate. But one thing I never did. I never went to him for the information that I had come to Haiti to seek. One reason for this was that everyone who goes to Haiti to find out something makes a bee line for Dr. Reser and tries to pump out of him all that they can in a few weeks and then they sail off and write as if they had seen something. Be it said right here that Dr. Reser tells no more than he wants to, so what they get is bound to be limited first by Dr. Reser's own information, which is bound to be limited by the nature of Haiti's vastly complicated and varigated lore, and second by what he chooses to give out to the lazy mind-pickers who descend upon him. Since he has plans of his own for the future, he gives out nothing of any great importance. Thus they waste their time in Haiti on him. But the most important reason why I never tried to get my information second-hand out of Dr. Reser was because I consider myself amply equipped to go out in the field and get it myself. So my association with him was fifty per cent social and fifty per cent a study of the man himself. I wanted to know all I could about this educated, widely travelled man, this ex-navy man who could so completely find his soul and his peace in the African rituals of Haiti. I have seen him in the grip of the African loa (spirits) known as possession: that is, the spirits have entered his head and driven his own consciousness out. I have seen him reeling as if he were drunk under the spirit possession like any Haitian peasant and I was trying to reconcile the well-read man of science with the credulous man of emotions. A man who could break off a discussion of Aristotle to show me with child-like eagerness, a stone that he had found which contained a loa. So I spent as much time as I could spare from other things on his porch sprawled upon one of his bed-swings. Besides he is a very fine and generous person; and then again, so many things happened around his place.

He is very kind and tender with the unfortunate people in the asylum. Though many have applied for his job, he is still considered by the Chief of the Service d'Hygiène the best man for the place. Of course, the criminally insane and the violent ones are strictly confined, but the harmless have a measure of liberty. And some days they hang around Dr. Reser's porch and say things and say things. He never drives them away nor speaks to one of them harshly.

One afternoon on the porch I fell to wondering what part of the United States Dr. Reser came from. I had tried to place him by his accent but I was not sure. So I asked, "Where are you from, Dr. Reser."

"I am from Lapland, Zora."

"Why, Dr. Reser, I thought you said you were an American."

"I am, but I am from Lapland just the same."

I fell to wondering if Lapland had become an American colony while my back was turned. He saw my bewilderment and chuckled.

"Yes, I am from Lapland—where Missouri laps over on Arkansas."

Naturally I laughed at that and he went on in the brogue of the hill-billy reciting about folk-heroes: "Yes, I'm the guy that chewed the wad the goat eat that butted the bull off the bridge!"

Just then the Syrian hurried up to the porch and called:

"Dr. Reser! Dr. *Reser!* The soldiers of Monte Carlo killed the Dead Sea, then they built the Casino!"

"Thanks for the information," Dr. Reser replied.

The patient who spent all of his waking hours quoting Fontaine's fables came to the porch too. I had laughed heartily at

Dr. Reser's quotations from the folk lore of the Ozarks, and perhaps our merriment attracted them. Another patient came up and began to babble the Haitian folk tales about Brother Bouki and Ti Malice.

Dr. Reser went on: "Raised on six shooters till I got big enough to eat growed shotguns. I warm up the Gulf of Mexico and bathe therein. I mount the wild ass and hop from crag to crag. I swim the Mississippi River from end to end with five hundred pound shot in my teeth! Airy dad gummed man that don't believe it, I'll hold him by the neck and leave him wiggle his fool self to death."

"Dr. Reser! Dr. *Reser!*" The Syrian attracts attention to himself. "They have horse racing in Palestine. The horses have contracts in Jewish and Arabic and English and the Jewish horse *must* be second. It's political."

The man who recited Fontaine pointed his stagnant eyes on the porch and babbled on as if he raced with the man who was talking about Ti Malice and Bouki, but he had a weaker voice. So we heard very distinctly:

"Of course, Bouki was very angry with Ti Malice for what he had done and Ti Malice was afraid, so he ran away very fast until he came to a fence. The fence had a hole in it, but the hole was not very big, but Malice tried to go through—"

"Dr. Reser! Dr. *Reser!* Never speak to person with tired physinomic! I drive car five years without license and the United States Government was very content."

"Are they annoying you?" Dr. Reser asked me. "They never worry *me* at all."

"Oh, no," I answered. "It is very interesting. Let them go on."

"All right, then. It will soon be time for them to go to bed anyway."

The Syrian was very close to the screen now. "When you write to the president, every amigo here remember you," he was advising us. "Dr. Reser, what is love?"

"I really don't know," Reser replied. "What is it?"

"Love is the heart. And what is the heart? It is the communication of the body."

The sun was setting and I lifted my eyes as the father of worlds dropped towards the horizon. In the near distance a royal palm flaunted itself above the other foliage with its stiff rod of a new leaf making assignation with life.

"Dr. Reser, I know love what it is," the Syrian went on. "I go in Cuba once and they have a house there. The bell ring 'ting!!' and you go in and they shake you like this and in the morning you come out and you know about life."

The Syrian turned suddenly and walked over to the shrubbery and began to gather hibiscus blooms. Dr. Reser sent the man who always quoted Fontaine to stop him from denuding the plants. Then we could hear the other one still telling his story of Malice and Bouki. "—Malice was stuck in the hole in the fence and he could not go forward neither could he back out. His behind was too big to pass through. So Bouki found him there but he did not know it. He saw this great behind stuck in the fence but he was impatient to overtake Malice so he slapped it and said:

" 'Behind, have you seen Malice?'

"The behind said, 'Push me and I'll tell you.'

"So Brother Bouki gave a great shove and bushed Ti Malice through the hole and he ran away. It was only after he was gone that Bouki knew it was Malice, so—"

He received the signal that supper was being served so he abruptly left us. In a short while we saw a file of men being conducted through the grounds to their sleeping quarters. Several women stood about within their enclosure, which was fenced in by heavy chicken wire. As the line of men came abreast of the space where the women were standing, one of the women walked up to the fence, suddenly lifted her skirts up around her waist and presented herself. Instantly one of the men broke from the line and ran to her. It was all unplanned, simple and instinctive. Presently the guard who was marching in front heard the commotion and looked around. He rushed back and dragged the man away with the help of two others.

The woman stumbled back to a stool and drooped down in a sort of apathy. The man was forced to his cell and could be heard cursing and howling all night long.

As for us, we waited outside until the black curtain ran all the way around the hoop of the horizon. Then Telemarque announced and we went inside and ate the delicious bits of lean cured pork that Telemarque knows how to cook. We ate jean-jean and rice, which is Haiti's most delicious native dish. Jean-jean is a little wild mushroom that grows there and Mme. Jules Faine prepares jean-jean and rice better than anyone else in Haiti.

Dr. Reser was discussing tides and the movement of ocean current for a while. Then somehow we got off on determining the sex of children before birth. He stated positively that it could be done by means of a gold ring suspended on a chain. From there he went precipitately into the occult and the occult in Haiti. He offered as justification for his firm belief in the power of the Voodoo gods several instances of miraculous cures, warnings, foretelling of events and prophecies. Some of them were striking. He told of visions of Prepti. He promised to introduce me to Prepti but we never did arrange it. Prepti was secretary to Charlemagne Peralt, one of the leaders of the Caco rebellion. Prepti was an educated and cultivated man and had no desire to perform any such service for Charlemagne Peralt, but he was kidnapped by Peralt and tortured and forced to serve him for three years as his secretary. He was forced to accompany Peralt during all of the fighting in the rebellion. Running away from an engagement with the Marines, Prepti fell over a cliff into a crevice from which he could not extricate himself. The sides were too sheer and steep. He struggled until he realized that escape was impossible. Then he cried out but there was no one to hear him. He grew hungry and thirsty and after the second day resigned himself to die. But during the night as he lay against the rocks in his extremity, came a vision of Ogoun with his red robes and long white beard. He assured Prepti that he would not die there, and that he would be found and rescued. Then came a vision of Erzulie, the goddess of love, who comforted him and also promised him that he would be rescued. Prepti stayed there several days. He was dried up and starved when they found him, but so much alive he completely recovered from his exposure and starvation. He had another vision also in which God sent two angels with needles and thread to make dolls and the movement of these figures showed him what would happen. And it all happened that way.

Dr. Reser began to tell of his experiences while in the psychological state known as possession. Incident piled on incident. A new personality burned up the one that had eaten supper with us. His blue-gray eyes glowed, but at the same time they drew far back into his head as if they went inside to gaze on things kept in a secret place. After awhile he began to speak. He told of marvelous revelations of the Brave Guedé cult. And as he spoke, he moved farther and farther from known land and into the territory of myths and mists. Before our very eyes, he walked out of his Nordic body and changed. Whatever the stuff of which the soul of Haiti is made, he was that. You could see the snake god of Dahomey hovering about him. Africa was in his tones. He throbbed and glowed. He used English words but he talked to me from another continent. He was dancing before his gods and the fire of Shango played about him. Then I knew how Moses felt when he beheld the burning bush. Moses had seen fires and he had seen bushes, but he had never seen a bush with a fiery ego and I had never seen a man who dwelt in flame, who was coldly afire in the pores. Perhaps some day I shall visit his roomy porch again and drink his orangeade and listen to him discourse on Aristotle, but even in the midst of it, I shall remember his hour of fire.

Ah Bo Bo!!

CHAPTER 18

✥

GOD AND THE
PINTARDS

With all of their ineptitude for certain concepts that the Anglo-Saxon holds sacred, the Haitian people have a tremendous talent for getting themselves loved. They are drenched in kindliness and beaming out with charm. They are like the pintards of God that Dr. Reser told me about. That is a Haitian folk tale that somebody told to him. A pintard is a guinea-fowl.

God planted a rice field one year. It was a rice field that was equal to His station and circumstances. It began to ripen and God began to look forward to the day of reaping.

One day a message came to God saying, "God, the pintards are eating up all of your rice. If you don't do something about it, there won't be any rice to reap."

So God called the Angel Michael and told him, "Here, Michael, you take this gun and go down to my rice fields and kill those pintards. They are eating up all of my rice and I did not plant rice for them. Go and shoot enough of them to scare off the rest. I meant to have a great crop this year."

The Angel Michael took the gun and went on down to God's rice fields to shoot the pintards as he had been told.

When he was about there the pintards saw him coming with God's gun and they all flew up into a huge mimbon tree and began to sing and clap their wings together in rhythm. Michael came up to the tree and pointed the shot-gun at the great mass of pintards crowded into the tree singing and making rhythm. But the song and the rhythm were so compelling that he forgot to pull the trigger. With the gun still pointing he began to keep time with the wing clapping. Then he went to dancing and finally he laid the gun down and danced until he was exhausted. Then he took up the gun and went away and told God saying, "God, I could not shoot those pintards. They were too happy and made too beautiful a dance-song for me to kill them." With a shamed face, because he had not done what God sent him to do, Michael put the gun down and went away.

God called Gabriel and said, "Gabriel, I don't aim to have all of my rice eaten up by those pintards. You take this gun and go down there and shoot them, and otherwise drive them away from my rice fields. I sent Michael and he never did a thing. Now you go and hurry up. I want some rice this year."

So Gabriel took the gun and went on down to God's rice field to shoot the pintards, but they saw him coming too and flew up into the mimbon tree and began to clap wings and sing, and Gabriel began to dance and forgot all about God's rice field for a whole day. When he saw the sun going down he remembered why he had been sent and he was so ashamed of himself that he couldn't bear to face God. So he met Peter and handed him the gun and said, "Please take God His gun for me. I am ashamed to go back."

Peter took the gun and told God what Gabriel had said. So God sent Peter and told him, "You go and *kill* those pintards! I do not plant rice for pintards and don't intend to have my crop all ruined by them, either. Go and clear them out." Peter took the gun and went down in a hurry to do God's will. But he got all charmed by the song and the dance and when he went back with the gun he was too ashamed to talk.

So God took the gun and went down to His rice fields

Himself. The pintards saw Him coming and left the rice and flew up into the tree again. They saw it was God Himself, so they sang a new song and put on a double rhythm and then they doubled it again. God aimed the gun but before He knew it He was dancing and because of the song He didn't care whether He saved any rice or not. So He said, "I can't kill these pintards—they are too happy and joyful to be killed. But I do want my rice fields so I know what I will do. There is the world that I have made and so far it is sad and nobody is happy there and nothing goes right. I'll send these pintards down there to take music and laughter so the world can forget its troubles."

And that is what He did. He called Shango, the god of thunder and lightning, and he made a shaft of lightning and the pintards slid down it and landed in Guinea. So that is why music and dancing came from Guinea—God sent it there first.

APPENDIX

MAITRESSE ERSULIE

Ersulie nain nain oh! Ersulie nain nain oh!
Ersulie ya gaga gaaza, La roseé fait bro-
dè tou temps soleil par lévé La ro seé fait bro-
dè tou temps soleil par lévé Ersulie nain nain oh!
Ersu lie nain nain oh! Ersulie ya gaza.

FÉRAILLE

Féraille oh! nan main qui moun ma quité baquiya
laquain moin ré tem songéogoun Fé raille ma conso
lé ma prendconrail oh! relé nan qui
temps ron sima lade oh cor wa non yé nan qui
temps nan qui temps oh! Cor wa nonyé ma con so
lé ma prend con rail oh! so bé guim as sura.

Fé - raille oh!.... nan main qui moun ma qui - té.... ba - qui - ya

la - quan moin ré tem songé - - o - goun Fé raille... ma con-so

lé ma prend - con - rail oh!...... re - lé nan qui

temps ron si - - ma lade oh cor wa non yé nan qui

temps nan qui temps.... oh! Cor wa non - yé ma con so

le' ma prend... con rail oh!..... so bé guim as su - ra.

Coté ma prend Coté ma prend Médi
oh! Aanago Coté ma prend Coté ma
prend Médi oh! Ana go Cotéma go.

Co - té ma prend..... Co - té ma prend Mé - di
oh! An - a - go....... Co - té ma prend.... Co - té ma
prend Me - di oh! A - na - go...... Co - té - ma go.......

RADA

Bonjour papa Legba bonjour timoun moin yo Bonjour papa Legba bonjour ti moun moín yoma pé man dé
ou con man non yéma pé man dé on con man non
yé bonjour pa pa Legba bonjour ti moun moin yo Bon.

Bon - jour pa - pa Leg - ba bon - jour ti - moun moin - yo Bon -
jour pa - pa Leg - ba bon - jour ti moun moin yo...... ma pé man dé
ou con man non yé - - ma pé man dé on con man non
yé bon - jour pa pa Leg - ba bon - jour ti moun moin yo..... Bon.

JANVALO (JEAN VALDO)

Adia ban moin zui potó tou félé
Adia ban moin zui poté tou félé Adia ban moin
zui zui ya ma qué félé Adia ban moin zui zui
ya ma qué félé Adia ban moin zui poté tout félé.

No. 5.

A - dia ban moin zui po - tó..... tou fé - lé

A - dia ban moin zui po - té.... tou fé - lé A - dia ban moin

zui zui ya ma qué fé - lé A - dia ban moin zui zui

ya ma qué fé - lé A - dia ban moin zui po - té..... tout fé - lé.

JANVALO

Adi bon ça ma dit si ma dènié oh! ga-
dé mi sè ya cé pon do moins adi bon ça ma
dit sit ma dénié oh! gade mi sè ya cé pon do moins.

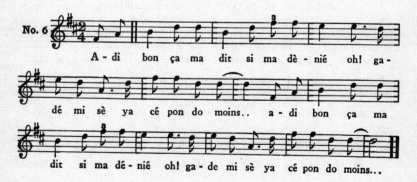

No. 6

A - di bon ça ma dit si ma dè - nié oh! ga-

dé mi sè ya cé pon do moins.. a - di bon ça ma

dit si ma dé - nié oh! ga - de mi sè ya cé pon do moins...

SAINT JACQUES

St. Jacques pas là St. Jacques pas là St. Jacques pas là
cé moin qui là St. Jacques pas là oh! chien ya modé moin.

PETRO

Nous vley wè Dan Pétro Nous vley wé oh!
Nous vley wè si ya qui té caille la tom bé
Nous vley wè Dan Petro Nous vley wè oh! Nous vley wè
oh! Si ya quité caille là tom bé elan oh!

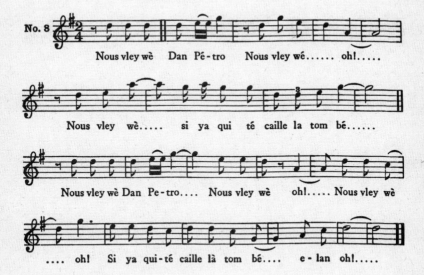

PETRO

Salut moin oh! Sa lut moin oh! Salut moins
Nous sé vi lan rent nan caille là oh! Salut moins.
oh a diě salut moins oh Salut moins oh Salut moins
nous sè vi lan rent nan caille la oh! Salut moins Salut.

Sa - lut   moin   oh! Sa lut   moin.... oh! Sa-lut   moins

Nous sé   vi lan   rent   nan caille là oh! Sa - lut   moins.....

oh.... a   diě sa-lut moins.... oh Sa-lut   moins.. oh Sa-lut moins

nous sè   vi lan   rent nan caille la   oh! Sa - lut moins...   Sa-lut.

IBO

Ibo Lélé Ibo Lélé Iyanman
ça ou gain yen çonça I bo Lélé cé con
ça moin danté Ibo Iyanman oh! Anan Iyanman
Con çam danté I bo Iyanman oh! An an Iyan man.

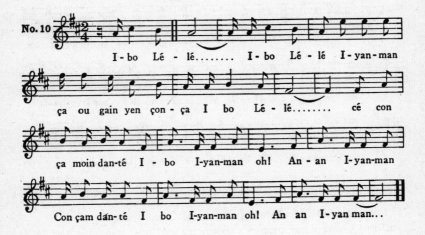

I - bo Lé - lé........ I - bo Lé - lé I - yan - man

ça ou gain yen çon - ça I bo Lé - lé........ cé con

ça moin dan - té I - bo I - yan - man oh! An - an I - yan - man

Con çam dan - té I bo I - yan - man oh! An an I - yan man...

IBO

Ibo moin youn oh! Ibo moin youn oh! I—
bo moin youn oh! m'pa gan guin man man gindémoin Grand
Ibo moin youn oh! m'pa gan guin man man gindé moins.

I - bo moin youn oh! I - bo moin youn oh! I -

bo moin youn oh! m'pa gan guin man man gin - dé - moin Grand I -

bo moin youn oh! m'pa gan guin man man gin - dé moins.

271

DAMBALLA

Fiolé por Dambalá Dambala wè do Fiolé oh! Dambala Wè do Fiolě por Dambala
Dambala Wédo Fiolé por Dam ba la.

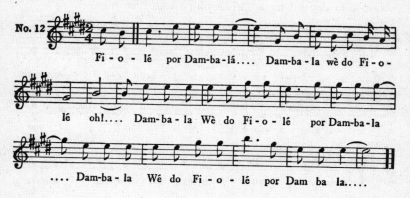

OGOUN

Ogoun tra vail oh! Ogoun por mangé Ogoun tra-
vail oh! Ogoun por mangé Ogoun tra vail tout nan nuit por O-
goun por mangé yiěre soi Ogoun dor mi sans sou per.

SALONGO

Zin zin zin zin zin zin Ba yan min oh! Saya Pim ba
zin zin zin zin zin zin Ba yan min oh! Saya Pimba

SALONGO

Tousa Tousa rè lè Tou Salonggo Tou
sa Tou sa rè lè Tou Sa longgo Tousa Tou sa rè lè Tou Sa
longgo.

LOCO

Loco Mabia Ebon Azacan Loco Ma-
bia Ello oh! Loco Mabia Ello Azagan
Loco Mabia Ello oh! Jean valou Moin Jean valou
Moin Loco Loco Mabia Ello Loco Ma Lo.

274

MAMBO ISAN

Mambo Isan ma pralé Oh! Ma pralé quéléfré
m'pralé chaché fammil moin yo Mam bo Isan ma pralé
Oh! Ma pra lé quáléfré m'pra lé chaché fammil moin
yo Mam bo Isan oh! cé ron qui maré moin Mambo I san
oh! céron qui ma ré moin cé ron qua laqué'm oh!

No. 2

Mam-bo I - san ma pra - lé.... Oh!... Ma pra-lé qué - lé - fré

.... m'pra-lé cha - ché fammil - moin yo... Mam bo I - san ma pra - lé..

..... Oh!.... Ma pra lé qué - lé - fré... m'pra lé cha - ché fammil moin

yo... Mam bo I - sanoh! cé ron... qui ma - ré moin...Mam-bo I san

oh! cé - ron qui ma ré moin cé ron qua la - qué'm oh!.....

DAMBALA

Filé na filé fem Dambala Wèdo
Filé na filé Dambala Wèdo cá conclèv oh! lèv oh!

Fi - lé na fi - lé fem Dam - ba - la.... Wè - do

Fi - lé na fi - lé Dam - ba - la Wè - do cé con - lèv oh!.. lèv oh!..

Ad libitum

AGOË (AGOUÉ TE ROYO)

Aroquè si ou gain yen chanson nivo pon ou chan-
té wa chan té l'nan hounfort oud ronan hounfort ou Pi
ga on mon tre criole than son ni vo Pi Vo on criole
va ga té mo yen ou Agoë ta royo neg bas sin bleu neg dlo salé
   neg
coqui doré Si ou gain yen chanson ni vo pon ou chan-
té Wa chan télnan houn for ou Pi ga ou mon tré creole chan son
   nivo.

No. 4

A - ro - què si ou gain yen chan-son ni - vo..... pon ou chan-

té..... wa chan té...l'nan hounfort ou-d ro - nan hounfort ou Pi-

gaon mon tre cri-ole than son ni vo Pi-Vo on cri-ole

va ga té mo yenou.... A-goë ta ro˙yo neg bas sin bleu neg dlo sa-lé neg

co-qui do-ré...... Si ou gain yen chan-son ni vo...... pon ou chan-

té.... Wa chan têl-nan houn for ou Pi ga ou mon tré cre-ole cha n son ni vo.

SOBO

Gué Manyan man yanga dé hounfort wa
ga dé houn for wa Sobo gué ma yan
be! Gué Man hé O gui Manyan Man yanga dé houn
for wa Sobo Ga dé houn for wa So bo Gué Man yan bé!

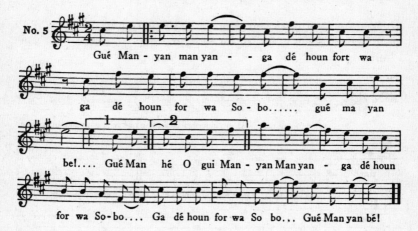

No. 5

Gué Man - yan man yan - - ga dé houn fort wa

ga dé houn for wa So - bo...... gué ma yan

be!.... Gué Man hé O gui Man - yan Man yan - ga dé houn

for wa So-bo.... Ga dé houn for wa So bo... Gué Man yan bé!

OGOUN

Alou man dia hé! Ogoun oh! ohsans yo oh!
aho! Alou man O sange ba conle qui man de dra-
po o Sane ba conlé qui man dé dra po lila O goun bare I baba.

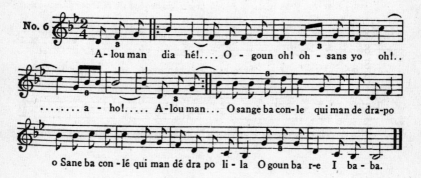

No. 6

A-lou man dia hé!.... O - goun oh! oh - sans yo oh!..

.... a - ho!..... A-lou man... O sange ba con-le qui man de dra-po

o Sane ba con -lé qui man dé dra po li - la O goun ba r-e I ba-ba.

278

SECTE ROUGE

Carrefour, tingindingue, mi haut, mi bas-é
Carrefour, tingindingue, mi haut, mi bas-é
Oun pralé, tingindingue, mi haut, mi bas, tingindingue
Oun pralé, tingindingue, mi haut, mi bas, tingindingue
Oun pralé, tingindingue, mi haut, mi bas,
tingindingue.

SECTE ROUGE

Sortie nan cimiterre, toute corps moin sentie malingue
Sortie nan cimiterre, toute corps moin sentie malingue
Sortie nan cimiterre, toute corps moin sentie malingue
Sortie nan cimiterre, toute corps moin sentie malingue.

CHANT BEGINNING ALL RADA CEREMONIES

Héla grand pere étérnel sin joé Heé-
la grand pere étérnel sin jozé do co agué Héla grand pere étérnel sin'nam min bon Diĕ o
Saint yen.

TUNE TO CALL THE "LOA"

LA MYSTÉRIEUSE, MÉRINGUE

A. L. Duroseau

ÉTONNEMENT, MÉRINGUE CARACTÉRISTIQUE

A. Herandez

—BONNE HUMEUR—
MÉRINGUE HAITÏENNE

à Miss Zora Neale Hurston

Arthur L. Duroseau

OLGA, MÉRINGUE PAR

Arthur Lyncie Duroseau

Arthur Lyncíe Duroseau

No. 5

CHANSON DE CALICOT

284

LA DOUCEUR

Méringue Haïtienne par Arthur L. Duroseau

—PETRO—

—IBO—

RADA

—JANVALHO—

AFTERWORD

❖

ZORA NEALE HURSTON: "A NEGRO WAY OF SAYING"

I.

The Reverend Harry Middleton Hyatt, an Episcopal priest whose five-volume classic collection, *Hoodoo, Conjuration, Witchcraft, and Rootwork,* more than amply returned an investment of forty years' research, once asked me during an interview in 1977 what had become of another eccentric collector whom he admired. "I met her in the field in the thirties. I think," he reflected for a few seconds, "that her first name was Zora." It was an innocent question, made reasonable by the body of confused and often contradictory rumors that make Zora Neale Hurston's own legend as richly curious and as dense as are the black myths she did so much to preserve in her classic anthropological works, *Mules and Men* and *Tell My Horse,* and in her fiction.

A graduate of Barnard, where she studied under Franz Boas, Zora Neale Hurston published seven books—four novels, two books of folklore, and an autobiography—and more than fifty shorter works between the middle of the Harlem Renaissance and the end of the Korean War, when she was the dominant black woman writer in the United States. The dark obscurity into which her career then lapsed reflects her staunchly independent political stances rather than any deficiency of craft or vision. Virtually ignored after the early fifties, even by the Black Arts movement in the sixties, an otherwise noisy and intense spell of black image- and myth-making that rescued so many black writers from remaindered oblivion, Hurston embodied a more or less harmonious but nevertheless problematic unity of opposites. It is this complexity that refuses to lend itself to the glib categories of "radical" or "conservative," "black" or "Negro," "revolutionary" or "Uncle Tom"—categories of little use in literary criticism. It is this same complexity, embodied in her fiction, that, until Alice Walker published her important essay ("In Search of Zora Neale Hurston") in *Ms.* magazine in 1975, had made Hurston's place in black literary history an ambiguous one at best.

The rediscovery of Afro-American writers has usually turned on larger political criteria, of which the writer's work is supposedly a mere reflection. The deeply satisfying aspect of the rediscovery of Zora Neale Hurston is that black women generated it primarily to establish a maternal literary ancestry. Alice Walker's moving essay recounts her attempts to find Hurston's unmarked grave in the Garden of the Heavenly Rest, a segregated cemetery in Fort Pierce, Florida. Hurston became a metaphor for the black woman writer's search for tradition. The craft of Alice Walker, Gayl Jones, Gloria Naylor, and Toni Cade Bambara bears, in markedly different ways, strong affinities with Hurston's. Their attention to Hurston signifies a novel sophistication in black literature: they read Hurston not only for the spiritual kinship inherent in such relations but because she used black vernacular speech and rituals, in ways subtle and various, to chart the coming to consciousness of black women, so glaringly absent in other black fiction. This use of the vernacular became the fundamental framework for all but one of her novels and is particularly effective in her classic work *Their Eyes Were Watching God,* published in 1937, which is more closely related to Henry James's *The Portrait of a Lady* and Jean Toomer's *Cane* than to Langston Hughes's and Richard Wright's proletarian literature, so popular in the Depression.

The charting of Janie Crawford's fulfillment as an autonomous imagination, *Their Eyes* is a lyrical novel that correlates the need of her first two husbands for ownership of progressively larger physical space (and the gaudy accoutrements of upward mobility) with the suppression of self-awareness in their wife. Only with her third and last lover, a roustabout called Tea Cake whose unstructured frolics center around and about the Florida swamps, does Janie at last bloom, as does the large pear tree that stands beside her grandmother's tiny log cabin.

> She saw a dust bearing bee sink into the sanctum of a bloom; the thousand sister calyxes arch to meet the love embrace and the ecstatic shiver of the tree from root to tiniest branch creaming in every blossom and frothing with delight. So this was a marriage!

To plot Janie's journey from object to subject, the narrative of the novel shifts from third to a blend of first and third person (known as "free indirect discourse"), signifying this awareness of self in Janie. *Their Eyes* is a bold feminist novel, the first to be explicitly so in the Afro-American tradition. Yet in its concern with the project of finding a voice, with language as an instrument of injury and salvation, of selfhood and empowerment, it suggests many of the themes that inspirit Hurston's oeuvre as a whole.

II.

One of the most moving passages in American literature is Zora Neale Hurston's account of her last encounter with her

291

dying mother, found in a chapter entitled "Wandering" in her autobiography, *Dust Tracks on a Road* (1942):

> As I crowded in, they lifted up the bed and turned it around so that Mama's eyes would face east. I thought that she looked to me as the head of the bed reversed. Her mouth was slightly open, but her breathing took up so much of her strength that she could not talk. But she looked at me, or so I felt, to speak for her. She depended on me for a voice.

We can begin to understand the rhetorical distance that separated Hurston from her contemporaries if we compare this passage with a similar scene published just three years later in *Black Boy* by Richard Wright, Hurston's dominant black male contemporary and rival: "Once, in the night, my mother called me to her bed and told me that she could not endure the pain, and she wanted to die. I held her hand and begged her to be quiet. That night I ceased to react to my mother; my feelings were frozen." If Hurston represents her final moments with her mother in terms of the search for voice, then Wright attributes to a similar experience a certain "somberness of spirit that I was never to lose," which "grew into a symbol in my mind, gathering to itself . . . the poverty, the ignorance, the helplessness. . . ." Few authors in the black tradition have less in common than Zora Neale Hurston and Richard Wright. And whereas Wright would reign through the forties as our predominant author, Hurston's fame reached its zenith in 1943 with a *Saturday Review* cover story honoring the success of *Dust Tracks.* Seven years later, she would be serving as a maid in Rivo Alto, Florida; ten years after that she would die in the County Welfare Home in Fort Pierce, Florida.

How could the recipient of two Guggenheims and the author of four novels, a dozen short stories, two musicals, two books on black mythology, dozens of essays, and a prizewinning autobiography virtually "disappear" from her readership for three full decades? There are no easy answers to this quandary, despite the concerted attempts of scholars to resolve it. It is clear, however, that the loving, diverse, and enthusiastic responses that Hurston's work engenders today were not shared by several of her influential black male contemporaries. The reasons for this are complex and stem largely from what we might think of as their "racial ideologies."

Part of Hurston's received heritage—and perhaps the paramount received notion that links the novel of manners in the Harlem Renaissance, the social realism of the thirties, and the cultural nationalism of the Black Arts movement—was the idea that racism had reduced black people to mere ciphers, to beings who only react to an omnipresent racial oppression, whose culture is "deprived" where different, and whose psyches are in the main "pathological." Albert Murray, the writer and social critic, calls this "the Social Science Fiction Monster." Socialists, separatists, and civil rights advocates alike have been devoured by this beast.

Hurston thought this idea degrading, its propagation a trap, and railed against it. It was, she said, upheld by "the sobbing school of Negrohood who hold that nature somehow has given them a dirty deal." Unlike Hughes and Wright, Hurston chose deliberately to ignore this "false picture that distorted. . . ." Freedom, she wrote in *Moses, Man of the Mountain,* "was something internal. . . . The man himself must make his own emancipation." And she declared her first novel a manifesto against the "arrogance" of whites assuming that "black lives are only defensive reactions to white actions." Her strategy was not calculated to please.

What we might think of as Hurston's mythic realism, lush and dense within a lyrical black idiom, seemed politically retrograde to the proponents of a social or critical realism. If Wright, Ellison, Brown, and Hurston were engaged in a battle over ideal fictional modes with which to represent the Negro, clearly Hurston lost the battle.

But not the war.

After Hurston and her choice of style for the black novel

were silenced for nearly three decades, what we have witnessed since is clearly a marvelous instance of the return of the repressed. For Zora Neale Hurston has been "rediscovered" in a manner unprecedented in the black tradition: several black women writers, among whom are some of the most accomplished writers in America today, have openly turned to her works as sources of narrative strategies, to be repeated, imitated, and revised, in acts of textual bonding. Responding to Wright's critique, Hurston claimed that she had wanted at long last to write a black novel, and "not a treatise on sociology." It is this urge that resonates in Toni Morrison's *Song of Solomon* and *Beloved,* and in Walker's depiction of Hurston as our prime symbol of "racial health—a sense of black people as complete, complex, *undiminished* human beings, a sense that is lacking in so much black writing and literature." In a tradition in which male authors have ardently denied black literary paternity, this is a major development, one that heralds the refinement of our notion of tradition: Zora and her daughters are a tradition-within-the-tradition, a black woman's voice.

The resurgence of popular and academic readerships of Hurston's works signifies her multiple canonization in the black, the American, and the feminist traditions. Within the critical establishment, scholars of every stripe have found in Hurston texts for all seasons. More people have read Hurston's works since 1975 than did between that date and the publication of her first novel, in 1934.

III.

Rereading Hurston, I am always struck by the density of intimate experiences she cloaked in richly elaborated imagery. It is this concern for the figurative capacity of black language, for what a character in *Mules and Men* calls "a hidden meaning, jus' like de Bible . . . de inside meanin' of words," that unites Hurston's anthropological studies with her fiction. For the folklore Hurston collected so meticulously as Franz Boas's student at Barnard became metaphors, allegories, and performances in her novels, the traditional recurring canonical metaphors of black culture. Always more of a novelist than a social scientist, even Hurston's academic collections center on the quality of imagination that makes these lives whole and splendid. But it is in the novel that Hurston's use of the black idiom realizes its fullest effect. In *Jonah's Gourd Vine,* her first novel, for instance, the errant preacher, John, as described by Robert Hemenway "is a poet who graces his world with language but cannot find the words to secure his own personal grace." This concern for language and for the "natural" poets who "bring barbaric splendor of word and song into the very camp of the mockers" not only connects her two disciplines but also makes of "the suspended linguistic moment" a thing to behold indeed. Invariably, Hurston's writing depends for its strength on the text, not the context, as does John's climactic sermon, a *tour de force* of black image and metaphor. Image and metaphor define John's world; his failure to interpret himself leads finally to his self-destruction. As Robert Hemenway, Hurston's biographer, concludes, "Such passages eventually add up to a theory of language and behavior."

Using "the spy-glass of Anthropology," her work celebrates rather than moralizes; it shows rather than tells, such that "both behavior and art become self-evident as the tale texts and hoodoo rituals accrete during the reading." As author, she functions as "a midwife participating in the birth of a body of folklore, . . . the first wondering contacts with natural law." The myths she describes so accurately are in fact "alternative modes for perceiving reality," and never just condescending depictions of the quaint. Hurston sees "the Dozens," for example, that age-old black ritual of graceful insult, as, among other things, a verbal defense of the sanctity of the family, conjured through ingenious plays on words. Though attacked by Wright and virtually ignored by his literary heirs, Hurston's ideas about language and craft undergird many of the most successful contributions to Afro-American literature that followed.

IV.

We can understand Hurston's complex and contradictory legacy more fully if we examine *Dust Tracks on a Road,* her own controversial account of her life. Hurston did make significant parts of herself up, like a masquerader putting on a disguise for the ball, like a character in her fictions. In this way, Hurston *wrote* herself, and sought in her works to rewrite the "self" of "the race," in its several private and public guises, largely for ideological reasons. That which she chooses to reveal is the life of her imagination, as it sought to mold and interpret her environment. That which she silences or deletes, similarly, is all that her readership would draw upon to delimit or pigeonhole her life as a synecdoche of "the race problem," an exceptional part standing for the debased whole.

Hurston's achievement in *Dust Tracks* is twofold. First, she gives us a *writer's* life, rather than an account, as she says, of "the Negro problem." So many events in this text are figured in terms of Hurston's growing awareness and mastery of books and language, language and linguistic rituals as spoken and written both by masters of the Western tradition and by ordinary members of the black community. These two "speech communities," as it were, are Hurston's great sources of inspiration not only in her novels but also in her autobiography.

The representation of her sources of language seems to be her principal concern, as she constantly shifts back and forth between her "literate" narrator's voice and a highly idiomatic black voice found in wonderful passages of free indirect discourse. Hurston moves in and out of these distinct voices effortlessly, seamlessly, just as she does in *Their Eyes* to chart Janie's coming to consciousness. It is this usage of a *divided* voice, a double voice unreconciled, that strikes me as her great achievement, a verbal analogue of her double experiences as a woman in a male-dominated world and as a black person in a nonblack world, a woman writer's revision of W. E. B. Du

Bois's metaphor of "double consciousness" for the hyphenated African-American.

Her language, variegated by the twin voices that intertwine throughout the text, retains the power to unsettle:

There is something about poverty that smells like death.
Dead dreams dropping off the heart like leaves in a dry
season and rotting around the feet; impulses smothered too
long in the fetid air of underground caves. The soul lives
in a sickly air. People can be slave-ships in shoes.

Elsewhere she analyzes black "idioms" used by a culture "raised on simile and invective. They know how to call names," she concludes, then lists some, such as 'gator-mouthed, box-ankled, puzzle-gutted, shovel-footed: "Eyes looking like skint-ginny nuts, and mouth looking like a dishpan full of broke-up crockery!"

Immediately following the passage about her mother's death, she writes:

The Master-Maker in His making had made Old Death.
Made him with big, soft feet and square toes. Made him
with a face that reflects the face of all things, but neither
changes itself, nor is mirrored anywhere. Made the body of
death out of infinite hunger. Made a weapon of his hand to
satisfy his needs. This was the morning of the day of the
beginning of things.

Language, in these passages, is not merely "adornment," as Hurston described a key black linguistic practice; rather, manner and meaning are perfectly in tune: she says the thing in the most meaningful manner. Nor is she being "cute," or pandering to a condescending white readership. She is "naming" emotions, as she says, in a language both deeply personal and culturally specific.

The second reason that *Dust Tracks* succeeds as literature arises from the first: Hurston's unresolved tension between her double voices signifies her full understanding of modernism. Hurston uses the two voices in her text to celebrate the psychological fragmentation both of modernity and of the black American. As Barbara Johnson has written, hers is a rhetoric of division, rather than a fiction of psychological or cultural unity. Zora Neale Hurston, the "real" Zora Neale Hurston that we long to locate in this text, dwells in the silence that separates these two voices: she is both, and neither; bilingual, and mute. This strategy helps to explain her attraction to so many contemporary critics and writers, who can turn to her works again and again only to be startled at her remarkable artistry.

But the life that Hurston could write was not the life she could live. In fact, Hurston's life, so much more readily than does the standard sociological rendering, reveals how economic limits determine our choices even more than does violence or love. Put simply, Hurston wrote well when she was comfortable, wrote poorly when she was not. Financial problems—book sales, grants and fellowships too few and too paltry, ignorant editors and a smothering patron—produced the sort of dependence that affects, if not determines, her style, a relation she explored somewhat ironically in "What White Publishers Won't Print." We cannot oversimplify the relation between Hurston's art and her life; nor can we reduce the complexity of her postwar politics, which, rooted in her distaste for the pathological image of blacks, were markedly conservative and Republican.

Nor can we sentimentalize her disastrous final decade, when she found herself working as a maid on the very day the *Saturday Evening Post* published her short story "Conscience of the Court" and often found herself without money, surviving after 1957 on unemployment benefits, substitute teaching, and welfare checks. "In her last days," Hemenway concludes dispassionately, "Zora lived a difficult life—alone, proud, ill, obsessed with a book she could not finish."

The excavation of her buried life helped a new generation read Hurston again. But ultimately we must find Hurston's

298

legacy in her art, where she "ploughed up some literacy and laid by some alphabets." Her importance rests with the legacy of fiction and lore she constructed so cannily. As Hurston herself noted, "Roll your eyes in ecstasy and ape his every move, but until we have placed something upon his street corner that is our own, we are right back where we were when they filed our iron collar off." If, as a friend eulogized, "She didn't come to you empty," then she does not leave black literature empty. If her earlier obscurity and neglect today seem inconceivable, perhaps now, as she wrote of Moses, she has "crossed over."

HENRY LOUIS GATES, JR.

SELECTED BIBLIOGRAPHY

WORKS BY ZORA NEALE HURSTON

Jonah's Gourd Vine. Philadelphia: J. B. Lippincott, 1934.

Mules and Men. Philadelphia: J. B. Lippincott, 1935.

Their Eyes Were Watching God. Philadelphia: J. B. Lippincott, 1937.

Tell My Horse. Philadelphia: J. B. Lippincott, 1938.

Moses, Man of the Mountain. Philadelphia: J. B. Lippincott, 1939.

Dust Tracks on a Road. Philadelphia: J. B. Lippincott, 1942.

Seraph on the Suwanee. New York: Charles Scribner's Sons, 1948.

I Love Myself When I Am Laughing . . . & Then Again When I Am Looking Mean and Impressive: A Zora Neale Hurston Reader. Edited by Alice Walker. Old Westbury, N.Y.: The Feminist Press, 1979.

The Sanctified Church. Edited by Toni Cade Bambara. Berkeley: Turtle Island, 1981.

Spunk: The Selected Short Stories of Zora Neale Hurston. Berkeley: Turtle Island, 1985.

WORKS ABOUT ZORA NEALE HURSTON

Baker, Houston A., Jr. *Blues, Ideology, and Afro-American Literature: A Vernacular Theory,* pp. 15–63. Chicago: University of Chicago Press, 1984.

Bloom, Harold, ed. *Zora Neale Hurston.* New York: Chelsea House, 1986.

————, ed. *Zora Neale Hurston's "Their Eyes Were Watching God."* New York: Chelsea House, 1987.

Byrd, James W. "Zora Neale Hurston: A Novel Folklorist." *Tennessee Folklore Society Bulletin* 21 (1955): 37–41.

Cooke, Michael G. "Solitude: The Beginnings of Self-Realization in Zora Neale Hurston, Richard Wright, and Ralph Ellison." In Michael G. Cooke, *Afro-American Literature in the Twentieth Century,* pp. 71–110. New Haven: Yale University Press, 1984.

Dance, Daryl C. "Zora Neale Hurston." In *American Women Writers: Bibliographical Essays,* edited by Maurice Duke, et al. Westport, Conn.: Greenwood Press, 1983.

Gates, Henry Louis, Jr. "The Speakerly Text." In Henry Louis Gates, Jr., *The Signifying Monkey,* pp. 170–217. New York: Oxford University Press, 1988.

Giles, James R. "The Significance of Time in Zora Neale Hurston's *Their Eyes Were Watching God." Negro American Literature Forum* 6 (Summer 1972): 52–53, 60.

Hemenway, Robert E. *Zora Neale Hurston: A Literary Biography.* Chicago: University of Illinois Press, 1977.

Holloway, Karla. *The Character of the Word: The Texts of Zora Neale Hurston.* Westport, Conn.: Greenwood Press, 1987.

Holt, Elvin. "Zora Neale Hurston." In *Fifty Southern Writers After 1900,* edited by Joseph M. Flura and Robert Bain, pp. 259–69. Westport, Conn.: Greenwood Press, 1987.

Howard, Lillie Pearl. *Zora Neale Hurston.* Boston: Twayne, 1980.

————. "Zora Neale Hurston." In *Dictionary of Literary Biography,* vol. 51, edited by Trudier Harris, pp. 133–45. Detroit: Gale, 1987.

Jackson, Blyden. "Some Negroes in the Land of Goshen." *Tennessee Folklore Society Bulletin* 19 (4) (December 1953): 103–7.

Johnson, Barbara. "Metaphor, Metonymy, and Voice in *Their Eyes.*" In *Black Literature and Literary Theory,* edited by Henry Louis Gates, Jr., pp. 205–21. New York: Methuen, 1984.

————. "Thresholds of Difference: Structures of Address in Zora Neale Hurston." In *"Race," Writing and Difference,* edited by Henry Lewis Gates, Jr. Chicago: University of Chicago Press, 1986.

Jordan, June. "On Richard Wright and Zora Neale Hurston." *Black World* 23 (10) (August 1974): 4–8.

Kubitschek, Missy Dehn. " 'Tuh de Horizon and Back': The Female Quest in *Their Eyes.*" *Black American Literature Forum* 17 (3) (Fall 1983): 109–15.

Lionnet, Françoise. "Autoethnography: The Anarchic Style of *Dust Tracks on a Road.*" In Françoise Lionnet, *Autobiographical Voices: Race, Gender, Self-Portraiture,* pp. 97–130. Ithaca: Cornell University Press, 1989.

Lupton, Mary Jane. "Zora Neale Hurston and the Survival of the Female." *Southern Literary Journal* 15 (Fall 1982): 45–54.

Meese, Elizabeth. "Orality and Textuality in Zora Neale Hurston's *Their Eyes.*" In Elizabeth Meese, *Crossing the Double Cross: The Practice of Feminist Criticism,* pp. 39–55. Chapel Hill: University of North Carolina Press, 1986.

Newson, Adele S. *Zora Neale Hurston: A Reference Guide.* Boston: G. K. Hall, 1987.

Rayson, Ann. *"Dust Tracks on a Road:* Zora Neale Hurston and the Form of Black Autobiography." *Negro American Literature Forum* 7 (Summer 1973): 42–44.

Sheffey, Ruthe T., ed. *A Rainbow Round Her Shoulder: The Zora Neale Hurston Symposium Papers.* Baltimore: Morgan State University Press, 1982.

Smith, Barbara. "Sexual Politics and the Fiction of Zora Neale Hurston." *Radical Teacher* 8 (May 1978): 26–30.

Stepto, Robert B. *From Behind the Veil.* Urbana: University of Illinois Press, 1979.

Walker, Alice. "In Search of Zora Neale Hurston." *Ms.,* March 1975, pp. 74–79, 85–89.

Wall, Cheryl A. "Zora Neale Hurston: Changing Her Own Words." In *American Novelists Revisited: Essays in Feminist Criticism,* edited by Fritz Fleischmann, pp. 370–93. Boston: G. K. Hall, 1982.

Washington, Mary Helen. "Zora Neale Hurston: A Woman Half in Shadow." Introduction to *I Love Myself When I Am Laughing,* edited by Alice Walker. Old Westbury, N.Y.: Feminist Press, 1979.

———. " 'I Love the Way Janie Crawford Left Her Husbands': Zora Neale Hurston's Emergent Female Hero." In Mary Helen Washington, *Invented Lives: Narratives of Black Women, 1860–1960.* New York: Anchor Press, 1987.

Willis, Miriam. "Folklore and the Creative Artist: Lydia Cabrera and Zora Neale Hurston." *CLA Journal* 27 (September 1983): 81–90.

Wolff, Maria Tai. "Listening and Living: Reading and Experience in *Their Eyes.*" *BALF* 16 (1) (Spring 1982): 29–33.

CHRONOLOGY

❖

January 7, 1891	Born in Eatonville, Florida, the fifth of eight children, to John Hurston, a carpenter and Baptist preacher, and Lucy Potts Hurston, a former schoolteacher.
September 1917– June 1918	Attends Morgan Academy in Baltimore, completing the high school requirements.
Summer 1918	Works as a waitress in a nightclub and a manicurist in a black-owned barbershop that serves only whites.
1918–19	Attends Howard Prep School, Washington, D.C.
1919–24	Attends Howard University; receives an associate degree in 1920.
1921	Publishes her first story, "John Redding Goes to Sea," in the *Stylus,* the campus literary society's magazine.
December 1924	Publishes "Drenched in Light," a short story, in *Opportunity.*
1925	Submits a story, "Spunk," and a play, *Color Struck,* to *Opportunity*'s literary contest. Both

	win second-place awards; publishes "Spunk" in the June number.
1925–27	Attends Barnard College, studying anthropology with Franz Boas.
1926	Begins field work for Boas in Harlem.
January 1926	Publishes "John Redding Goes to Sea" in *Opportunity.*
Summer 1926	Organizes *Fire!* with Langston Hughes and Wallace Thurman; they publish only one issue, in November 1926. The issue includes Hurston's "Sweat."
August 1926	Publishes "Muttsy" in *Opportunity.*
September 1926	Publishes "Possum or Pig" in the *Forum.*
September–November 1926	Publishes "The Eatonville Anthology" in the *Messenger.*
1927	Publishes *The First One,* a play, in Charles S. Johnson's *Ebony and Topaz.*
February 1927	Goes to Florida to collect folklore.
May 19, 1927	Marries Herbert Sheen.
September 1927	First visits Mrs. Rufus Osgood Mason, seeking patronage.
October 1927	Publishes an account of the black settlement at St. Augustine, Florida, in the *Journal of Negro History;* also in this issue: "Cudjo's Own Story of the Last African Slaver."
December 1927	Signs a contract with Mason, enabling her to return to the South to collect folklore.
1928	Satirized as "Sweetie Mae Carr" in Wallace Thurman's novel about the Harlem Renaissance *Infants of the Spring;* receives a bachelor of arts degree from Barnard.
January 1928	Relations with Sheen break off.

May 1928	Publishes "How It Feels to Be Colored Me" in the *World Tomorrow*.
1930–32	Organizes the field notes that become *Mules and Men*.
May–June 1930	Works on the play *Mule Bone* with Langston Hughes.
1931	Publishes "Hoodoo in America" in the *Journal of American Folklore*.
February 1931	Breaks with Langston Hughes over the authorship of *Mule Bone*.
July 7, 1931	Divorces Sheen.
September 1931	Writes for a theatrical revue called *Fast and Furious*.
January 1932	Writes and stages a theatrical revue called *The Great Day,* first performed on January 10 on Broadway at the John Golden Theatre; works with the creative literature department of Rollins College, Winter Park, Florida, to produce a concert program of Negro music.
1933	Writes "The Fiery Chariot."
January 1933	Stages *From Sun to Sun* (a version of *Great Day*) at Rollins College.
August 1933	Publishes "The Gilded Six-Bits" in *Story*.
1934	Publishes six essays in Nancy Cunard's anthology, *Negro*.
January 1934	Goes to Bethune-Cookman College to establish a school of dramatic arts "based on pure Negro expression."
May 1934	Publishes *Jonah's Gourd Vine,* originally titled *Big Nigger;* it is a Book-of-the-Month Club selection.

September 1934	Publishes "The Fire and the Cloud" in the *Challenge*.
November 1934	*Singing Steel* (a version of *Great Day*) performed in Chicago.
January 1935	Makes an abortive attempt to study for a Ph.D in anthropology at Columbia University on a fellowship from the Rosenwald Foundation. In fact, she seldom attends classes.
August 1935	Joins the WPA Federal Theatre Project as a "dramatic coach."
October 1935	*Mules and Men* published.
March 1936	Awarded a Guggenheim Fellowship to study West Indian Obeah practices.
April–September 1936	In Jamaica.
September–March 1937	In Haiti; writes *Their Eyes Were Watching God* in seven weeks.
May 1937	Returns to Haiti on a renewed Guggenheim.
September 1937	Returns to the United States; *Their Eyes Were Watching God* published, September 18.
February–March 1938	Writes *Tell My Horse;* it is published the same year.
April 1938	Joins the Federal Writers Project in Florida to work on *The Florida Negro*.
1939	Publishes "Now Take Noses" in *Cordially Yours*.
June 1939	Receives an honorary Doctor of Letters degree from Morgan State College.
June 27, 1939	Marries Albert Price III in Florida.

308

Summer 1939	Hired as a drama instructor by North Carolina College for Negroes at Durham; meets Paul Green, professor of drama, at the University of North Carolina.
November 1939	*Moses, Man of the Mountain* published.
February 1940	Files for divorce from Price, though the two are reconciled briefly.
Summer 1940	Makes a folklore-collecting trip to South Carolina.
Spring– July 1941	Writes *Dust Tracks on a Road*.
July 1941	Publishes "Cock Robin, Beale Street" in the *Southern Literary Messenger*.
October 1941– January 1942	Works as a story consultant at Paramount Pictures.
July 1942	Publishes "Story in Harlem Slang" in the *American Mercury*.
September 5, 1942	Publishes a profile of Lawrence Silas in the *Saturday Evening Post*.
November 1942	*Dust Tracks on a Road* published.
February 1943	Awarded the Anisfield-Wolf Book Award in Race Relations for *Dust Tracks;* on the cover of the *Saturday Review*.
March 1943	Receives Howard University's Distinguished Alumni Award.
May 1943	Publishes "The 'Pet Negro' Syndrome" in the *American Mercury*.
November 1943	Divorce from Price granted.
June 1944	Publishes "My Most Humiliating Jim Crow Experience" in the *Negro Digest*.
1945	Writes *Mrs. Doctor;* it is rejected by Lippincott.

March 1945	Publishes "The Rise of the Begging Joints" in the *American Mercury.*
December 1945	Publishes "Crazy for This Democracy" in the *Negro Digest.*
1947	Publishes a review of Robert Tallant's *Voodoo in New Orleans* in the *Journal of American Folklore.*
May 1947	Goes to British Honduras to research black communities in Central America; writes *Seraph on the Suwanee;* stays in Honduras until March 1948.
September 1948	Falsely accused of molesting a ten-year-old boy and arrested; case finally dismissed in March 1949.
October 1948	*Seraph on the Suwanee* published.
March 1950	Publishes "Conscience of the Court" in the *Saturday Evening Post,* while working as a maid in Rivo Island, Florida.
April 1950	Publishes "What White Publishers Won't Print" in the *Saturday Evening Post.*
November 1950	Publishes "I Saw Negro Votes Peddled" in the *American Legion* magazine.
Winter 1950–51	Moves to Belle Glade, Florida.
June 1951	Publishes "Why the Negro Won't Buy Communism" in the *American Legion* magazine.
December 8, 1951	Publishes "A Negro Voter Sizes Up Taft" in the *Saturday Evening Post.*
1952	Hired by the *Pittsburgh Courier* to cover the Ruby McCollum case.
May 1956	Receives an award for "education and human relations" at Bethune-Cookman College.

June 1956	Works as a librarian at Patrick Air Force Base in Florida; fired in 1957.
1957–59	Writes a column on "Hoodoo and Black Magic" for the *Fort Pierce Chronicle.*
1958	Works as a substitute teacher at Lincoln Park Academy, Fort Pierce.
Early 1959	Suffers a stroke.
October 1959	Forced to enter the St. Lucie County Welfare Home.
January 28, 1960	Dies in the St. Lucie County Welfare Home of "hypertensive heart disease"; buried in an unmarked grave in the Garden of Heavenly Rest, Fort Pierce.
August 1973	Alice Walker discovers and marks Hurston's grave.
March 1975	Walker publishes "In Search of Zora Neale Hurston," in *Ms.,* launching a Hurston revival.